The Edge of Life

Louise Croft

Linellen Press
265 Boomerang Road
Oldbury, Western Australia
www.linellenpress.com.au

Dedication

To my dear daughter-in-law, Jo,
who sadly died during the completion of my novel.

Contents

Acknowledgments

My heartfelt thanks go to my husband Ian who has provided love, ongoing support and encouragement during the writing period of three years. He has re-read the story multiple times and always given worthwhile suggestions and ideas for enhancement.

Elena

This Italy so dry, so hot down here
Rocks and stones, baked sky
Small villages, bells I fear
Not always good news to ring
Small children play. Harm
Does not come to them, it's not yet near
But black is the colour as closer it flirts
For now at least the children sing.

A life as carefree is not to be
Times changed by dark forces
Lives are taken and villages lost
She flees across the hills
Escapes! But life has changed for good.
Tragedy follows, a love dies
Years would pass and still a love dies
This world, this life, this pain.

All she felt, all she loved
Her protection taken from her

The little she wanted was never to be
Her body now crippled but not so her face
All has been taken but the light in her eyes
Her beautiful smile is for all to see
The pianist's notes in the right key
Oh Elena, Elena please dance with me.

Ian Allison

Caterna, Puglia. May 2004

The ancient church bells are clanging the hour, the harsh sound resonating against the stone buildings of the hilltop village, disturbing the pigeons crowded on the spire. The noise resounds across the valley and is faintly echoed by the monastery church bells situated on a distant hilltop. The air is still and scented with thyme and dry stone. Between the closely packed buildings are glimpses of the Puglian countryside with small cultivated fields surrounding the ruined stone walls. Rampant fig trees grow in small patches of soil and some buildings have tiny gardens and terraces filled with clinging roses, pots of geraniums and petunias.

Leaning against the rough stone of the shadowed archway built into the village wall, Elena closes her eyes as the bells bring back tragic memories. It's midday, and she pushes on, walking slowly into the bright piazza, the spring sun's warmth on her shoulders, the stored heat of the cobblestones under her feet. Her heart feels heavy when she visits this village; fills with horror, regret, intense sadness and guilt.

Her eyes stretch involuntarily across the piazza to where the ancient stone church stands, to the faint scattering of bullet marks on the right-hand wall. Here, a large brass plaque reflects the sunlight and she remembers with terrible clarity the morning in 1942 when some of the villagers, including the priest, were shoved across the piazza by the occupying German soldiers, made to stand against the wall where they were shot. The sound of their screams and cries for mercy have never left her. Elena remembers the women clinging to their husbands; still sees the two old people stumbling hand in hand. The blood stains on the piazza cobblestones and the church wall have long since been eroded by the weather, the only evidence of that terrible day the brass plaque engraved with twenty-five names of the men and women shot by German soldiers in World War II and the dents in the stones from bullets.

She shudders as the memory grips her of being imprisoned for a long dark night with these innocent people in the Mayor's cellar. She can still remember the smell of the underground room, dank and airless. During the night two old people, terrified, shaking and unable to control themselves, added to the smell with their urine. The priest helped Elena escape but the other unfortunate villagers were shot with no trial or chance to defend themselves.

Tall, slender Elena sits on a bench at the edge of the piazza, enjoying the sun's warmth and the tiny birds twittering as they fly between the buildings; she watches with large, dark, deep-set eyes as a pair of doves land on the cobblestones near her feet and peck around her; they coo softly. She lays down her cane on the stone bench, rests her brown, elegant, long-fingered hands – a pianist's hands – on warm, broad, prominent cheekbones, aware now that the soft brown skin is lined with age, much like her clearly marked eyebrows that have turned white with time. She pats her dark, tinted hair which is pulled back from her high, broad forehead and tied into a knot. Today she wears a bright silk shirt and cool linen skirt, her favourite style of clothing which are always of quality. Her expressive face is creased with laughter lines around her eyes and mouth, but grooves of sadness run from nose to chin.

Returning to Caterna in her home province of Puglia always brings memories of her adolescent years back into focus, a time when she was beautiful. She had grown up in a different hilltop village some twenty kilometres across the valley, and had made this pilgrimage to Caterna only once before as a widow. She knows that this is the last time because she is finding the air travel to and from Australia increasingly strenuous and tiring.

She had come by taxi from a hotel in the valley to this village, never returning to her home village of Mitorna, which was partially destroyed by a stray bomb in World War II. Mitorna is now overgrown with vegetation and deserted, apart from a few old people. Many villagers emigrated after the Second World War either to America or Australia in search of a better life for their families.

Elena rests for a few minutes and enjoys the serenity of the piazza – the surrounding buildings comfort her in their centuries-old permanence. Most of the ancient walls have crumbling plaster, exposing bare stone which gives an impression of the modern trend for the distressed look. Some buildings are adorned with washing lines, and pots of bright red geraniums crammed onto window sills and in stone troughs around the yards.

A few old men sit outside a tiny cafe shaded by a striped awning, the aroma of espressos drifting across to her. She sees a couple of dark-clad women come out of a shadowy alley and walk across to the few shops by the cafe, followed by a child tugging a small dog. A bicycle with a front basket leans against a wall. She notes the few rotting lettuce leaves and trodden tomatoes on the cobblestones left from the market held that morning and the smell of crushed basil floats on the warm air.

The stones are worn and uneven but brightly reflect the sun shining from a deep blue sky – no shadows clouding the old buildings. The air is filled with the perfume of potted geraniums and the buzzing of furry bees hovering in and out of the flowers. The scene is peaceful and calm with the permanence of an ancient settlement. A young couple saunter arm in arm across the piazza followed by their small children, two girls in bright cotton dresses, the boy in tidy shorts and shirt.

Despite the idyllic scene, Elena can't prevent the memories seeping into her mind like a leaking roof. She feels the familiar clenching of her stomach. Her eyes close tightly, the thin lids filtering the strong sunlight; her hands grasp her cane. The sheen of fear spots her forehead and perspiration glistens on her hands and back. Glancing to the left, she sees the schoolhouse and Mayor's office where she had worked before the war. The Italian flag flaps in the light breeze to the left of the door and the European Union flag with the circle of stars hangs on a metal pole on the opposite side.

So deep in her memories, she is not aware of other people around her. She does not hear the chatter of voices drifting from the café tables, or childish footsteps approaching, and shudders as a small warm hand touches her arm. Her eyes flicker open, blinded by sunlight.

'*Buongiorno*,' says a childish voice. 'Are you feeling well?'

As her eyes focus, Elena sees a small girl about six years old looking at her curiously, and has an urge to touch the child's mop of curly black hair. The girl's large dark eyes sparkle with mischief. Dressed in a faded, floral cotton dress and worn leather sandals, with hooped silver rings in her ears and a red ribbon in her hair, the child smiles broadly, brightening her soft, round, olive face.

'Si, grazie,' replies Elena, her native Italian with its distinctive Puglian dialect instantly flowing onto her lips. 'Do you live here?'

'Si,' says the child waving her arm to the right, 'that's my mamma hanging out the washing there.'

Elena looks across the piazza to a tall stone building with cracked plaster where a young woman is leaning out of the window, pegging her clothing on a line suspended from the window frame.

'What's your name?' Elena asks.

'Maddalena,' the child responds.

'That's a pretty name.'

'Papa says it suits me but Mamma says it's too long to be used every day so she calls me Lena.'

'How old are you? Do you go to school here?'

'I'm six years old and I go to the school behind the church. I like it there. I have lots of friends. The Padre teaches us to read and write and love Jesus,' replies Lena.

'Is the church open? I would like to look inside and say a prayer for my friends.'

The child nods vigorously. 'The Padre says everyone must be able to talk to God all the time.'

Elena smiles. 'Will you take me there?'

The child holds out her plump and slightly grubby hand. Elena eases herself off the stone bench, takes the child's hand and walks across the uneven cobblestones; strolls to the church wall on the right and pauses a moment, head bowed in front of the shining brass plaque with its twenty-five engraved names. Elena glances again over the many bullet holes surrounding the plaque and runs her fingers carefully over the indentations in the stone, some are deeper than others … but thankfully no blood stains them now. She trembles as the memories flow again of the German invasion and the murder of innocent people. It has taken decades of effort to enable her to pull a shutter down over the traumatic past. She must bring herself back to the sunny piazza, to the child's sticky hand in hers and the serenity of the village.

The child tugs her hand impatiently and Elena looks down at Lena and smiles.

'I would like to go into the church on my own. Will you wait for me?'

'Si,' says Lena, unclasping her hand. 'Shall I ask Mamma if you can come for lunch? It's pasta funghi as we picked them this morning in the valley. There's only a smelly cafe filled with old men in the village.'

Elena demurs slightly but the child laughs and excitedly runs over to her home in the old building, leaving Elena to walk slowly into the ancient church with its intricately carved wooden door. She pauses as her eyes adjust from the bright sunlight of the piazza to the soft gloom of the building; she automatically dips her fingers into the consecrated water of the font and crosses herself before carefully sitting down in the last row of wooden chairs. It feels cool after the midday heat outside, and the sun shining through the old stained-glass windows casts soft luminous colours on the worn paving stones. The church is peaceful now, its bells silent. The tranquillity comforts her as here there is no echo from the old stone walls of the war-time tragedy outside, or of earlier human tragedies. She gazes at the carved wooden cross with Jesus impaled on it; it hangs over the cloth-covered altar and her eyes wander further, round the walls, taking in the old oil paintings depicting the Stations of the Cross.

The church smells of warm wax and incense, and the gilded icons glitter in the flickering light of the eternal flame. The church door opens with a rusty creak and a few rays of sunlight cast a golden glow over the ancient stone floor. A small group of black-clad women walk to the font, bow to the altar and cross themselves. They separate and sit on either side of the aisle. Some kneel in prayer, and an old woman fingers her rosary beads. An old man wearing a dark cap and walking with a cane limps slowly past Elena to light a candle at a side chapel. A young woman holding a baby sits a few rows in front, softly crooning her prayers to the child as it sleeps at her breast.

As she shifts on the hard chair, Elena wonders where the years have gone and reflects on the periods of happiness and tragedy that have indelibly marked her life. She knows no-one in Caterna now and has no family in either Italy or England. During her long life, she has lived in several countries including Italy and England but now lives alone and at peace in Western Australia, in a vibrant Italian emigrant community. She has been married twice, the first time to an English airman she met in Naples at the end of the war, with whom she had a son.

A tug on her hand breaks her reflections: Lena has returned and is standing expectantly waiting for Elena to open her eyes. She smiles and asks, 'Mamma says the pasta is ready and can I bring the lady now?'

Touched by the invitation, Elena longs for homely pasta. She remembers her Nonna's favourite dish was spaghetti with herbs and garlic. How long ago her childhood feels now — it was a different world and seems to belong to another person.

'Si grazie,' Elena replies and takes the child's soft hand to be led across the piazza and up the cracked cement stairs to the third floor. The stairway smells of cleaning fluid but the inhabitants of the building have tried to soften its bleakness by putting small tubs of plastic flowers on the landings.

'Mamma, she's here,' Lena shouts excitedly as she opens a faded blue door and pulls Elena into the kitchen.

A young woman with long black hair, pushed back with clips, appears from another room.

She is slender, has high cheekbones and dark brown eyes, and is dressed in faded jeans and a blue cotton T-shirt. Wearing gold hoops in her ears, and red and blue strappy leather sandals, Elena instantly sees the family likeness. The woman welcomes her with a smile and holds out her hand.

'*Buongiorno. Benvenuto a mia casa.* I am Maria. The orecchiette is freshly made. We don't get many tourists here as there are no famous frescos or paintings in the church and only a ruined castle on the edge of the village. Please sit down then you can look over the piazza.'

They sit at a scratched wooden table in the centre of the spotlessly clean kitchen, the aroma of freshly cooked pasta surrounding them. On the old plastered walls are wooden shelves packed with labelled storage jars and crockery. Saucepans and ladles hang from nails amidst a string of rosary beads, a plait of garlic and a faded framed postcard of the Madonna. Gauze, striped curtains of red and yellow float around in the breeze coming through the open window. The wooden chairs are slatted, and a handmade multi-coloured cotton rug lays on the floor. The ceiling is heavily beamed and the terracotta tiled floor gleams with polish. Maria ladles the hot pasta into blue pottery dishes, puts them on the table then lays down cutlery and a small glass dish of grated parmesan.

'Would you like a drink of water?' Maria asks.

'Grazie,' replies Elena. The kitchen reminds her of the happy childhood spent in her Nonna's house in Mitorna. She dips her fork into the pasta, feeling hungrier than she has been for years. It tastes delicious, flavoured with mushrooms and herbs, and she savours the contrasting bite of the grated parmesan sprinkled on top. Tiny chopped pieces of red chilli adds a spicy flavour.

The kitchen is quiet, only the distant sounds of neighbours drifting through the window on the hot afternoon wind. A clock chimes nearby and the church bells ring the hour. Elena starts and shifts nervously in her chair as if she is leaving. Her right hand trembles as she lifts the pasta to her mouth. She is aware that both Maria and Lena have paused in their eating.

'How do you know about Caterna?' Maria asks to keep Elena talking.

Elena lifts her head and gazes out of the window. There is an expectant silence in the kitchen as Maria and Lena look up from their meal.

'Many years ago, when I was seventeen, I was encouraged by the local priest to leave my family village and work here in the Mayor's office, and assist the school teacher. The village where I was born and spent my childhood is Mitorna. It was similar to Caterna, built on a hill with surrounding stone walls for protection but it is ruined and deserted now.'

Elena stops for a minute, unable to continue, her memories, both happy and tragic, flooding her mind. She puts down her spoon, dips her head and wipes a tear from her cheek. The visit to the church and the hospitality of this woman and her child unsettle her.

'I'm sorry, I don't mean to upset you,' Maria says softly, turning away to refill the glasses with water. 'My father always said my curiosity would be my undoing.'

'Is it about the war and the bullet holes in the church wall?' Lena asks with the innocent curiosity of a child.

Maria frowns at her but says, 'My parents told me very little about this village before and during the war. They have been dead several years. If you don't wish to talk about the past, I understand as none of the old people living here discuss their wartime experiences.'

Elena pushes away another tear, pulls her hands into fists in her lap and tries to calm herself by taking a few deep breaths. She looks down and sits quietly for a few minutes, asking herself the unending question. *How can I explain the terrible things that happened here? It will spoil my time with Lena and*

Silence envelops the kitchen for several more minutes as Elena reflects on the tragic years of 1942 and 1943. Maria and Lena continue eating, allowing Elena time to regain her composure, giving her a chance to change the subject. When they have all finished, Maria clears the plates and takes them to the sink.

Lena fidgets a little and looks out of the window, longing to go out into the sunshine and play. Maria nods her agreement and Lena slides off her seat, pats Elena's hands then runs out of the room and down the steps.

'Would you like a coffee?' Maria asks gently.

'Si, grazie. I haven't lost my taste for Italian expresso. Lena is a delightful child. She guided me to your apartment and several people greeted her. She says she goes to the church school here.'

'Lena is my only child; she's special and has a happy nature. Her father went to America about a year ago to make money for us to emigrate there. There is very little work here. Andrea worked in the local vineyard but he was poorly paid and it was physically hard work. He wanted to better himself and improve Lena's prospects. It gets lonely without him, though we talk on the phone when we can. Lena misses him greatly.'

Elena says, 'My father emigrated to America when I was very young, soon after my mother died giving birth to my little brother who also died. I was looked after by my grandparents from the age of four until I was fourteen. I loved my Nonna and grandfather very much. They protected and cared for me and I knew I was everything to them as they had no other family. Although they worked hard on the land, they gave me all their love and found time to share simple games with me. They were poor but we never went hungry. Their strong Catholic faith sustained them as life was very hard before World War II.'

'The village of Mitorna was a close community and people helped each other where they could. The men worked on local farms but it was seasonal labour and poorly paid. Many small children died of hunger and were clothed in rags or cast-offs. Housing was basic, with beaten earth floors or stone paving with a small wood fire laid in the centre of the single room with a metal container hung on a chain which was used for cooking, usually simple soups and stews. If the menfolk were handy with wood, there might be a table and settle. Women wore black – skirts, jumpers, shawls and head scarves with heavy working shoes.'

Elena sighs.

'There was no work for me when I left school at sixteen. I helped in the local café but I needed to earn money after my grandparents had died. The priest arranged for me to move to Caterna where the Mayor needed help in typing letters and I was good with English at school.'

Elena unclenches her fists and shifts her feet under the table. She takes a deep breath, picks up her cane, leans on it then hesitantly starts to talk, trying to describe those events from so long ago that changed and damaged her life forever. As she recounts what happened to her, she relives the horror, feels again the abandonment and deep sadness she experienced back then. Maria sits quietly but Elena can see she too is emotionally affected. She pauses and sips her coffee, her hand trembling as she reaches out to replace her cup in the saucer on the table. The cup rattles on the plate and she cannot catch it quick enough – it clatters to the floor and shatters into tiny pieces.

Maria quickly clears it up.

German Invasion of Caterna 1942

'I was born in the small isolated village of Mitorna, and raised by my grandparents. We lived in a two-roomed cottage built into the stone walls of the village. I accepted my life and the hardships for lack of knowledge of anything different. My grandparents were generous with their love even though they were poor. Their only furniture was a wooden table and a bench in the kitchen. They slept in the other room using a straw pallet on an old metal bed and hung their clothes on nails in the wall. They collected wood when and where they could, and cooked over an open fire in the centre of the kitchen. Their tin cups, plates and pans were stored on wooden wall shelves, along with tin cans of pasta and flour.

'We spoke a dialect more like the Franco-Provencal language than the Italian-Tuscan spoken today.

'The hilltop town of Mitorna was surrounded by crumbling stone ramparts; the streets were narrow and cobbled with tall stone buildings on either side. From the top of the hill, in the market square, the view of the Puglian countryside was stunning, a landscape of small cultivated fields, olive groves and farm buildings. Once, the village was protected by a castle but time had pushed it to ruins before I lived there.

'At one end of the piazza stood an old stone church, its wide steps leading to a carved, solid wooden door. A round stained-glass window overlooked the entrance. The church, which dated back to the tenth century, had been used as a watchtower in medieval times, and the villagers sheltered there when marauding gangs of bandits and invading Turks threatened the village.

'Every Sunday morning, I went with my grandparents and our neighbours to early morning mass. I sat on the pew and dangled my legs; held my Nonna's hand until I grew tall enough to put my feet on the floor. The mass seemed long and boring to me as a small child, although I remember watching the sun's rays shining through the plain glass windows illuminating insects and dust that floated in the light. I was allowed to stay on my seat when the adults knelt to pray.

'On market days, the piazza filled with stalls: livestock, birds in cages, and people selling produce from the villages and surrounding areas. We wandered through after mass, greeting neighbours, buying goat's cheese and occasionally cheap meat like a sheep's head, tripe or giblets, which Nonna made into a delicious stew, adding our own vegetables or wild herbs and mushrooms.

'The nearest villages were Faeto and Celle di San Vito. The nearest large towns were Trani and Bari on the Adriatic coast and Foggia in the northeast. Rarely did we or our neighbours leave the village as we had no transport, except when a local farmer drove his cart into Trani once a month and took passengers.

'In 1932, when I was six years old, the village was invaded by a gang of Blackshirt soldiers. They shot my grandfather. No-one knew about the fascist party that had been established by local police in the town of Bari. Several other villagers were killed at the same time. It was terrifying for the inhabitants of Mitorna, especially the children, to see such violence and bloodshed outside their homes. The Blackshirts left after the shootings, loading all the animals into a truck and marching proudly down the lane.

'I continued to live with my Nonna until she died in 1940, worn out by hard physical work and a broken heart. I lived alone in the stone cottage for another couple of year.

'I was sixteen then and determined to leave the sadness of Mitorna and find work in another town. Padre Stepano, the local priest, encouraged me as I was his best pupil in the village school and ambitious enough to want work other than farming. He inquired of his friend, Padre Pietro, the priest in

Caterna, who told him the school teacher and the Mayor could both offer me clerical work and accommodation. Padre Stepano told me the Mayor, Signor Marco Bastia was a local man who lived with his family in the farming community and was voted Mayor because of his popularity with the villagers.'

'Were you nervous about leaving Mitorna and your friends and moving to a different village to find work?' asks Maria. 'It seems a brave thing to do. Did you have any family in Caterna?'

'I had no alternative,' replies Elena. 'I needed to earn a living and use my education so I could leave the tragedies of childhood behind. I didn't have any family left in Italy so I packed a few things into a hessian sack and hitched a ride on a donkey cart delivering vegetables to the surrounding villages. The carter took me to the Mayor's office where I was met by the school teacher and his wife who rented me an attic room in the school house.'

Elena smiles a little as she remembers Signor Bastia and Padre Pietro. Both men were suited to their vocation and had a strong sense of civic duty to their village. Signor Bastia kept in touch with the world outside Caterna by listening to the daily news on his radio. He posted weekly bulletins on the noticeboard outside his office.

'Signor Bastia had been Mayor of Caterna for ten years before he heard on his radio that the Germans had invaded the north of Italy, and south into Sicily. I overheard the Mayor and Padre Pietro agree to keep any news about the war situation to themselves as they thought Caterna was isolated and of no strategic value to the Germans, although German planes had been seen flying from the airfields around Foggia, the large town to the northeast.'

'I was seventeen when, during the Saturday market, the distant roar of motorbikes and heavy vehicles was heard outside the village. Within minutes, two motorbikes roared through the main arch into the piazza, followed by four brown trucks filled with uniformed German soldiers. Their commanding officer followed in a jeep flying the Hakenkreuz flag. I remember seeing sunlight flashing on the metal fittings of the vehicles and smelt the truck exhaust in the air.'

'Signor Bastia had been peering through the shutters and gaped at the soldiers as the Germans climbed out of their vehicles. He hastily stepped out of the mayoral building and held out a hand to the commanding officer who exchanged a few words with his aide-de-camp.'

'I could see through the open door the villagers standing speechless and stunned, fearfully watching the soldiers disembark. They assembled under the command of their officers and marched into the piazza. The soldiers were trim and smart in their spotless grey-green uniforms. The sound of booted feet as they hammered into line for the 'Heil Hitler' salute was threatening; it echoed around the piazza and reverberated off the stone buildings. The soldiers held their rifles on their shoulders, the rims of their helmets shadowing their eyes. There had been no resistance as no-one was aware the Germans were in the area.'

Elena pauses, overcome with emotion. She sips a mouthful of water; she gazes out the window, but doesn't see the sun-drenched piazza with people enjoying coffee and chatting with neighbours, only the ranked German soldiers. She feels vulnerable now she has started to describe the past, stripping off the layers she had carefully constructed to bury her terrifying wartime experiences. They were buried beneath happier memories of married life in England and migration to Australia.

She takes another mouthful of water and clenches her hands in her skirt trying to control her emotions. She is frightened to unleash the past but knows the history of Caterna must be told.

As a visitor, she can walk away and keep her memories locked down, whereas the local families would continue to live with the horror that engulfed this village in the war. Elena takes a deep breath and, in a broken voice, continues to relate the events she had lived through in Caterna back in 1942. Her body shakes despite the warmth of the kitchen. To Elena, it feels like peeling an onion – as each layer is torn away, the tears fall slowly at first then flow down her face. But she continues.

'There was no shouting or shooting as the Captain commandeered the Mayor's office, ordered the Italian flag to be lowered and replaced by the obtrusive swastika. Standing on the steps he identified himself as Captain Hoffner and ordered his troops to line up in front of him. He was in full dress uniform with the golden badge of the Nazi Party on his left arm and medals glinting on his chest. He was tall, lean and upright, his face pale and immobile, clean-shaven and distinctive looking with a sharp nose, his eyes hidden under the peak of his hat. He smiled often with no warmth, showing his immaculate white teeth. Facing the assembled villagers, the Captain raised his right hand and proclaimed, 'Heil Hitler. His commands were precise and slow as if he was deliberating what words to use in halting Italian, the lilting melody of the language lost in the clipped short sentences. I will never forget his threatening manner as he calmly stated his control over the village.

"I am Capitano Hoffner. With immediate effect from today I assume absolute control over Caterna with full military powers. We are using the Mayor's building for the purposes of the war effort. I and my two officers intend to live and work in the Mayor's house. My soldiers will camp outside the village walls. There will be a nightly curfew between 8 pm and 6 am. Church services can be continued but the bells must not be rung under any circumstances.'

'Then the Captain lifted a clenched fist, beckoned to the Mayor to stand next to him and continued.

"Further commands will be posted outside the Mayor's office over the next few weeks. You must surrender all weapons and ammunition to me at the Mayor's office within twenty-four hours. Anyone with a radio must also deliver it to this office. My soldiers will search your homes during the week and anyone found in possession of firearms or a radio will be immediately shot and your home destroyed if you are caught. There will be no uprising here and no communication with the outside world. Every villager who obeys has nothing to fear. Anyone who openly or covertly acts against my orders will be executed! *Capisco?*"

Elena stares out at the empty, bright piazza, breathing down the emotions stirred by those frightening events. 'Shortly after the Captain's announcement, the Mayor posted a proclamation outside his office confirming the military powers of the Germans. We stood silently in huddled family groups, stunned and unable to understand the complete and sudden capitulation of the village to the Germans on this bright summer's day. Until then, I believed that everything was safe and certain. There'd been no time to toll the church bell as a warning that the village was threatened. The Notice stated in German and Italian that we were to be formally identified by queuing in front of two desks removed from the Mayor's office and placed in the piazza.

'The queues formed slowly as people tried to edge towards the back. Two officers sat behind desks in the shade cast by the tall buildings with notebooks open to register us. The people shuffled forward slowly, the old and infirm being helped by their family to register. Questions of identity and literacy confused the older villagers. There were delays as mothers with children wrote the family names or lifted children to give thumbprints. As each person walked away from the registration process a palpable feeling of relief showed on their faces. They hurried across to the apparent safety of their homes, dragging crying children, locking and barring their doors where they could.

'I stood in line with the school teacher and his wife, Andrea and Lucia, the hot sunshine beating down on us. Sweating with fear and heat, I whispered my name to the officer and my place of birth. He frowned as he wrote down the unfamiliar Italian names and, without looking at me, told me brusquely to leave when my details were taken.

'It was midday by the time everyone was registered, but no friendly church bells stirred the torrid air in the piazza. The Captain and his officers marched out through the town archway to the main road where their trucks were being unloaded. A field of brown tents was quickly erected for the soldiers outside the walls, with ditches dug for sanitary purposes. That evening, target practice shattered the normally peaceful dinners of the villagers who remained inside to obey the curfew.

'I remember sitting at Andrea and Lucia's kitchen table, clenching my hands, almost forgotten memories of the terrifying Blackshirt invasion of Mitorna overwhelming me. The air was filled with threat and the village eerily silent after the proclamation.

'Lucia continuously rubbed her hands down her skirt, worried whether the school needed to close down. Andrea advised us to stay indoors and eat the pasta and vegetables that Lucia had bought at the market. He suggested I move downstairs from the attic and sleep in the kitchen for safety. He helped me get my clothing and bedding from the attic and re-arranged the furniture in the kitchen.

'The hot, airless day dragged by. That evening a sack of firearms collected by the villagers and two radios were deposited on the steps of the Mayor's office as commanded and promptly removed by the soldiers. No-one left their homes the next day, the piazza remained eerily silent and empty, the remains of the market produce rotting in the sun that beat down mercilessly.

'In the evening of the second day, heavy storm clouds shadowed the sun and darkened the piazza. Huge drops of rain splattered the cobblestones and the roofs. Thunder crashed and echoed around the village and the valley below, lightning crackling viciously as though a raging gunfire battle was taking place in the fields outside the village. The villagers remained indoors, sheltering from the storm and the Germans.

'I hardly slept that night, disturbed by the storm, and terrified the soldiers would burst into the kitchen, although the stout old wooden door had been firmly barred and locked. At dawn I remember getting up and washing my face, smoothing down my crumpled clothes. Andrea made coffee and sliced bread for breakfast. Lucia appeared soon after. They both looked heavy-eyed and had obviously slept little over the two nights. We ate in silence. The storm had disappeared, and the sky was clear blue, the sun drying the cobblestones. These memories are indelibly printed on my mind and difficult to erase.'

Elena shudders and takes a deep breath, brushes her skirt nervously. 'The village continued to be eerily silent and withdrawn, the café and shops closed, and no-one walked into the piazza.'

Maria places her hand on Elena's shoulder and asks if she would like coffee or another glass of water. 'If you feel able to continue I would like to hear more but I am deeply saddened that you were so young when all this happened.'

'I would like a glass of water please,' Elena replies as she runs her fingers through her hair, preparing herself to relate the horrific events the Germans had perpetrated in Caterna.

She shifts in her chair and continues. 'The German officers sat outside the café to drink beer most evenings and the proprietor had to serve them, helped by Sophia, his pretty young daughter. Her father warned her not to speak with any of the hated Germans when she cleaned the tables and washed the glasses, and to avoid eye contact. On one occasion we heard that an officer sitting at the café had drawn his gun and threatened the café owner even though the soldiers had been warned not to bring guns into the village. The Captain confiscated the gun.

'The villagers avoided the café, and the old men who used to meet every day to chat and read newspapers, stayed out of sight. Even on market days a sullen silence reigned instead of the normal sounds of people greeting each other while standing on doorsteps or hanging out of windows. The market stallholders did not encouraged people to browse, and the enormous cauldrons of stew and pasta were absent. People no longer popped into the Mayor's office and he avoided the market.'

'From the first day, the Mayor's attitude was different. He was ingratiating to the Germans, seeking out their company at the café, quickly providing official documents to their Captain. I think he was drawn like a magnet to the Captain's power and confidence. Signor Bastia had told me in confidence one hot afternoon that he had been born to an illiterate tenant farmer on land belonging to an ancient noble family. He had tried all his life to improve his station in life with self-education and minor positions of authority like school teacher, and now Mayor.

'After a week, Captain Hoffman made another announcement from the steps of the Mayor's office.

"Normal life will continue and the school and shop will open. You can tend the vegetable plots, but the church bells must not be rung. I have received many firearms and radios, but my warning is still valid. I will personally shoot anyone found harbouring these items.'

'The villagers cautiously crossed the piazza, going to the shop for food, but never using the café. Some soldiers bought from the market stalls and, although they were polite, their presence was threatening. Attendance at Sunday morning mass had been an important part of village life and now the only occasion when people met family and friends. A few weeks later, I was eating breakfast with Andrea and Lucia when we saw Michello, the grocer, being dragged from his shop by two German soldiers, his wife clinging to them, pleading for her husband.

"He never had any firearms as he was wounded in the Great War and his right arm is useless,' she pleaded between sobs.

'We saw that Michello was handcuffed and dragged to stand against the church wall with his eyes bound. Padre Pietro pleaded with Captain Hoffner for the grocer's life, his wife kneeling in front of him, sobbing piteously and begging him to save her husband.'

'Captain Hoffner shouted at them that Michello had been hiding a gun and the village was under military command. 'Shoot him,' he yelled. Five soldiers were lined up in front of Michello and loaded their guns. They sighted the victim and fired a fusillade of shots into Michello's body which jerked to the ground, blood pouring from the multiple wounds. The Captain and his soldiers walked away. 'Pick him up and bury him outside the walls,' he commanded harshly, looking over his shoulder.

'Peering out through the school door, we could see Michello's son and his friends wheeling a small hand-cart. They bound the grocer in a tablecloth and lifted him onto the cart then wheeled it to the cemetery. They buried Michello quickly without any ceremony, only a few words said over the grave by Padre Pietro. The villagers collected a few wildflowers to scatter over the burial ground but, not wanting to bring danger to themselves, quickly returned to their homes, leaving his grievously sobbing wife and son to mourn.'

'We did not understand why Michello had hidden an old gun that he couldn't use. The villagers were warned of the consequences of not handing in arms to the Germans. There was no way to find out as the grocer's shop was shuttered and his wife consoled by her son and friends. After that tragedy, the locals hardly dared look at each other and there were no visits to other homes. There was a palpable air of mistrust in the village as no-one knew who had informed on Michello. It could have been anyone, but they were suspicious of the Mayor who was ostentatiously working with the enemy.

'The warm community atmosphere disappeared and it was unsafe to walk outside at night. Group meetings were forbidden by the Germans and even in the market there was little conversation between people. The Germans were polite and disciplined but did not mix. There was no more shooting but the burden of their presence affected the vitality of the village. People hurried with bowed heads across the piazza to mass, the school or the shop. The Mayor did not issue any news bulletins.

'We had no knowledge about the progress of the war. I heard that someone managed to retrieve the Mayor's radio in the confusion on the day of the occupation and hid it in a cow barn outside the walls. During the afternoon siesta, various men sauntered outside the walls as if going to their vegetable plots and crept into the barn. They tuned in and listened to the crackling announcements from the Italian government.

They heard that the Allied Forces had landed in Sicily, overthrown the Germans, and were heading to Messina. Whispered comments were passed around, but the grim reality of daily life had removed all thoughts of release from the German occupation.

'The Mayor moved his office to the dining room in his home and no longer needed my assistance. The German command made all the decisions and I noticed the Mayor shared information and drank with them in the evenings at the café. Signor Bastia pretended that he was fraternising with the Germans to help the people of Caterna but, in reality, he was only interested in sharing power and preserving his comfortable life.

'A few months later, I was woken early by screaming and shouting in the piazza. I looked out of the tiny attic window and saw three village men, hands tied behind their backs, pushed across the piazza by a group of armed German soldiers. Other villagers were dragged from their homes, men and women. A thundering knock on the kitchen door made me quickly withdraw from the window but I heard Andrea and Lucia shouting as they were pushed out into the piazza. About twenty villagers, hands tied behind their backs, were huddled in the middle of the piazza, including my closest friend. Signor Bastia, the Mayor, was standing in the shadow of the archway watching, a sly smile on his face.

'Captain Hoffner stood in front of them and calmly said, 'My soldiers found a confiscated radio in a barn outside the village after they saw men slipping through a barn door. I warned you that the perpetrators would be shot if this happened. You will be held in the Mayor's cellar overnight, during which time the identity of the informer will be evident. Tomorrow morning at dawn, you will be brought out to the church and executed. Take them away.'

'Screams and shouts filled the air as the condemned were pushed across the piazza and down the steps to the cellar below the Mayor's office. I stood in the schoolhouse doorway shaking with fear, biting my lips in terror until they bled, clenching my fists so hard my fingernails dug into the palms of my hands. I was frozen in place, unable to move inside.

'I saw, as if in a nightmare, a soldier walking towards me shouting, but my senses had shut down. I was unable to understand him. He pointed his finger at me accusingly and yelled, 'Take her too. She must have known about the hidden radio.' He grabbed hold of me and pushed me down the steps into the Mayor's cellar.'

'The heavy wooden door was slammed shut and locked. Two soldiers stood outside all that day and night. The atmosphere inside the cellar was despairing, and threatening, as neighbour stared at neighbour, wondering who the informer was. Family feuds and neighbourly disputes were common in a small isolated village. People were pushing and shoving each other in that cramped enclosed space, pointing accusing fingers. There was little room to sit and only a small barred window provided air and light. Most of the villagers sat slumped on the floor or leant against the walls, too stunned to realise this was the last hours of their life. Some asked the priest to listen to their last confession, mumbling their sins into his ear. I crept over and stood in a corner alone but Padre Pietro managed to reach me.

"Try to stay calm, my dear. I must give my benediction to these poor people before they are shot. I have been thinking that in the confusion of the soldiers dragging these people out of the cellar, I will try to distract the Germans by falling down the steps as I am saying my prayers,' he had whispered gently taking my hands. 'I am old and have lived a full life. You have only just started. If you wait till last, I hope my distraction will allow you to slip into the alleyway next to the cellar steps. Then run as fast as you can out of the village and into the hills.'

'I could only nod, too shocked to reply. In between taking confessions, the priest stayed by me that night as we waited for the dawn light to pierce the tiny barred window. The villagers had sobbed and cried, huddled on the dirty floor or crouched in a corner. The priest continued to pray, requesting God's mercy to mitigate the fear and pain. A strong smell of urine had filled the cellar as an old couple, clutching each other in fear, had no longer been able to control themselves.

'After an endless night, the cellar door was unlocked and the villagers pushed outside into the sunlight. It had rained overnight, the cobblestones were gleaming and the air was crystal clear and bright, all sounds and smells amplified. They stumbled up the outside steps, clutching members of their family or clinging to the handrail.

'Slowly the cellar emptied leaving only Padre Pietro and me. I can vividly recall his whispered words as he bade me to stay hidden in the corner until I heard him crying out as he lost his footing on the steps. I heard the soldiers yelling as they herded the villagers across the piazza. I could see the soldier drag the priest up the steps, shouting at him as he stumbled and fell to his knees, bumping his head on the next step. The soldier continued to drag him up by his arms and pushed him to the villagers. The Padre lost his balance again and fell to the ground.

'I waited behind the cellar door, peering through the cracks in the wood, shivering with fright, my shawl wrapped around my shoulders for warmth and comfort. I saw someone help the Padre to stand up and wipe the blood on his head with a dirty rag. The soldiers were jabbing the points of their rifles into the backs of the prisoners outside to get the condemned crowd moving towards the church.

'I crept up the dark steps, and out of the cellar door left open in the confusion. I moved cautiously along the damp wall and peered over the last step. The condemned crowd had been roughly pushed away, the soldiers with their backs to me intent only on doing their cruel work. Their shouting and swearing covered any other noise as I crept up the last step, slid around the corner of the building and into the shadow of the alleyway.

'I remember stumbling down the stone steps outside the crumbling ramparts and hearing shouted commands, pleading voices and screams of terror. I was terrified and heartbroken, my body shaking with sobs of despair. A dog's howl pierced the torrid air. I heard a controlled volley of rifle fire and frantically scrambled into a muddy ditch. I knew then for certain that the priest and my friends had been killed. I cringed lower in the shallow water that filled the ditch, my arms huddled at my side, shivering uncontrollably, too frightened to move as I heard the dogs howling their fear.

'Hours later, when the sun had set behind the hills on that terrible day, I cautiously raised my head. I saw a few lights in the blackness that surrounded the village. I climbed out of the ditch, muddy and wet, slowly turned my back on the village, closing the door on my adolescent life. I stumbled down a goat track, unsure where I was going in the dark. I was shaking, exhausted and stunned and gasping so hard I thought it would be heard in the village.

'Hours later my legs were unable to support me and I sank to my knees on the edge of the track. I can still feel the tears and mud mingled on my face. In the deep silence of the countryside, I heard a dog howling again and again. An owl brushed past my head, its wings beating strongly as it rose from a nearby stone wall into the darkness. I was alone, homeless and terrified. I had lost my friends, my home, my job and had no idea how to continue living with the guilt, terror and sorrow. I could only think of the hopelessness of my future.'

Elena finishes speaking, the echoes of the terrifying past filling the silent kitchen. Several times Maria's disbelief and compassion shows on her face as she listens to the tragic story. She places her arm around Elena's shoulder to provide a measure of comfort and hands Elena a glass of water. Elena realises that the horror of these events has eased and that for many years now she has lived her days without constantly thinking of the family and friends she'd lost in Puglia. Their memory will always be in her mind but their faces have faded with time like old photographs.

'When I escaped from Caterna, I had nothing except the clothes I was wearing and an old blue cotton shawl. Everything I had was muddy and wet from lying in the ditch outside the village. I scrambled over the stony ground, running and stumbling, crouching at times to listen for any pursuit, my heart battering in my chest like a loose shutter. The low scrubby bushes scratched and tore my legs and the hem of my dress had been ripped. I looked up at the sky and saw it was clear, the stars, planets and the Milky Way whirling above, but no moon. I had no sense of direction or any clear thoughts other than to escape from the horror I had experienced. I sank down to my knees and prayed.'

Elena stops talking and looks up at Maria as she slowly emerges from the story of those dark days; she blinks in the late afternoon sunshine drifting through the window, and shakes herself to restore the present. Her back and knees ache with tension, and she grasps her cane tightly in her hands; feels tears moisten her cheeks.

'I can still remember every painful detail of the day of my escape, the dank odour of the cellar, the smell of the gunfire, the stink of the ditch I hid in, the texture of the mud that clung to my body and clothes as I slithered lower into it. I remember the dense silence after the gunfire stopped, my heart thudding so loud I thought I would be discovered.

'The next day I subconsciously walked back to my home village but there was no welcome or help there as my friend's family rejected me for fear the Germans would invade Mitorna and shoot them for sheltering me. I walked alone for days after that until I found shelter one night in a ruined stone hut. I was woken at dawn by the sound of sheep munching and crowding around the doorway. A farmer and his dog appeared in the middle of the flock, surprised to find me, a young girl sleeping alone and unprotected in that unpopulated area. He asked me what I was doing.

'I had difficulty understanding his dialect but managed to explain I was escaping from my village where the Germans had invaded and I needed to rest. The farmer allowed me to stay on his farm for three months, cautioning me to keep out of sight but there were no visitors. I started to feel stronger and calmer, able to think about a future. My muscles developed with the physical work and I became brown from the sun. I still had nightmares of being imprisoned in the Mayor's cellar and of being shot. The traumatic events in the village would never leave my head but slowly I learnt how to calm them. I grew from innocent adolescence to adulthood whilst I lived at the farm but still feel the burden of guilt that I escaped and have had the opportunity to live a long life with all its ups and downs, contentment and sadness.'

Maria gently reaches out and covers Elena's arm with her work-worn hands as they sit in silence. 'Why should you feel guilty?' she asks quietly.

'I don't really understand myself,' Elena sighs, swallowing several times. 'I have learnt to live with it and to block out memories of the past. Everything I experienced has made me stronger and more able to cope with the difficulties of life. '

Maria nods and replies, 'It has taken a lot of courage for you to live with your miraculous survival when others close to you have not, and to persist in living a normal life. Thank you for telling me about the tragedy of this village and your life. I understand how hard it is to talk about it. I am honoured that you feel able to confide in me. It explains much about the people in the village and their relationships with each other. They are so distrustful of strangers.

'My parents weren't shot but moved out of the village as they couldn't cope with the tragedy and sadness. I returned about 10 years ago when I met my husband at the market in a nearby town. I was not welcome here for many years. I felt uncomfortable and thought the locals did not like me. My husband tried to explain but he knew little about the past, having grown up elsewhere.

'In these ancient villages and buildings, the dead leave an echo, a substance that is almost tangible.' Maria stops talking and squeezes Elena's hand to show her understanding.

Exhausted from talking about the past, Elena wipes away a tear and rises slowly from the kitchen chair, arthritic bones clearly giving her pain as she stands. She smiles at Maria, 'I must leave now and return to my hotel. I arranged for a taxi to meet me outside the main archway. Thank you for sharing your pasta with me and your patience in listening to my memories. I fly back to my life in Australia in a few days so may never see you again.'

Maria leaves her chair; moves closer to envelop Elena in a warm embrace and kiss her cheeks.

'*Arrivederci. Andare con Dio,*' she says as she guides Elena out of the door and watches as she walks down the steps and over to the archway. The taxi is waiting and the driver opens the passenger door. Elena turns and waves to Maria and Lena who has just returned from playing in the piazza.

Childhood in Mitorna

In the hotel restaurant that evening, Elena eats a small dinner with a glass of local red wine then returns to her room. Though tired, she is unable to sleep. She piles the pillows behind her to support her back and lies staring into the darkness of the impersonal room. The present no longer feels real. Her mind drifts through the memories of her childhood in Mitorna. They are a jumble of words, feelings, images and scents. The misty faces of people she knew, some beloved, others unpleasant or threatening. In some ways it seems as if these experiences happened to another person, the things she'd done feeling unbelievable. Those experiences had changed the pattern of her life and set her on a completely different course, often lonely, sometimes frightening.

She remembers playing outside Mitorna in a deserted farmyard when she was six years old and hiding behind an old stone wall to avoid the village children, about nine or ten girls and boys of different ages who chased each other in and out of the ruined farm buildings, their natural playground. She was frightened of them for they tugged her hair and called her names, their non-malicious but persistent teasing because she had no family other than her grandparents who were old. Her mother died when she was three giving birth to her brother, who also died. Her father then emigrated with other villagers so she lived with her grandparents.

Elena remembers that, when the church bells rang at midday disturbing the stillness of the air and echoing the monastery bells across the valley, the children ran back to the village for their lunch. They leapt and jumped and tumbled over each other as they left the old buildings and clambered up to the hilltop village. She always stayed in hiding and waited until they had left the farmyard. In the echoing silence she recalls peering around the wall and, seeing that they had gone, scampering after them, hiding in a herd of goats. She was often late for lunch and her grandparents gently scolded her even though it was usually only pasta and herbs. Nonna made a weekly batch of orecchiette, the small shell-shaped pasta native to Puglia, and dried it in the sun on wooden trays. She served a sauce with it using seasonal vegetables like courgettes, aubergines, onions or broad beans which they grew themselves. Occasionally, in summer, there were small sweet tomatoes but in winter it was just herbs with the pasta or turnip tops.

Elena's grandparents cultivated two small fields outside the village walls, drying any spare produce in the sun or storing them in the cottage loft. Several olive trees in the fields yielded small green fruit which were bottled by Nonna. The earth was fertile in the valley below the village, a mixture of red and deep brown soil. Grandfather dug in chicken and cow manure to improve the soil.

In summer, it was dry and hot, the heat bouncing off the rocks. The ground was stony and parched, with thyme and sage plants scenting the air but struggling to grow. She usually sat in the shade of an old olive tree, the cicadas chirruping around her as she maybe teased an ant with a grass stalk. Other tiny insects chased each other over the stones and dried goat droppings. In the valley below, endless groves of olive trees survived despite the summer heat and the arid soil.

She reached the village, running very fast and surefooted across the piazza, down a shady alley and out the back to the remaining village walls where her grandparents lived in a small two-roomed cottage. It was cooler in the shadow of the walls and Elena cautiously entered the cottage. Tin spoons were laid on the table outside and the rough wooden benches pulled up either side.

'I'm back,' Elena shouted into the cottage.

'OK, OK,' Nonna replied grumpily. 'You're late.'

'I had to hide from the other children before I could come home.'

'Grow up, girl! You'll get worse treatment than they give you when you're older. Sit at the table and I'll call your grandfather. Let's eat, the pasta's hot.' Despite her brusque words, Nonna looked fondly at her granddaughter, patting the tousled dark curls that framed a plump childish face and scared dark eyes. Elena's clothes were, as usual, crumpled and dirty, a large hole in the elbow of her worn cardigan, grass and mud stains on her cotton dress with its small collar and flared skirt. Her dark stockings had slipped down into her muddy buttoned shoes. Nonna bent and kissed Elena's head as she pushed her towards the bench.

Elena scrambled into her place on the bench and picked up her spoon, her hands still grubby and sticky. Nonna's chickens scattered and the cow tethered at the side of the cottage lowed mournfully. Nonna brought out a steaming metal bowl of pasta with a few slices of salami and fennel. She spooned helpings onto the tin plates and filled the earthenware cups with fresh well water, calling to her husband as she did.

Elena's grandfather limped out, ruffled her curls with his calloused hand and placed his arm lightly on her shoulders. Although he smiled affectionately at her she noticed his eyes were shadowed and his lined forehead had a deep frown. He was tanned, stocky and wore heavy, laced, leather boots, checked shirt open at the neck, brown cotton trousers and a dusty beret. In winter, he draped an old blanket around his shoulders. His life was one of continual hard labour, struggling to grow vegetables in the stony soil, and finding fodder for their cow despite heat-filled days, thunderstorms and cold winter winds. His back was bent with the unrelenting physical work in the fields, carrying water, fodder and wood. As he waited for his meal, he picked at a piece of loose skin on his thumb and rubbed his hands together with a sound like sandpaper.

He didn't talk much but in her memories Elena felt there was always an aura of warmth and kindness surrounding him. He never complained but cheerfully accepted his life despite having arthritic knees, shoulders and hands. He cared deeply for her and took his responsibility for her upbringing seriously, sharing this with Nonna. He had a resonant voice and loved church music and his voice rang out clear and powerful in church services. They had sometimes all sung together in the evenings and Elena sang joyfully with him for she had a clear pure voice and had inherited his love of music.

Nonna seemed old to her as she was growing up. She wore her dusty black cotton dress that reached down to her scuffed leather boots, and a cardigan covered her shoulders. In summer, she replaced the boots with tattered sandals. She was thin and bony, her white hair scraped back under a black head scarf. Her brown, lined face had high cheekbones with bright black eyes surrounded by folds of skin. She had been very proud of her long-fingered hands when young but the nails were broken and dirty through gardening, the skin scratched and torn. Her hair had been night black until Elena's mother died, then it turned white as limestone. Her shoulders and back were bent, also through age and hard work, the skin on her arms and hands wrinkled and marked with scars, some not healing well as she aged.

Grandfather told Elena: 'When we were first married, she walked out to the fields and sang when her chores were finished. Sometimes I saw her skipping along in time to the music, her pretty face lifted to the sky, her dark hair swinging on her shoulders. I met her at the church choir as she loved religious songs, and she had a sweet voice and a deep feeling for music. She loved to sing nursery songs at your bedtime and encouraged you to clap the rhythm.'

Elena remembered sadly that, as she grew older and had less energy, Nonna stopped singing. Maybe there was less to sing about. Nonna was patient with her except when she deliberately hurt an insect, animal or child. Then she shouted, raised her hands and asked God to advise her how to deal with a naughty, unkind child. Kindness was the most important quality in Nonna's world, and God was remembered and evoked in all aspects of life. She was polite to the neighbours but never gossiped. Nonna's opinion was, as she often told Elena, 'You keep your private life to yourself and don't listen to gossip. In a close community, gossip can be a problem that leads to shouting matches or trouble between families.'

Nonna was born in the village to a family who owned a large piece of land outside the town walls. They had an olive grove, and a herd of goats. Her mother brought up six children single-handedly as her husband and five adult sons worked all daylight hours in the fields, but her sharp tongue kept them in order. Nonna helped her mother with the goats, milking them and making cheese.

Nonna told Elena that the family gathered in the olive grove at harvest time. 'We laid sheets on the ground and collected the fruit shaken down by my father and brothers who climbed into the trees. There was a picnic afterwards with scrawny chickens cooked on open wood fires served with raw vegetables and freshly cooked bread. There was rough local red wine for the men and watered down for the women. Someone would bring an accordion or a flute and everyone danced in and out of the trees.'

Nonna's family had lived in the same cottage where Elena grew up. It had two rooms and a loft reached by a steep wooden ladder. The loft had planks nailed across the beams and Nonna told Elena that the youngest children slept on floor mats. It was lit by a gap in the roof tiles which was covered in bad weather by a wooden shutter. One room was used as a kitchen and eating room for the family.

Her parents slept in the other room on an old brass bed with a crocheted, multi-coloured blanket and a prickly straw mattress. Nonna said the older children preferred to sleep in the fields in summer and in the goat shed during the winter. There was no glass in the two tiny cottage windows and only handmade wooden shutters to protect from the winter weather. It was dark inside as the only light came from the constantly burning fire used for cooking, and one kerosene lamp. An iron frame for the cooking pot hung over the fire.

Meals were basic: sometimes a wild rabbit stew or a piece of bread spread with oil. A few tomatoes and withered apples stored over wintertime finished the meal. There were no toilets or washing facilities in or near the cottage. The children washed irregularly in tin baths filled from the nearby village pump. The water was cold even on hot summer days. Laundry days and bathing days were avoided as much as possible. There were several water pumps in the village where local women queued each morning to gossip and collect water in tin bowls or buckets.

Over time, Nonna's siblings married and left the village. Nonna, as the youngest, was expected to look after her aged parents and the land. When they died she remained in the cottage and married Elena's grandfather. They had two daughters, one of whom moved away from the village. The youngest had been Elena's mother who died in childbirth.

Elena remembers Nonna had said her mother was a sweet-natured girl. 'She liked to help me in the kitchen and had a joyous sense of fun. She played tricks on us, like putting salt in my coffee or changing Grandfather's socks so they didn't match. She even stuffed his shoes with a handful of messy olives. He wasn't amused as the juice stained his feet for days. She was the sunshine in my life and when she died I cried for weeks. Grandfather was very sympathetic as he had lost a brother in a childhood accident. He said that the sadness became bearable over time.'

Lost in her past life, Elena hardly notices the large cloud obliterating the sun and darkening the hotel bedroom. It has been an emotional day talking to Maria and Lena and now she is tired. She goes out to the balcony and sits watching the sun go down, listening to the sounds of children playing and dogs barking. She misses the exuberance of Italian family life, the murmur of distant voices as the old men gather in the local café. As darkness falls, the streets fill with people shopping, meeting friends, laughing and drinking. The delicious smell of onion and garlic cooking for the evening pasta meal makes Elena feel hungry so she orders room service and a glass of local red wine. She wants to spend the evening with her memories of childhood, cherish the good and exorcise the bad.

The Blackshirt Invasion of Mitorna 1932

Her birthplace, Mitorna, was in a very poor area that never recovered from the Great War and the emigration afterwards when many local inhabitants left for a new life – any life – in America or Australia. After World War II, wealthy landowners employed gangs of day labourers, *braccianti*, including children as young as eight. Peasants and day labourers didn't earn enough for basic sustenance; meat was rare and only local vegetables available. A life of dire poverty was the norm, and many children died young of starvation or disease from malnourishment.

Throughout the 1930s, this poverty became worse due to the world economic depression. In the 1920s, scattered uprisings of peasants prevailed but these were destined to fail as they carried only spades and had no weapons. In Puglia, landowners joined together to fight the violence in the name of Fascism in order to purge their lands of peasant leaders. Bari was a Fascist stronghold and Blackshirt gangs freely roamed the countryside.

Elena remembers one summer day in her childhood, when her family were eating their midday meal outside the cottage. They heard shouting and tramping of booted feet which shattered the heavy torpid silence. She was seven when the Blackshirts invaded Mitorna. Nonna had told her, 'Run and hide in the hills … quickly now. Gangs of Mussolini's Blackshirt soldiers have been seen in this area. They have been burning down villages. The priest said they are vicious.'

Elena had scooped the last of her pasta into her mouth, gulped greedily and scooted along the walls and down the outside steps. She peered round the archway then slid down the hillside into some bushes, and crouched there panting and trembling with fear. She heard breaking glass, crashing, shouting and screaming in the village. She pushed her fists into her mouth and bit down to stop crying out.

A squad of Blackshirts had attacked the village, intent on humiliating and terrorising the villagers. They smashed and destroyed property. Elena heard a fierce argument, followed by a gunshot and a piercing scream. She crouched down lower in her hiding place; saw other children scramble away from the village to various hiding places. Two more gunshots echoed around the village followed by harsh laughter, then booted feet were heard crunching over broken utensils and glass as the squad departed down the hill.

Elena could just see them as she cowered in the bushes. They were clean shaven, tall, muscular young men with grim faces and clenched jaws. They marched with a military posture in a tight column and wore black shirts embellished with a badge that reflected the sunlight, black loose jodhpurs held up with a wide belt and buckle and tucked into black leather jack boots. Some of the men had guns on the belts fastened around their hips; others carried wooden clubs, banners and flags. They were led by a man wearing a military peaked cap.

She waited a long time after they had marched away, hot and thirsty, trembling and too frightened to move, bitten by ants that had ran over and left small red marks on her legs while she crouched so still. Her bare shoulders and arms were sunburnt and scratched by the prickles of the bushes; her tummy churned with the half-eaten pasta.

Finally, the heated air had settled into its normal summer tightness, as if all the flora and fauna were melded together; not even a leaf had shaken or a grass stalk waved. Two birds of prey were circling over the village. The sun continued to beat mercilessly down on her head and the cicadas clattered endlessly and unfeelingly. Elena glimpsed a small boy creep from his hiding place and crawl over the rough stony ground to the village archway where he disappeared inside. The silence was disturbed by a low keening sound drifting from the village.

Soon other children crept cautiously out of their hiding places and crawled up the stones and into the archway. A pall of black smoke drifted up from the village. Still Elena waited and waited as she felt so frightened. After a long time, she crawled out from the bushes and cautiously slid up to the village walls and the steps. As she peered out of the archway, the full horror of what had happened spread out before her.

In the piazza lay three bodies, her Nonna bent over one, wailing with horror and despair. The relatives of the other bodies knelt around her, wiping tears on their sleeves, keening their grief. Dead chickens had been bashed against the walls until their feathers were loosened and fluttered to the ground, a dead dog and two dead pigs lay by the church. One building had been set on fire, the flames viciously leaping up through the dry timber roof structure and reaching into the sky, then leaping across to the adjoining building. The air was filled with sparks and embers, the metallic smell of gunshot and blood, and the faint odour of putrefaction as the heat trapped in the piazza started to decompose the bodies.

Children crowded together inside the archway, hands over their mouths, tears pouring down their cheeks, unable to express their horror. The older ones had grabbed hold of the smaller children to still their shaking and comfort them. Elena sidled across and the oldest girl held out her hand to take hers. Elena was unable to move. It was impossible for her to walk across the piazza to Nonna. The body she was keening over was no longer her laughing, spirited grandfather.

Huddling together for a long time in the shadow, the children watched as villagers stood up and brought cloths to cover the bodies. The dead animals were collected in a wooden cart. The men lifted each of the cloth-covered bodies in turn and carried them into the family home to be washed and prepared for burial and mourning.

A line of women filled buckets with water from the nearby pump to throw onto the blazing building. The fire seemed to lose its fury as the wood was consumed and the next building seemed fairly intact except for the roof – there was no wind to fan the flames. When the piazza was cleared, the women brought pails of soapy water and brushes and tried to clean the cobblestones under the merciless sun as it sank behind the buildings.

Dark shadows blurred the scene when the children's parents walked slowly across to the archway, took their hands and led them inside their homes. Nonna had walked across to Elena and hugged her briefly. She had changed, her brown, lined face settled into deep grooves of grief around her eyes and mouth, her eyes cloudy and wet. Her dress was stained with blood and dirt and her hands shook.

'We'd better get you home,' she said, laying a gnarled hand on her shoulder to guide her across the piazza.

Nonna pulled her roughly into their cottage where Grandfather was placed on the table covered by a sheet from head to toe. She tersely told her to go to bed and stay there.

'Are you hurt?' Nonna asked.

Elena shook her head.

'I'll talk to you in the morning.'

Shocked into silence, comfortless and trembling, Elena climbed the ladder; lay on her pallet and pulled the single cotton cover over her head. She tried to shut out the memory of the bodies in the piazza. Somewhere in the distance, she heard the hysterical barking of a dog and the wailing of a small baby.

She knew her grandmother was awake, that Nonna sat at the table in the dim lamplight, head in her hands, shoulders shaking. The frightening, long night ended for Elena when Nonna woke her at dawn, drained of emotion, her face stained with tears. Nonna took her hand and explained what had happened. Her grandfather's body had been removed from the kitchen and the table covered in oilcloth.

'Your grandfather was trying to reason with the Blackshirts to prevent them shooting other villagers. He was always a proud man and yesterday he was very brave. We had known each other all our lives; we depended on each other as we had no other family.'

Nonna clutched Elena to her, trying to control the desperate grief that shook her body. They sat together in silence on the old wooden bench Grandfather had made years before, Elena feeling hollow inside; she placed her head on the table, tears streaming on her arms. Nonna placed her arm around Elena's shoulders and patted her gently.

'We have to manage by ourselves now,' she said, wiping away the tears. 'There's no other way. Let's get some water from the well to wash.'

Elena remembers sadly that, after the Blackshirt massacre, a long period of grieving ensued before the village calmed down. The faint blood marks on the cobblestones were a constant reminder, as was the huge gap where the building had burned down. The Marconis who lived there moved away to live with family in a nearby town. The Benecottis who lived next door could not stay in their damaged home so had taken their few undamaged possessions to the nearby ruined farm buildings and made a primitive shelter with stones from a crumbling wall and a rough slatted roof.

The old men still gathered and smoked in the café yet there was little laughter and no joyful cries to each other for Elena's grandfather had been the life and soul of the group with his silly stories and jokes. Many young men emigrated to search for a safer and better life, and never returned with their vigour and money.

Elena and Nonna continued living day to day, missing the grandfather in every job, every day their souls saddened by the loss of his presence. His pointless death had cut into the whole fabric and purpose of their lives and, for Nonna, opened the door to old age. Her bright eyes dulled and the stoop of her shoulders became more pronounced. Every evening at dusk they visited the tiny cemetery outside the village walls and sat by his grave.

Elena told him about her day and what she had learned at school. Nonna had rested her head on Elena's shoulder and softly cried.

'It has been so very hard without him, Elena. But I have thanked God every day that I have you beside me for company and comfort. You always remind me so much of your mother but you have an aura of sadness around you that she never had.'

Nonna took a long deep breath as her voice broke with sorrow. She squeezed her eyes to stem the flow of tears that came so readily to her these days.

Elena cried, 'Oh, Nonna, it's so unfair and hard. Every day I want Grandfather to put his arms around me and wink at me. The cottage is empty and sad without him and he is not around to help me with my school work.'

Elena, at this time, started hating her father for deserting her and causing Nonna additional suffering by providing no financial support. She could hardly remember him. Vivid dreams frightened her so much she woke screaming and trembling, thinking that a Blackshirt soldier was in the room, bending over her, pointing a gun at her head. Nonna clutched Elena to her breast, patting her back to soothe her, humming a soft lullaby to calm her into sleep.

The summer passed and their sorrow filled the air around them. Autumn brought chill winds and showers to the parched land. Then winter arrived with frosty nights and cold rain, and the threat of another invasion by the Blackshirts receded. The villagers continued with their daily lives, planting winter vegetables in the fertile land.

Elena helped her grandmother feed their chickens and the cow. She worked in their vegetable garden as Nonna became more weary and frail – she never regained her zest for life after her husband was shot. Yet Nonna still encouraged Elena to learn everything at school and she bargained for old books with spare vegetables at the local market. Elena found comfort in her books and searched for something that would give purpose to her life, as without her grandfather, school work seemed pointless and her future bleak.

Mitorna 1932-1942

Growing up in a small village, Elena had been aware of the pity of parents and the other schoolchildren as well as the snide comments about her old clothes. The children were unkind and excluded her from their street games. She seemed to be always searching for an authoritative father-figure after her grandfather was killed.

She longed to be normal like the neighbours' children who welcomed their papas when they returned home from the fields with shouts of glee, asking to play football in the street. Nonna was the centre of Elena's life and the only example to follow. She had no male role model. Their meals were silent and hurried with none of the warmth and laughter of their neighbours. Occasionally Sophia, a neighbour, brought a pot of soup to share with them and talked with Nonna about the old days.

A feeling of insecurity and inadequacy developed in Elena as she grew. She clung to her Nonna when they left the village and visited the nearest town, riding in the village donkey cart to buy boots and material to make Elena new clothes.

In the early spring a new family moved into the village with a girl named Marina who was Elena's age. They became good friends and ran hand in hand around the village, giggling and laughing. Soon the crying of a new baby was heard as Marina's family had their second child. The two girls enjoyed minding the baby. Pietro and Angelina were kind to Elena, often inviting her to eat with them.

Padre Stepano provided the younger children with a basic education in the church school. When they were eight, they were taken every day in the donkey cart to the next village, Barga, where a small school provided further education for several years until family circumstances made their parents withdraw them to work on the land. Additional education cost money and time.

When Elena was eight, she joined on the donkey cart to Barga. The boys wore short trousers and heavy boots, and sat on the back of the cart swinging their skinny legs. The ride was great fun for the children as they tumbled and pushed each other when the cart rocked from side to side on the stony path. Some days they sang popular tunes, although not the bawdy ones that the carter bawled out when he'd had a glass or two of wine at lunch.

After finishing her dinner in her room, Elena rises to gaze out the hotel window into the darkness of the Puglian countryside. Few lights glimmer nearby and a dog barks roughly, disturbing the peaceful night. She finds it hard to sleep some nights and at home plays her opera discs. Her favourite is *Tosca*, and she remembers explaining to Bill, her first husband, 'The painter sings to Tosca in the last hour of his life – it is so passionate. My favourite tenor is Franco Corelli. He sings the aria with so much feeling.'

Elena hums the aria quietly as she returns to her bed, still unable to sleep after the exhausting but cathartic day in Caterna. She hears the dawn chorus of birds through her unshuttered hotel window and memories of her childhood swirl thick and fast back into her head. It seems that talking to Maria has opened all the barriers she had built to shut out the past. The shadowy faces and figures of her friends drift by as she tries to capture the special memories of her childhood, attending baptisms and weddings, singing a solo in church or at a wedding.

She remembers that, as a child, life in the village was mostly pleasant and uneventful. She made friends with the other children going to school in Barga and recalls playing games in the streets. The villagers eked out a living off the land or sold handicraft and produce at the local village markets. Most of the families had chickens and a cow. Food was scarce, mostly self-grown. Occasionally, the old men went shooting in search of rabbits.

Elena's mouth waters when she remembers the rich taste of rabbit stew, flavoured with wild garlic and herbs. Other memories she had pushed into the recesses of her mind begin to emerge, the images clear and vivid as if they had happened only weeks before. She is surprised how these memories bring a feeling of comfort and warm familiarity, and reflects back to the hilarious time with the donkey cart.

The carter had bought a young donkey in Barga and tied it to the back of the cart. When the children clambered into the cart for their ride home from school, it had bucked and brayed, tugging at the rope round its neck. Halfway through the ride, the donkey had bitten through the rope and cantered away, kicking up its hooves as it galloped across the stony plain.

'Stop, stop! The donkey's got loose!' shouted Marco, the eldest boy as he tapped the sleeping carter on the shoulder – the man had been drinking as usual.

The carter stopped the cart, lumbered down from the front seat and set off in pursuit of his donkey, swearing vociferously.

The children raced after him, leaving their school bags on the cart, the carter, fat and old, soon overtaken as he shouted, 'Try and head him off. Some of you run in front and others go to one side. I don't want a broken leg as I've just paid good money for it.'

He sweated copiously and wiped his face with his shirt. The children, enjoying the fun, tried to turn the donkey around and pull it back to the cart. After about ten minutes the carter gave up and collapsed onto a boulder, breathing heavily, leaving the children to chase the donkey.

'Look, there's a stone wall. Let's chase him to there,' shouted Marco.

The donkey, seeing the wall ahead, stopped abruptly, brayed loudly and put his head down to butt the wall, then kicked up its hooves.

'Now, some of you circle him and the others get behind the wall to try and catch him with this rope noose,' the carter gasped as he caught up. After much jostling and shoving, the eldest boys edged round to encircle the donkey while
others crept behind the wall with the rope.

The carter followed and after several attempts managed to get the noose around the animal's neck. The boys helped tug the donkey back to the cart where the carter re-tied the rope. The children scrambled up onto the cart, avoiding the kicking hooves and biting mouth. When they arrived back at the village their mothers were waiting anxiously in a group near the archway.

'Mamma, mamma, the donkey got loose and we had to chase it around the plain. It was fun and the carter nearly fell over. It took such a long time to catch it,' Marco explained.

'Nonna, I got my new boots dusty in the chase but it was fun,' Elena called with a laugh. Her dress was dirty and her hair untidy.

The mothers' relieved smiles were plastered on their faces and they marched their kids off to wash and eat.

Old Francesco had lived in the village all his life and loved to carve wood to make small flutes for the village children. He taught them how to breathe into the mouthpiece, cover the holes with the tips of their fingers and produce a pleasant sound. At the beginning, the wailing sound of the children practising their flutes filled the evening air after school.

'Take a deep breath and then ease it out gently into the mouthpiece,' Francesco coached patiently. 'Place your fingers like this.'

Marco, Elena and several other children soon became adept at making a tune with Francesco's tuition. As Marco improved, he started leaping around playing the flute like the Pied Piper. He echoed Francesco's words 'Breathe in, breathe out gently, put your fingers just like this,' he cried between songs, whirling around the piazza. They improvised and tried to copy the songs they'd heard on the radio with much hilarity and discordant notes.

'It's dreadful,' Marco yelled after their first attempt. 'It sounds more like wailing cats than music.' He mimicked the sound, prancing around like a cat, howling at the sky. Soon about five or six children were seen most evenings winding around the alleyways, through the piazza, chasing each other and trying to flick the drips of moisture from the flutes around. Elena loved playing the flute to her Nonna who sang with her.

One evening the carter brought back an old wooden guitar. Pietro, the grocer, repaired it and after weeks of trial and error, managed to strum a simple tune. Using some old tin cans with cured goatskin stretched across to make simple drums, the children now had a small band. One winter they were asked to play in the church for Christmas and visited Barga to play with their school band.

Travelling by donkey cart, the children joined the school band to walk through the village playing traditional songs. A crowd of followers soon gathered. Women set up tables in the piazza with cloths and candles and made hot chocolate and biscotti – it was a magical time for Elena and the children. The night was cold and crisp and the arc of the sky above the village filled from end to end with glittering stars. A few flakes of snow fell and dusted the stone walls. The children rode home in the cart, singing songs, a few stray flakes of snow caught on their coats and hair.

At this time, Nonna encouraged Elena to grow her black curly hair so it could flow over her shoulders. She made new clothes for her as Elena's slender body developed womanly curves. Her eyes remained dark brown and bright, her face shaped by high cheekbones and a pointed chin. She had inherited her Nonna's long-fingered hands.

Elena remembers how she enjoyed being with Marina's family, feeling the comforting warmth of a real home, how the family took pleasure in mothering her and teaching her simple tasks such as sewing and cooking, which Nonna was too tired to do after her hard labouring. She was, however, grateful that her granddaughter received education in home and academic subjects.

Some evenings, Elena and Marina played ball in the piazza with the other children, shouting and encouraging each other to score goals by kicking the ball through the archway.

'You girls aren't too bad at football,' Marco told them. He was always the leader of their group.

'You boys need to be more careful of kicking too high and breaking windows,' Elena retorted, giggling. She liked Marco with his good looks and sense of fun.

'The problem with girls is that they're always worrying about their dresses getting dirty and torn. It's impossible to tackle them,' Pietro shouted.

'At least they don't cry when they fall over,' Marco replied. 'Come on … we have half an hour before the sun goes down.'

At times, the children wandered around outside the village playing hide and seek, or treasure hunts searching for unusually shaped or coloured stones, or wild flowers. Once, Marco found part of a rusty old sword which he pretended was Roman.

Marco's father, Antonio, was an educated man and taught Science and Maths at the school in Barga. He paid a tutor living in Barga to give Marco extra tuition on Saturdays to extend his education. Nonna encouraged Elena to participate and they cycled to and fro, swapping tales and keeping each other company.

'I love the stories about the Romans, their battles, armour and chariots, and how they conquered Italy and France, and their engineering ability. I can imagine them marching over the hills to the sea, getting in wooden boats and rowing to the south coast of France,' Marco said enthusiastically on the way home.

'I prefer the descriptions of their clothes and food and how they lived. They had water plumbing and proper toilets,' Elena mused with envy.

The peaceful years passed and, although her friendship with Marina continued, she spent a lot of time with Marco, singing and dreaming about the future. They often sat on the stone village walls in the evenings and talked about where they would go and what work they could find in other villages.

The village population continued to decline over the years as moving between villages was discouraged by the Government in Rome and there were few work opportunities on the land. The young men who emigrated rarely returned and, if they did, they just collected their family members and left again.

At this time, after a short illness, Nonna died in her sleep and Elena was alone. She had nowhere else to live so continued to sleep in the stone cottage, but she ate most of her meals with either Marina's family or Marco's. She was determined that one day she would leave Mitorna and find work in another village or town. This she had talked over with Marina's and Marco's families.

Marco's father, Antonio, suggested, 'I could ask at the school where I work or maybe a local shopkeeper wants some help.'

Marina's father said, 'I will speak with Padre Stepano. He knows you are intelligent and have an ongoing curiosity in life and in new ideas. The Padre knows many of the priests in the villages around here. He might know of some clerical work for you.'

Caterna 1942

A knock on her hotel bedroom door rouses Elena and she is surprised to see the morning sun is rising in a bright blue sky, shedding a rosy light on small drifting clouds. She must have slept a little despite her vivid memories. She rises to open the door; takes the tray laden with croissant, fruit and orange juice from the waiter. She opens the French doors and places the tray on the balcony table, savouring the view of wooded hills and the sun's rays highlighting the land's gentle curves. In the street below, children are running to school, shouting at each other, and the mumble of voices drifts up from the hotel café.

As she eats her breakfast, she remembers the evening in 1942 when she talked about her future with the local priest.

She had been sitting on the wooden bench outside her cottage, mending a cotton shirt in the last of the sunlight. Her black hair was tied back with string, her bare brown legs she stretched out. Padre Stepano, frail and uncertain in his walking, thoughtfully flapped across the piazza in his dusty worn sandals, his black soutane crumpled and creased with age, his hat pressed on his head. He had little hair on his head but abundant growth on his face, and always had a welcoming smile for the villagers.

He collapsed on the old wooden bench next to her.

As his breathing steadied, he said, 'My dear, sad as I am that you want to leave our village, I understand and encourage you. I think there is an opportunity for you to work in Caterna. My priest friend there told me the head teacher and the Mayor can offer you clerical work and you can live in a small room in the school house. This is your chance to set out into the world. You leave no family behind and your friends may leave the village too as they seek work. What do you think?'

Elena stopped sewing and sat in silence, too stunned to reply immediately, and fully aware of the great gulf of the unknown future ahead of her. She knew Barga because of attending school there but found it hard to imagine how she would manage without her friends and their families in a new town. And could she do the work?

Padre Stepano, sensing her uncertainty, patted her hand, shuffled his sandaled feet and said, 'I understand this will be a significant change in your life. My parents sent me to the local monastery to study and become a priest when I was sixteen. Life was so dramatically different, strange and scary.

'For the first time I slept, ate and spent my days with other young people. Not once have I ever regretted the opportunity for a better future. Please take this chance, my dear, as you are too capable and intelligent just to remain in this village and marry.'

Elena gulped several times after listening to the priest. She looked over the priest's shoulder into the piazza and knew that she was ready to start a new life.

'Can I think it over tonight, please?' she asked.

'Of course. I will come tomorrow morning for your answer.'

After a sleepless night, Elena decided this was her best chance to leave Mitorna and poverty behind and earn some money. She told the Padre next morning that she would take the work.

'I will leave here and make a success of it so you and everyone in this village will be proud of me.'

'Bene, bene and you know my thoughts and blessings go with you. I suggest that you start in a week's time. You can go in the donkey cart and take your bicycle with you and your clothes. That way you have little time to change your mind but time to clear your house, pack your belongings and say goodbye to your friends,' he said.

Elena hugged the old priest and, after he had left, sat a while longer on the old wooden bench her grandfather had made, feeling excited about the future and sadness for the life she was leaving behind.

A week later, Elena lifted her tapestry bag filled with clothes into the back of the donkey cart and placed it alongside the cardboard box containing personal items that Nonna had left her. A few neighbours kissed her and wished her good luck then she climbed into the back, sat on a hay bale and pulled her bag and box around her. While she felt sad saying goodbye to her friend Marina and her family, who had supported her after Nonna died, she was excited at the opportunity to move to a new town and improve her clerical skills while working for the Mayor and a schoolteacher. Marina gave her a tiny, carved wooden box to keep treasures in and promised to visit when she could.

As the donkey pulled the cart away, Elena looked back at her friends, waved and wiped away her tears.

The cart stopped at the village archway and a man in dark clothing and a felt hat jumped into the front seat beside the carter. Even though it was early morning, the sun was warm and a gentle breeze blew. Elena knew it would take about two hours to reach Caterna.

The cart lurched from side to side on the rough track, and she hung on to her bag and put the box between her feet to keep it from sliding around. As the countryside rolled on, she noted the crumbling stone walls lining the track, the few isolated farms, fields cultivated with ground crops such as beans and tomatoes, and others that were abandoned to wild olive and cactus. Fig and almond trees bordered the roadside and small bright green lizards skittered swiftly over lichen-covered rocks and dry, stone walls.

Puglia was a feudal farming region, rearing sheep and keeping cattle for working at the plough, and for providing milk and cheese until Mussolini decreed the production of grain, olives and wine must be increased to meet his policy of self-sufficiency in the 1920s. The area grew most of the wheat used for producing Italy's pasta, olive oil and red wine. Before this period, many Pugliesi families had emigrated north, abandoning their smallholdings and homes in search of food and paid work. Young men left towns and villages to escape the brutal life of basic farming or to fight for their country in the two world wars.

After an hour, the cart stopped in front of a *masseria* (farmhouse) surrounded by cultivated vineyards and olive groves. The carter climbed down, swigged from a stone bottle, and wiped his mouth with a dirty hand. The other traveller sat still, head down, face hidden by his hat. He did not look around or acknowledged her.

Wanting to stretch her legs, Elena jumped down from the cart also and walked about, stood gazing at walled village on a hill in the distance, its church spire and tower rising above the closely packed rooftops. A few minutes later, the carter returned and told her to get back on the cart, then he climbed into the front seat, shouted at the donkey and waved a stick to encourage it to move. The cart churned up the dusty track and the wind blew bits of sand and grit over Elena. She pulled a scarf over her mouth to protect it.

Doubts about what she was doing mixed with nervous anticipation of her future. By noon, the carter pointed to Caterna in the distance. Small market gardens and rows of vines surrounded its base and a few bent figures worked in the fields. A stone wall surrounded most of it with a ruined castle to the north east. Many of the buildings had flat roofs and were closely packed together on the hillside, probably for protection from invaders. The castle was small compared to the string of defensive castles built in the area by the Holy Roman Emperor, Frederick II in the thirteenth century. Caterna dated back to the colonisation by the Mycenaen Greeks in the eighth century BC. It continued to be lived in over the centuries by the Romans and, in the Middle Ages, had flourished as a small trading post for the harvesting of olives and citrus fruits. At this time merchants financed the building of a distinctive church in the centre of the village as proof of their wealth. It had local limestone walls, carved door arches, a high wooden roof and stained-glass windows. From the top of the town the surrounding Murge plateau sloped down to the narrow coastal plains of the Adriatic Sea.

The donkey cart stopped at the entrance to the town to allow the other passenger to alight. He'd not spoken a word throughout the journey, his wide brimmed hat hiding his face. The carter, who recognised Elena from taking her on school trips, shook his head and muttered, 'An unpleasant traveller, but he paid me well and that's what matters most.' He smiled at Elena and said he would take her direct to the Mayor's office.

The cart wound its way up narrow cobbled streets lined with tall stone buildings, some with flower pots placed on window ledges or in doorways. The route was just wide enough for the cart to pass through as it had deep stone gullies on either side for drainage. Doors opened straight onto the street with a stone cover for house occupants to walk over the drainage gullies.

Flights of stairs disappeared into the gloom and lines of washing hung overhead. Two women leaned out of upstairs windows to gossip; three children ran down the stairs in one building, almost colliding with the cart, and jumped over the gully. The smell of garlic and onions mixed with sewage pervaded the alleys. A rusty bicycle was propped against an open door and a cat lay stretched out in the sunshine.

The carter was familiar with the town and the donkey trudged slowly up the cobbled lanes ignoring the washing hung overhead between the buildings. It was airless and the carter constantly wiped his face with a dirty cloth and flapped at flies clustering round the donkey's eyes. After fifteen minutes the road opened out onto a cobbled, square piazza surrounded by tall buildings with ancient stone arcades underneath. The stone church, with its tall tower and a distinctive porch, sat imposingly on the opposite corner, stone pots of flowers placed randomly in front of it and around the piazza.

The carter turned the cart to the right and stopped outside a three-storey building where an impressive set of steps led to the main entrance. The Italian flag hung outside and waved in the breeze. A young woman stood on the steps of the Mayor's office and walked to the cart when it stopped.

'*Buongiorno*. Are you Elena Rossi from Mitorna? My father is the Mayor and I'm married to the school teacher. You will be working for them. My name is Lucia. I'll help you unload your belongings and take you to the Mayor.'

Elena handed her tapestry bag and cardboard box to Lucia then jumped down from the cart. She looked around the piazza with interest, thanked the carter and held out her hand to Lucia.

'*Buongiorno*. I am pleased to meet you.' Elena followed Lucia up the steps and into the Mayor's office where she was introduced to the Senor Bastia.

He explained that he needed clerical assistance with administration tasks such as typing letters and village bulletins. Senor Bastia said he could provide her with a room in the school house next door where Lucia lived with Andrea, her husband, the school teacher. Elena thanked him, picked up her belongings and followed Lucia next door. Lucia pushed open the front door and showed Elena the steep wooden stairs that led to a bright airy room in the attic. A small dormer window in the eaves, that was fitted with battered wooden shutters, was pushed open to let in the warm breeze. Elena had to duck her head where the ceiling slanted against the roof line.

The room was simply furnished with a single iron bed and a thin mattress. A clean sheet and a bright cotton cover lay on the bed. A scratched wooden table and chair was placed under the window that overlooked the piazza, and a rickety brown cupboard for clothes leaned against one stone wall. The plain calico curtains wafted in the breeze coming through the open window. A small, framed print hung over the bedhead, and a wooden crucifix sat on the opposite wall. A cloudy mirror on the wall nearby reflected the doorway. The bedsprings creaked when she sat on it, and so did the floorboards under the blue and white striped cotton rug. Lucia had placed a tiny jar of wild flowers on the table so the room looked fresh and welcoming.

'I'll leave you to unpack and then come down to the kitchen. Andrea is at school and will be back for lunch. We'll take a little walk after the afternoon siesta to show you the village and introduce you to the neighbours. I hope you'll be happy here,' Lucia said cheerfully.

'Grazie, Lucia. I'm looking forward to starting work with Signor Bastia and your husband. It will be nice to meet some locals.'

'Most mornings I work in our fields and we eat our own vegetables. We have chickens and a cow, and get fresh water from the village pump in the centre of the piazza for washing. I have put a washbowl and towels in your room. Do you need soap?' Lucia asked.

Her nervousness returning, her excitement having dissipated during the uncomfortable journey, Elena hoped the Mayor would find the quality of her work acceptable. Padre Stepano had assured her his friend, the priest, would help her settle in and meet some townsfolk. Elena unpacked her belongings from the tapestry bag and put them in the wardrobe; she washed the dust from the road from her face and hands and descended the stairs to the kitchen where Lucia was cooking.

'Will you be comfortable here?' Lucia asked and Elena nodded.

Andrea had moved a school bench and table outside the house for Elena to sit and sew in the evenings. Across the piazza stood the ancient church whose old bells rang at 7 am, midday and 6 pm.

Elena enjoyed working two days per week for Signor Bastia. He was cheerful and took his duties lightly. He told her he disliked the constant paperwork and found the government rules and regulations tedious. He needed Elena to type official letters and public notices, correct his grammar and spelling, arrange postage, file the documents and manage the stationery. The only problem was that Signor Bastia liked to place his hand on her back as she worked or put an arm around her shoulders. He watched her as she sat down and pulled her skirt over her knees. And she was always asked to stop work and wait outside when he received calls on the old wind-up telephone that sat on his desk.

Middle-aged and plump, with thick dark hair shading to grey at the sides, he kept his hair long to give him the look of an artist. A local school teacher for many years before being elected as Mayor, he enjoyed the social prestige of being Mayor and wearing smart clothes. He ensured his hands and nails were always clean for when he shook hands with government officials, and he encouraged Elena and the villagers to participate in local events such as religious fetes and parades, cake and bread-making competitions for which he was the judge.

The other important person in the village was Padre Pietro, the village priest for over fifty years. Almost as round as tall, with very little hair on his head, he was a cheery man with bright eyes and a great sense of fun. In his younger days, after he had delivered a particularly meaningful sermon, he had skipped from the church to his house when he thought no-one was watching.

He had endless patience when hearing people's problems, chiding them gently rather than allocating a religious penance. And he firmly believed that goodness and kindness brought out the best in people, and it did in his parish. Occasionally he had been heard to use a swear word to describe a particular problem but never to his God. He was always involved in Caterna events and festivities.

A sly competitiveness existed between the Mayor and Padre Pietro regarding whose public notices were grammatically correct and the most interesting. The Padre's notices were pinned weekly to the church door and often contained repetitive or conflicting information on local affairs compared to the Mayor's.

Two days a week Elena worked in the school with Andrea teaching the little children to read and write. The school was a stone building with one large room, tall windows on the sides, a high vaulted roof, and an oak floor. The room was cold in winter despite the wood burning stoves placed at each end, but in summer, with some of the shutters closed, the room was pleasantly cool and shady. The younger children sat with Elena at one end while Andrea instructed the older ones in maths and basic science. Most of the children left school at eleven years of age to work in the fields with their parents, learning to plough and plant crops. Each family owned a few strips of land outside the village in which they grew vegetables and grain. Most plots had chickens, a pig or two, and a cow.

After lunch, at the end of the school day, Elena taught the small children to sing folk tunes. She wrote the words of the songs on the blackboard and encouraged them to join in and clap. Some days she taught the children to dance the tarantella, the local folk dance – traditionally used to cure the bite of a spider called the *lycosa tarentula*. Remembering the fun she had as a child playing in the Mitorna brass band, Elena talked with Andrea about starting one in Caterna.

'I know there is a tradition for brass bands in Puglia. In Mitorna some of the instruments we played were home-made like a drum and a whistle. We could talk to Enrico, the carpenter, and ask him to help us?' Elena asked Andrea at dinner that evening.

'I think that's a great idea as many of the children enjoy music at church. Matteo has an old guitar he could repair. I'll ask him and Enrico on Saturday when they're at the cafe.'

'And I'll ask Padre Pietro to contact the priest at Mitorna to speak with Marco, the leader of the brass band in the village, for advice. Maybe Padre Pietro could ask them to ride here on the donkey cart one weekend and give some training to our children,' Elena replied enthusiastically.

'I hope their parents encourage the kids to join in. If it goes well, the band can play at the Festa di San Nicola,' Andrea responded.

Elena enjoyed meeting Lucia's and Andrea's families and friends, or going on an occasional picnic in the hills. She made friends and felt contented and settled. She was introduced to many of the townsfolk through her work with Signor Bastia when they visited his office to pay bills, complain about their neighbours, or report problems.

Signor Bastia had a deputy – Fernando – who was old and bent but had a sparkling sense of fun. Fernando had been the former Mayor, and was well liked. He used an old donkey for transport around the town as his legs were weak with age but he needed help to get on and off. In retirement, he enjoyed helping with town problems and visiting old people needing company. He repeatedly told his favourite jokes and stories.

Another character in Caterna was Signor Compo who lived alone in an ancient one-room stone house built into the town walls. The floors of his home were beaten earth and he cooked over an open fire. His clothing was worn and dirty as he had no access to washing facilities. He spent his time in two fields outside the walls, in which he grew vegetables and kept chickens.

The old men had formed a group with Fernando to shoot rabbits and birds, dividing their spoils for neighbours to put into stews. They usually left the town at dawn and their hob-nailed boots were heard tramping over the cobblestones, their shouts and laughter echoing off the high stone buildings, hunting dogs barking at their heels. The men gathered after the shoot at an old tin hut below the town walls. There they butchered their kill, smoked their evil-smelling wooden pipes and swapped tales of hunting prowess. By midday, the aroma of meat stew wafted around the streets. This was always followed by a long siesta when silence reigned and young children's cries were muffled by their mothers.

At times Elena was asked to accompany Fernando on his visits to old women who needed advice on health problems. The town had no doctor as they had left to support the military, but there were two old women who served as midwives and gave basic first aid. Their ability to set broken bones was limited but they were knowledgeable about healing herbs. Elena spent time learning basic first aid, the medical uses of local herbs, and how to blend them. She enjoyed the visits as, having lived with her grandparents when a child, she empathised with the difficulties of growing old.

Life continued placidly in the town, dictated by the seasons of the year, religious days, and the annual festival of the local saint, San Nicola in late May. Caterna had adopted the patron saint of Bari when a relic had been brought to the town in 1087. The church in Caterna had been built a few years later by a group of travelling artisan monks sent out to the countryside by the bishop of Bari. The Padre told Elena the legend of the church's creation.

The townsfolk believed that a single finger bone of the saint had been brought by the monks to Caterna and buried in the foundations of the new church. A wooden, painted effigy of San Nicola had been placed in a dedicated side chapel. It was brought out for the Festa di San Nicola, and carried through the village streets by locals dressed in their best clothes and children dancing alongside. Signor Bastia informed Elena that he needed her help in organising the Festa with Padre Pietro.

'It's a special event that follows a traditional programme and everyone in Caterna is involved. There's a dawn mass in the church and a re-dedication of the effigy before the procession starts. The statue is placed on a *fercolo* which is a handmade wooden cart with ropes pulled by four men chosen by the Padre. The procession follows a special route through Caterna which is the same each year. The villagers crowd onto rooftops and balconies to view the procession or follow along behind it, many wearing something white – a shirt or shawl. Special candles are made for the re-dedication. I have photos of previous Festas I can show you.' Signor Bastia smiled and heaved a sigh.

'You can imagine how much work is involved but the Padre will help you. He enjoys the ceremony and writes a new sermon each year. Tables are set up in the piazza in front of the church and local people bring food for the feast which lasts all day. In the evening, the tables are cleared and musicians group on the church steps to play traditional music for dancing called the *taranta*. Balconies on the route are decorated with flowers and handmade paper shapes.'

Elena laughed. 'That sounds fun and I'll enjoy helping with the planning. Mitorna didn't have a special saint and the church had been dedicated to the Virgin Mary so we celebrated the birth of Jesus at Christmas with a special mass followed by a communal lunch. In the evening I played in the local children's brass band when we processed through the streets. The women served hot chocolate and honey cake. It was a magic time even if the weather was cold and wet.'

Signor Bastia smiled and replied, 'I'll ask the Padre to come to my office tomorrow morning to talk about the arrangements for this year. It will be a good opportunity for you to meet other people in Caterna.'

Elena walked to the school house and excitedly told Lucia and Andrea that the Mayor had asked her to work with Padre Pietro to plan for the Festa di San Nicola.

'Signor Bastia says it involves a lot of arranging and paperwork and he'll be glad to have help. He said he will show me photos of previous Festas but can you please tell me more about it?'

'The day before the Festa we go out to the fields and pick wildflowers and cherry blossom to decorate the church and our balconies. We make special ring biscuits called *taralli* using flour, olive oil and olives. They are baked in communal ovens. The children love to help because they can eat as they help their mammas. People wear their Sunday best clothes. Women decorate their hair and shirts with home-made flowers. This is the only time that children are made new clothes by their mothers,' Lucia said excitedly. 'We dance in the piazza all night and it's fun.'

'Can you help me make a new dress, Lucia? My Nonna showed me how to sew and mend clothes so I can do seams and hems but I need help cutting out the material. Can I buy material at the market?'

'I've saved a few lengths of summer cotton from my dowry. I'll get them out of the cupboard and you can make a choice. I think we can use my dress for a basic pattern as you are about the same size as me. Do you have any sandals to wear?'

'No. I only have these old shoes. Perhaps I can ask around the village if anyone has spare sandals. What do you think, Lucia?'

'OK, but people in the village are poor and don't give away clothing as it's so hard to replace because of the war. You can borrow a pair of my white socks and we'll sew some lace on the tops,' Lucia replied, smiling.

'Andrea and I are starting a school brass band which we hope can play at the Festa. We've asked Matteo to lend us his guitar and Enrico to help us make wooden whistles and drums. Maybe some of the parents will lend us other instruments. We're teaching the children to sing old folk songs and play the *taranta*.'

Elena chatted on eagerly, telling Lucia about the fun she had playing in the brass band in Mitorna.

She worked hard during the next few weeks, encouraging the school children with their music, discussing the route for the procession of San Nicola with the Padre. They drew a map and coloured in the route, asking people to decorate their balconies and tidy in front of their houses. Animals were banned from the streets so they were clean when the procession walked through. Some locals muttered about the fuss and moaned about the interruption to their lives by tethering their dogs in the back yards so they couldn't roam the streets.

All supplies were brought by donkey to the Mayor's office the day before the Festa so animal dung could be cleaned up that day. Elena and the Padre had so many notes and instructions which Elena had typed out in the Mayor's office then pinned to the notice board. The Padre put up the details of his mass on the church door.

Elena rose before dawn on San Nicola Festa day and excitedly dressed in her new clothes, tying her hair back with a strip of cotton material. She ate a hurried breakfast with Lucia and Andrea before they walked to the church for dawn mass. The church was packed with villagers who watched as the effigy of San Nicola was taken from its niche in the side chapel and re-dedicated by the Padre before being placed on the *fercolo*. The four men chosen to pull the hand cart assembled in place and tugged it carefully through the church door, lifting it down the steps onto the piazza where the crowds waited for the procession.

'Bravo, Bravo,' they cried and jostled into place behind the *fercolo*. The procession wound around every street, the Padre blessing the houses they passed. Children sprinted alongside the procession when the street was wide enough, jumping up and trying to touch the effigy. Elena was carried along by the crowd, walking down lanes she had never visited before.

The day shone brightly with the sun's rays lighting the tops of the close-packed tall buildings lining the route. Families waved from balconies and children dropped paper flowers onto the procession. There were frequent stops by the procession as people crowded out of houses onto the streets, cheering excitedly. The men pulling the *fercolo* were careful to avoid gutters and protruding stone steps, changing places frequently to rest their shoulders. They wore special caps and white tunics over their everyday clothes. It took about an hour for the procession to circle round the town and return to the piazza.

Meanwhile the women put out tables in the piazza, put white cloths and food on them. Under the side arches, tables were laid with wine and lemonade. Everyone brought their own mug and plate and waited until the effigy of San Nicola was taken back into the side chapel in the church. Many people lit candles and placed them in the sand tray in front of the effigy, crossing themselves before they left.

Elena waited on the church steps with the Mayor, scanning the arrangements in the piazza. Padre Pietro walked around the tables blessing the food then waved to Elena who guided the school band out to the church steps. They played enthusiastically, if not always correctly, and their parents sang along. A line of people queued along one side of the piazza waiting for the band to finish and the feasting to begin.

Elena clapped the band and kissed each of the children before taking their instruments to be stored in the church for safety. She laughed as their parents congratulated her and ran down the church steps into the crowd to find Lucia and Andrea. Many people patted her on the back and said they enjoyed the music and asked if the band would play again that day.

'No, we have an adult band for the dancing this evening. It was a lot of effort for the children to learn two songs. Luckily they had lots of support from their parents and the Padre. I think they've earned some fun and food now.'

She found Andrea and Lucia sitting on the bench outside the school house. They had saved some food for her and praised her for the band performance.

'Thanks for your help and encouragement, Andrea,' Elena said as she kissed them both on the cheek. 'There were some wrong notes but this is the first time the children have played to an audience and they were nervous. I think they played marvellously and I had fun too.' Elena's face flushed with heat and excitement as she sat down.

By mid-afternoon all the food was eaten, the tables cleared away and everyone returned to their houses for a siesta. The festivities continued at sunset with music and dancing, pasta cooked in great cauldrons, and fresh bread. Elena danced with Lucia, Andrea and others. She met a young man called Gennaro and enjoyed a glass of local wine with him. The dancing stopped at midnight and Elena kissed Gennaro on the cheek, agreeing to meet him at the weekend, then walked with Lucia and Andrea to their house.

'That's the best day I've had for ages. People are so friendly here and I feel happy and safe in the village.' She waved her hands excitedly and twirled her way up the steps into the house. 'I shall stay awake all night remembering the fun I had.' And she ran up the stairs to her attic room, humming a song she had danced to with Gennaro.

She woke at dawn to birds singing in the eaves; jumped out of bed, eager to get to work at the Mayor's office. She worked hard through the week, impatient for Sunday and her walk with Gennaro after mass.

Elena confided to Lucia about her agreement to meet Gennaro. 'Do you know the family? He said that he has several sisters and brothers still living at home. His father is a plumber and carpenter,' Elena asked Lucia the morning after the Festa. 'He dances well and is very handsome.'

Lucia nodded. 'Yes, I know his parents. They live behind the church. They are a large family – four boys and four girls. I met Gennaro, the eldest, when he and his father were doing repairs to the Mayor's house. The parents are respectable and regularly go to Mass. One of the girls is your age. The family have lived in this village for generations – many of them buried in the cemetery. I believe two of Gennaro's uncles died fighting in the First World War. He is a nice young man, hardworking and smart.'

'Gennaro suggested we walk down to the river after Mass on Sunday. He said he'll bring food for a picnic and a blanket.'

'That will be fun. It's beautiful along the river. In the summer, the children swim there as it's shallow and safe for them,' Lucia answered.

'I'm looking forward to it,' Elena replied. 'I'll wear my new dress.'

Saturday was warm and sunny and Elena wore her dark hair tied back. Her nervousness and excitement made her fidget during Mass. Gennaro waited outside the church for her and introduced her to his parents who were obviously eager to question her, but Gennaro caught Elena's hand and pulled her down the steps and across the piazza towards the river.

'I don't want to waste time talking with my parents on our first date,' Gennaro explained, holding Elena's hand tightly as they ran down the stone steps to the river bank. 'I told them that you work with the Mayor and come from another village in Puglia. My parents love to talk and have invited you to the family lunch but I told them we have arranged a picnic. Here's a sheltered place with flat ground and I've brought a rug. Mama made an onion pizza for us and we can drink the river water. Mama's pizzas are famous in the village and are favourites at the church festas.'

'My Nonna taught me basic cooking but not how to make pizzas so I'll enjoy your mamma's.'

Nervous, Elena sat on the rug and looked around at the river gliding by, the sunlight shining on tiny ripples. Small birds darted over the water chasing insects and dragonflies.

The peaceful scene calmed her somewhat and soon she was munching on pizza, laughing at Gennaro's comments on the Padre. He was a good mimic and imitated the Padre's mannerisms perfectly.

Gennaro pushed out his stomach and patted it, miming the Padre waving his arms and saying, 'Now let's kneel and thank God for his bounty to us before we go home and eat lunch with the family, taking a little red wine then a siesta.' Then he mimed the Padre sleeping and snoring loudly, patting his stomach again.

'Look at the swallows dipping over the river, and look, there's tiny fish in the shallows by my feet,' whispered Elena.

Gennaro placed his arm around her shoulders as he knelt beside her and looked into the river. 'This is a magical place, isn't it? My family come here on special occasions like birthdays to celebrate. The river is shallow and safe for the little ones. Sometimes Papa catches a few fish for dinner then lights a fire and cooks them over it. Delicious,' Gennaro mused on the closeness of his family. 'Maybe you'd like to come to lunch next Sunday with my family? We are a little cramped with eight children and my parents but we manage and help each other. You must feel very lonely at times.'

'Si,' Elena replied, 'but I am used to it most of the time. I grew up with my Nonna and grandfather and no other family. Now both of them and my mamma are dead … and I don't know where my father has emigrated to. He left when my mama died.'

Elena jumped up and caught Gennaro's hand. 'Come on, let's walk. It's too nice a day to be sad and we've only just met each other. I'll tell you about my family another day.'

She ran along the river bank, tugging Gennaro, avoiding the low trees branches and dancing like a woodland sprite. Her ponytail bounced on her shoulders and her new dress swayed around her legs as she skipped along. They both tripped over a large tree root and collapsed on the ground, laughing at each other.

Gennaro leant over and kissed her but Elena knew it was too early in their relationship. She lay with her arms behind her head looking up through the leaves and knew this was a special moment to be treasured.

'Can you see the hawk circling in the sky to the left of us?' Gennaro asked, pointing. 'It must be searching for mice in the grass. We get many of them here as the land is wild and sparsely populated. Look, it's diving and has caught a snake … Can you see it squirming in its beak? Now it's circling higher with its prey and flying over the village. I'd love to able to fly like that and see the country from on high.'

They walked back along the river bank, hand in hand, bathed in golden sunlight. 'It's time I went home,' Elena said. 'The sun will be setting soon and I need to be back before dark or Lucia will worry. What a wonderful day it's been. I shall never forget it.' Elena looked up at the sky and then smiled at Gennaro.

They continued to meet at weekends, falling in love, delighting in each other's company, and Elena found she often interrupted her work to gaze out the window in the Mayor's office, dreaming of Gennaro.

Two months later, Elena met Padre Stepano when he visited from Mitorno to ensure she was settled.

'How are you? It's good experience for you to live away from your home village.'

'I'm fine. I enjoy the work, although it was a little difficult to understand at first. The local people are friendly, but I miss Marco and Maria, and my friends at Mitorna.'

Elena talked it over with Lucia and Andrea one evening.

'I know the villagers are kind to me but I miss the friendship of Marco and Marina.'

'That's natural,' Andrea replied. 'It's a big adjustment to make after living in the same village for seventeen years. I'm sure it will become easier over the next few months and you have your new friend Gennaro. No promises, but maybe I can arrange for Marco and Marina and some of your old friends to come over in the donkey cart for your birthday. It's in two weeks' time, isn't it?'

'Oh, that would be wonderful. Thank you. I'll decide what we can eat, and ask the Mayor if we can set up some tables and benches in the piazza.'

A week later the older children from Mitorna visited with their musical band, arriving in the donkey cart. There were joyous greetings and much laughter as they were introduced to Lucia and Andrea, and Gennaro. The band played in the church that evening.

Marina and Elena exchanged news and talked softly about their boyfriends. 'Oh, I almost forgot to tell you, Elena … a man visited our house just after you left Mitorna. He asked where you were living. I told him you had moved to Caterna and was working here. He seemed pleased then left the village. I think it might have been your father. He was scruffily dressed and thin as if he had been travelling for a while. I've only met your grandparents so I'm not sure. Did the man come here?'

'No-one has come looking for me,' Elena said thoughtfully. She was a small baby when her father emigrated so had no memories of him. She felt sad that he hadn't come to Caterna as she had no other family.

But this sadness only lasted a few weeks as a terrible tragedy engulfed Caterna.

The Escape 1942

Elena takes a short walk round the town after breakfast, looking in the gift and ceramic shops and enjoying conversations in Italian. She wanders back to the hotel and finds a comfortable cane chair on the shady terrace to sit in. The terrace overlooks a swimming pool and she watches the children jumping and playing in the water; reflects how different life is now to when she was a child. The Italian economy has been boosted in the last few decades by tourism and membership of the European Union. Agriculture has become more productive, assisted by government grants; wheat, olive oil, wine, fruit and ground crops are intensively cultivated and exported to a range of countries. Elena has taken several drives in a private taxi through the surrounding countryside, noticing the renovations to old stone buildings and churches, the liveliness of villages and towns.

After escaping from the Germans in Caterna, Elena remembers skidding and slithering down a rocky ravine, clinging to branches as they lashed out at her. She skinned her elbows, bruised her legs and arms on rocks. She followed a goat track that twisted and turned as it wound down the hill to a wild, uncultivated plain where small stone huts had been abandoned, now overgrown with bushes and briars. Olive trees had spread their stunted shade overhead as she scrambled through the dense growth searching for a place to hide. Her chest hurt and breathing was difficult.

Again, and again, Elena now wonders how she found the strength to get up and run on. By mid-afternoon when the sun was at its hottest, her legs had given way with exhaustion and she had sat down suddenly on the rocky ground, heedless of the prickly plants and the myriad insects crawling around her. She had tried to calm her breathing, the dust of the track and the pollen of low-lying shrubs lying in her throat. She bent her head over her knees, trembling with fear. She was in the middle of nowhere with no-one to help her, abandoned by everyone she knew. The sun beat on her uncovered head and her body was exhausted. She had lifted her tear-stained face and looked around at the bleak and desolate landscape scattered with clumps of straggly bushes and hillocks of rough stone. Bright green lizards darted swiftly past her and large black ants, some carrying leaves, scurried purposefully around her legs. Large black beetles with iridescent backs shining in the brilliant sun edged their way past her feet.

Wherever she looked the grey-green and beige landscape stretched monotonously on all sides. Only insects and lizards lived here. It was too hard to survive in the hot dry summer, even native bushes and trees struggled to find liquid and earth to sustain them.

The only humans in this arid southern plain of Italy were goatherds moving their flocks between known water holes and shade provided by native olive groves and the occasional stone hut.

After a while, she wearily rose from the ground and trudged on. The sun was setting and she found shelter in a small crevice between a few rocks. She had nothing to light a fire with for protection and, as she had watched the sun sinking behind an olive grove, hugged her knees and wondered how much further she could go. She was bereft of family and friends, home and work. She had no-one to protect or help her in her desolate predicament. She had no idea how to survive in this countryside, how to find food or water, how to start a fire. She only had her will to survive and determination to start a new life somewhere safe, far away from the tragedy and horror of the past. She felt abandoned to the elements.

She dozed exhaustedly for a few hours squashed in the stone crevice and had then sat up, watching the whirling stars until dawn lightened the sky. The countryside became steeper as she continued to trudge all day along animal tracks. Often, they were hard to detect, straggling through heather and grasses. There was no shade and she was terrified of pursuit.

She reached a small peak, took a deep breath and looked around. There was nothing to see except deserted moorland and sky. Halfway across this plain the sun was setting and Elena had glimpsed an old goatherd in the distance. He called out to her but she ran away, not willing to trust anyone after her bitter experience. He called again and, breathless and stumbling, she stopped.

The old goatherd, stooped with a bent back, slowly walked across the stony ground towards her. The herd of goats, young and old, with brown and black coats, surrounded him. They bleated continuously as they grazed among the sparse vegetation. They moved towards her, milling and pushing her, causing her to stumble on the uneven ground. Her heart hammered in her chest and her hands were wet with the sweat of fear. The goatherd held out a leathery brown hand to steady her. He was clearly affected by the infirmities of old age. She looked up into his dark bright eyes and noticed the wisps of white hair sprouting from his ears and chin and beneath his battered canvas cap. He wore a stained leather jerkin over a crumpled brown shirt, and canvas trousers. His feet were clad in large scruffy boots with heavy rubber soles and no laces. Elena felt less frightened as he smiled at her, showing a few brown stained teeth.

'Buongiorno,' he said. 'Are you wandering these hills alone? Yesterday I heard screams and gunfire in the distance,' he asked.

She hung her head, twisting her hands and whispered, 'The Germans have invaded my village and shot many of the people, including the priest.'

'War does terrible things to ordinary people, but you escaped?'

'Si. The village priest took my place,' Elena stammered, still unable to believe that she was alive while the friends and neighbours she knew had been shot.

'You can rest here for a few hours and share my bread and cheese. No-one comes into these hills as the goats protect me and I can see anyone climbing here.'

She stood in the midst of the goats, hardly aware they were pushing her with their soft moist noses and poking her gently with their severed horns. She glanced around and saw a small aperture under a large overhanging rock with a small wood fire burning brightly, a battered metal pot balanced on top. She felt exhausted, so traumatised by the recent events and terrified to trust anyone, yet she needed shelter.

Elena took the goatherd's outstretched hand, feeling the calluses and knobs on his arthritic fingers. Nudging her out of the goats, he led her to a flat stone to sit near the fire, handed her a leather bottle and told her to drink the cool fresh water. She gulped thirstily, coughing as the liquid poured down her parched throat, reviving her.

'Careful or you'll choke and waste precious water,' the goatherd said. 'Have some bread and goat curd but eat it slowly as there is no need for haste here.'

The sun warmed the ground; the cicadas clicked, and a strong aroma of wild herbs mingled with the smell of goat droppings on the hot evening breeze. Slowly Elena relaxed as the goatherd sat on another rock, his hand clasped on the curved top of his wood cane. In his left hand he held a worn wooden pipe to his mouth. The smoke drifted lightly into the clear air. He was silent and contemplative, enjoying the tranquillity of his environment.

Elena ate the bread and curd but could feel her eyes closing, her shoulders slumping as she leaned to one side. She sensed the goatherd watching her and that he'd noticed her ragged clothes and tangled hair, the dirt on her hands and face.

He said, 'Lie down in the shelter for a while on the old goatskin. My name is Rico. I need no other name living as I do, but I have named the goats so I can gather them at night when they wander.'

Rico helped her from the stone seat into the shelter, a primitive hollow carved out in the rocky hillside. A huge gnarled olive tree spread its roots above the shelter, somehow finding enough soil to grow amongst the boulders. The goatherd pushed her to the back, calling to his goats to circle the rocks. It was cool and dark inside with shadows flickering on the rock walls from the wood fire. She slept a little, purely out of exhaustion, her arms folded protectively across her chest and her hip resting on the stony ground. When she awoke, it was dusk and the grim reality of her situation struck again that she was alone and her friends in Caterna were dead.

Elena crept stiffly out of the shelter. The old man was sitting in the same place on his rock seat, silhouetted against the rising moon, his legs stretched out in front. He smoked his wooden pipe and gazed across the bleak scrubland surrounded by his goats which bleated and called to each other. It was a comforting sound as the horrific events of the previous day crowded into her mind in nightmare scenes.

'Where are you going to? This area is barren and unpopulated – few people live here now. I heard that the Germans invaded some of the local villages but there's nothing of value or interest for them on this rocky arid plain. I am content to live here with my goats, far away from the damage of war. I fought in the First World War and experienced enough terrible things to last my lifetime. Yesterday, I heard gunshots echoing off the rocks. Were you running from that?'

'Yes,' she answered. 'The Germans shot my friends and neighbours. I hid in ditches last night.' Tears poured down Elena's dirty face and her shoulders shook.

Rico sat still and silent as she talked, his pipe puffing wisps of smoke into the breeze. She felt waves of desolation and despair overwhelm her – she had no safe place to go. Her life had been hard but she always had the comfort and care of her Nonna and friends, and the companionship of other villagers in Caterna.

All that had been torn from her in one tragic day, her life, home and work obliterated by a single barbaric and intensely cruel act. She was seventeen years old and entirely alone.

'Stay here overnight. I have little water and food but I'll share it with you,' Rico said. 'It's a long difficult walk to get anywhere from here. Do you have relatives elsewhere who could give you shelter?'

'No-one,' she cried. 'All my family are dead long ago and I was living with friends while I worked in Caterna. They were shot. Where can I go? What can I do?' she screamed in panic. 'My life is broken. I have no future. No place to feel safe and no-one I can trust.'

'We'll talk in the morning about where you can go to be safe. Do you think the Germans are searching for you?'

Elena shook her head, too stunned by tragedy to think about anything other than surviving the present. She and Rico ate the sparse food and sipped the brackish water, sitting by the fire under the vast canopy of starlight. Elena crept into the rock shelter again, leaving the goatherd to lie by the fire. She had a very disturbed and uncomfortable night, dreaming of the nightmare scenes she had seen. Next morning at sunrise Rico offered her some dry bread and water. He used a dry stick to draw a simple map on a flat rock showing the area he roamed with his goats and put crosses where water and shelter could be found.

'Take the path ahead as it leads to a tiny hamlet about two hours away. Ask someone for water and hide overnight where you can. Then walk west on animal tracks so you can avoid meeting anyone. Don't use the roads and avoid towns where Germans might be. The safest place to hide is a city like Naples. It's a long way from here but you might find work there. There won't be much shelter as I heard the city has been badly bombed. I will show you how to look for birds' eggs and which plants are safe to eat. Of course, there are plenty of olives, figs and occasionally wild apricots.'

He gave her a spare flint so she could make a fire and a disused tin can for boiling water. Then, with his kind wishes, Elena left the goatherd and climbed further into the hills, over rocky ground. She was scratched by thorns and bushes. The sun glared down and, without a hat, she was pounded by the heat. She was thirsty and could find only a few brackish pools hidden in the rocks.

Although Rico had suggested where she might go, her mind was too shocked and numbed by the events of the previous days to think clearly. She walked all day and realised that, unconsciously, she had gravitated towards her home village, Mitorna. Luckily, she met no one.

That night she slept in a hillside copse and woke abruptly as the sun rose and streamed across her face. She walked over the cultivated fields and grazing land outside Mitorna, stumbling on the ploughed earth. She entered through an arch in the town walls, walked up the cobbled streets to the church and the main square then decided to wait in the shadow of an archway near the village pump, knowing that her friend, Marina, would come to collect the day's water. Other women filled their terracotta pots, one trailing a small child clinging to her skirt. It looked so peaceful and normal it was impossible to believe that twenty kilometres away an invading army had shot innocent people without trial.

She pulled her torn and dirty clothing around her and ran her fingers through her tangled hair in an attempt to appear normal for Marina. The sun's rays rose over the stone buildings and reached into the archway. She felt desperately tired, hungry and thirsty. 'Please, please God, let Marina see me and help me,' she pleaded silently, making the sign of the cross in the air. Her feet hurt in the broken sandals and her bones ached from lying and walking on stony ground.

Then she saw her childhood friend going towards the pump, carrying two water containers. Elena whistled to attract her attention and quietly called her name. Marina looked around, her eyes widening, her jaw dropping on seeing Elena hiding in the archway. As Elena beckoned, Marina hesitated before walking over.

'What are you doing here? I thought you lived in Caterna now?' Marina whispered.

Elena tried to tell her quietly about the shooting and the German invasion, constantly looking behind her and whispering for fear of being overheard. Marina listened silently, clearly horrified and scared as Elena's tale unfolded. She put down her water carriers and covered her mouth with her hands. Shaking her head, she rested her arm on Elena's. Yet, while Marina seemed sympathetic, she was reluctant to take her to the family home and it took a few minutes to persuade Marina that the Germans hadn't followed her to Mitorna.

Marina collected her water and told her friend to follow her, Elena looking around carefully as she left the sheltering arch. They walked up the cement stairs to the family apartment and Marina opened the door.

'I found Elena hiding in the piazza. Her neighbours and friends have been shot by the Germans in Caterna. She managed to escape alone and walked here. She pleaded with me to help her as her clothes are torn and dirty and she hasn't eaten for a day. She has no family to help,' Marina pleaded with her mother at the door.

'Go away. You bring trouble to our home.' Marina's mother pulled her daughter inside; pushed Elena out and slammed the door in her face.

Stunned at this rejection by a family who had supported and cared for her after her Nonna died, Elena stared at the familiar door shut in her face and laid her head on her arms against the stairway wall. Tears flooded her face and moistened the plastered wall. She slowly slid down to the top stair, sat and cradled her head on her knees. Her body weak through lack of food and water, any youthful resilience and energy she had left dissipated. A door opened further down the stairs and an old woman poked her head out, enquiring what the noise was. She saw Elena's distress but went back inside her home and shut the door.

Elena's future seemed hopeless. She had no money, no clean clothes and no friends. She knew no-one outside Mitorna and Caterna. It was then, finally, that her grief and feeling of abandonment burst out and she wailed with sorrow, pain and deep sadness. She cried and cried as she mourned the loss of her youth, her friends and childhood. Terrible guilt of being a survivor assailed her, a feeling which was never to leave her.

After a while, she rose and walked slowly down the stairs and out of her home village. She followed the dusty track and found a sheltering stone wall where she collapsed with exhaustion and despair. The German soldiers might be hunting her. There was no safe place. What should she do? She imagined eyes watching her as she rose and ran along the dusty track. But where could she go? She shivered uncontrollably despite the hot sun. Her torn cotton dress was stained with copious tears, water and mud from the ditch, her sandals were broken, and she had no protection against the cold or rain. She knew that wild dogs roamed the scrub plain, attacking herds of goats.

The Lonely Trek from Puglia 1942-43

The setting sun reminded Elena she needed to get as far away from the two villages as possible. She dimly remembered Rico, the goatherd, had said that to the west was a vast rocky plain of scrubland and native olive groves. Far beyond that was Naples where maybe she could find work and somewhere to live. That night she lay on the bare ground staring up at the stars in the Milky Way, their dim light creating faint shadows of the bushes and rocks. She felt abandoned and bone achingly weary. A fleeting wind brought faint sounds of barking dogs but no church bell, no night birds called to each other as they nestled down in the nearby olive groves; there was not even the hoots of owls. A profound silence lay around, no animals moved. A great desolation of spirit and exhaustion of body overwhelmed her and she dozed fitfully, shifting her body to avoid stones.

At daybreak Elena forced herself to get up off the hard ground. She brushed her clothes and trudged down the deserted track. Where it petered out she stumbled over untended fields and drainage ditches, trying to reach the monastery across the valley. She saw no-one on that hot summer day, even the birds slept and the butterflies seemed drugged with the heat, balancing precariously on a twig in the shade of the few scrawny bushes. By midday, she no longer had the strength to climb up to the monastery and collapsed under a wild olive tree where she dozed for most of the evening and night.

Then, aimlessly, she followed another dusty featureless track flanked by dry stone walls, some of them crumbling into piles. The countryside was bleak, and she passed a single burnt farmhouse and roofless stone huts, the Germans having burned the crops surrounding the village and stripped the primitive stone dwellings of stored food. As the sunlight faded at dusk to a bright glow, clouds cast streaky black shadows over the deserted moorland; a flock of black birds soared on the thermals overhead searching for prey.

She found a ruined hut for shelter that night although it was dirty and smelly, and woke at dawn after a restless night, tormented by nightmares. She turned her back on the rising sun and hoped she was heading west; she drank from ponds in the rocks where she found them, bathing her tear-stained face and sore feet to remove the dust that clung to them. Her feet in the broken sandals were becoming blistered so she tore a strip from her dress to bind around them, and didn't walk far that day, exhausted by trauma and the difficulty of the terrain.

Just after midday, she collapsed in an olive grove and, with her back against a tree trunk, closed her eyes and let the tears of despair trickle down her face. The faces of her friends in Caterna and Mitorna resurrected themselves in her mind. She tried to take some comfort from the happy times she had shared with them. She heard Nonna's voice repeating what she had said when the Blackshirts invaded Mitorna, 'You have to go on and manage alone now. There's no other way.'

Elena heard a cart rumble in the distance but otherwise she was alone as she continued her trek, picking olives and wild figs to eat. Black clouds threatened on the horizon and she felt the wind becoming stronger. Within a few minutes, a rain storm lashed the plateau, bringing hailstones that clattered on the rocks. In the frequent lightning flashes she noticed a deserted farm building and ran to shelter inside the walls, the track and surrounding countryside no longer visible in the rain and sudden dimness.

When the storm abated, Elena realised the reddish-brown fields around the deserted farm were untended. A wild thicket of fig trees flourished in one corner of the yard with a crumbling goat pen in another. She scavenged something to eat from the weed infested vegetable garden, all the while smelling an overgrown orchard rank with rotting apricots and fallen almonds. She ate those that were visible amongst the vegetation.

As she set off again the next morning, an old woman clattered by driving a mule cart, laden with melons and vegetables. She was dressed in black, her head covered for protection against the dust. She stopped and asked if Elena was lost. Elena shook her head but accepted a ride to the outskirts of the next village and, cupping her hands, drank the cool water from the village pump. She could smell the tang of wood cooking fires but the streets were empty as most people worked in the fields until dusk. She used the last of her lire given by Marina to buy bread and cheese at a small café. The people sitting at tables eyed her strangely so Elena ate her food quickly and left.

She dreaded the night-time when it was time to find shelter from the many dangers and risks of travelling alone across the unpopulated countryside, but her depressed spirits were lifted by the glory of the red and golden sunset and the drifting purplish clouds. She found shelter in a small stone shepherd's hut, its broken wooden door hanging off its hinges. Dirty straw spread across the floor along with fragments of charred wood from a fire at the entrance. But the roof was roughly thatched and she decided to rest there for the night.

She pulled some straw into a rough mattress and slept heavily until she awoke suddenly in the darkness, dreaming of being captured and shot by German soldiers. Sitting bolt upright, she tried to calm her uneven breathing; listened intently to the night sounds outside – the distant howl of a stray fox and the hoot of an owl hunting for ground prey. She lay down and stared for a long time at the black shape of the hut and noticed a single star shining into the doorway.

As she set out the next morning, having stayed awake since her nightmare, Elena continued on her lonely trek, her legs covered in dust to her knees. She was hungry again and exhausted as heavy dark clouds gathered but there was no smell of rain in the air. All she could see was an unending rocky, barren plateau that reached in a gentle curve to the misty horizon where the sun was highlighting the dark clouds in gold. The air was clear, still and hot with the sun beating off the dry ground. She walked through deserted olive groves, their squat ragged shapes in need of pruning, the olives, dry and shrunken, hanging in clusters from the branches. She picked some and ate them as she walked.

By early evening, the distant hills took on a dark blue hue, their shapes piled in layers reaching into the coloured sky then fading into pale blue on the horizon. Little brown birds fluttered around the track and the clacking of the cicadas became a gentle background hum. She glimpsed a village church tower and headed towards it, hoping to find food and water. As she walked closer, she could see the houses piled on top of each up the hillside and the ancient stone church tower crowning the village. Faintly on the wind came the braying of a donkey and the evening crow of a cockerel, all the normal sounds of human habitation she had grown up with. The campanile rang the evening bells.

After an hour of stumbling over rough ground, she reached the crumbling walls. A couple of feral cats leapt off the wall, their long, sharp claws reaching for her face. One leapt onto her shoulder and tore at her dress, raising blood, and she screamed, flailed her hands wildly to dislodge it; the cat snarled at her, showing its blood covered teeth. Then the other cat leapt, tearing the skin on her arm. Elena flung up her arm in terror and managed to temporarily dislodge it. It landed on all fours and raised its head, snarling at her. Weak and faint with fear, she almost collapsed to the ground when a rough hand pulled her upright and supported her. She looked up as a peasant woman wielded a heavy stick at the feral cats.

'*Smamma*! *Vattene*!' she screamed, swiping at the cats with the stick. '*Stai bene*? Are you alright?' she asked as the cats leapt onto the wall and scurried, searching for another prey. 'You're bleeding – come with me to the village pump and I'll wash the scratches or they'll become infected.'

Feeling faint and shaking, Elena followed the woman into the village piazza, where the woman held Elena's arm under the flow of clear cold water for a few minutes then pushed her shoulder into the flow. Pulling her kerchief from her head, she wrapped it tightly around Elena's arm. A group of women clustered around and the woman asked for another kerchief to bind Elena's shoulder. Then she pushed Elena onto a nearby stone bench and indicated that she should put her head between her knees.

One of the other women ran back to her apartment and brought a small glass jar of lavender-smelling paste; gestured for Elena to put it on her scratches and wrap them again.

Though Elena had difficulty understanding their dialect, the kindness of the women was evident and she smiled briefly. Tapping her chest, she introduced herself. The other women followed suit and Elena understood that the peasant woman who had rescued her from the feral cats was Claudia. Using gestures and some common words, Elena explained why she had some to their village, and that she was hungry and thirsty. Claudia took a metal cup hanging on a string by the pump and filled it with water for Elena to drink.

'*Grazie, grazie. Sei molto gentile.* You are very kind.' Elena smiled as she thanked them.

'*Seguimi. Puoi dormire con me.*' Follow me – you can stay the night with me,' replied Claudia, helping Elena to stand. Holding her hand, she led her to some steep concrete steps built into the wall of an old building.

Claudia stopped at a wooden door with brown peeling paint and an old metal latch, which she lifted to open. She ushered Elena into a bright kitchen with a table in the centre and a warped wooden door on the left. Claudia laid out some dry bread, hard cheese and a few olives and indicated to Elena to eat them. The light was fading fast as Elena sat at the kitchen table and ate. Claudia offered her another cup of fresh water and indicated a stone alcove with a wooden ledge and a straw mattress. She mimed sleeping and gave Elena a rough blanket. Elena stumbled over and lay down, exhausted by her nasty experience with the feral cats. She slept soundly and was awoken at dawn by Claudia shaking her shoulder.

'I've put water and bread on the table for you. I must go and help in the fields now. *Va con Deo*'. Claudia opened the door and left Elena to eat.

The village was empty as Elena walked through it, moving on towards Naples, all the able-bodied people working in the fields. The scratches on her arm stung and her shoulder felt stiff, caution causing her to watch for the feral cats, but they had disappeared.

The air was clear and fresh and Elena's spirits rose. The bright indigo sky was empty of clouds and she could hear the twittering of birds and humming of bees in the village. Warmed by the kindness of the village women, she hummed a song Nonna had taught her, and flung back her head and let the breeze flow through her hair as she trod the dusty track. She had often sung at her grandparents' cottage, and enjoyed singing with her friends in Mitorna. This song was full of sweet tones and melancholy but her soft melodic voice invoked sad memories of her childhood which brought tears to her eyes. She brushed them away, felt the returning vigour of her young body overcome the depredations of the last days. She felt a lightening of her spirit and an optimism that had been missing since she'd escaped from the Germans.

As she rested that afternoon under an olive tree Elena knew she faced an uncertain and difficult future but the courage and willpower that had supported her through her adolescent years would, she knew, guide her to a better future. She had a long walk ahead of her to reach Naples, with the possibility of danger from humans and animals, but she needed to forget past tragedies and think positively about the prospects she could find there.

A bird of prey circled silently overhead searching for mice and rabbits as she walked across the countryside eating a few wild olives and plums with the dry bread Claudia had given her. She was alone again, amid uncultivated fields coloured ochre, amber and red, the blue sky above whitened by the heat. The dusty lane wound ahead to the horizon like a length of rope, bounded by ditches and crumbling walls. The only sounds were the crunching of her feet on the stones, the eerie cry of the hunting bird and a distant jangling of church bells.

After a few hours she noticed the heavy clouds massing in the sky, their dark ragged shapes fitting like jigsaw pieces, backlit by the rays of the sun. The shapes resembled birds and one looked like a leaping hare. By early evening the cloud cover acted like a blanket suppressing the heat of the day.

She came to a deserted villa, climbed over the gate which had warped with time, and walked up a path overgrown with wild plants and littered with dried twigs. She pushed open the front door, which squealed on its rusty hinges, and peered into the shadowy interior of a house with two floors, the wooden beams of the upper floor broken and hanging down.

There was a smell of years of neglect and rotting vegetation where creepers had invaded the broken windows and roof. Through the last rays of the sun she could see debris littering the stone tiles and a rusty old iron stove. In a corner was an alcove where a torn, stained straw mattress laid on a stone ledge, a dusty, ragged curtain hanging over it. She carefully checked it for snakes and insects then lay down on the bed and heaped straw for a pillow. Exhausted though she was, sleep was slow in coming as her thoughts of the future in Naples whirled around in her head.

Elena was woken by the sound of sheep munching and crowding around the open doorway, a shaggy dog nosing around her bed. A farmer appeared in the middle of the flock, surprised to find a young girl sleeping alone and unprotected in this isolated country.

'Why are you in this deserted place?' he asked, bidding his sheepdog to move away. Pushing his greasy, weather-beaten hat off his face with grubby hands, the farmer scratched his unshaven chin and squinted at Elena. He wore dark, stained trousers and a brown cotton shirt, and his nails were blackened and torn.

Elena sat up and looked around, scared of the sheep crowding in, frightened of the dog nudging her legs with his wet nose. She thought the owner of the house had returned and said nothing for a moment. Slowly, she realised the man had spoken in a local Puglian dialect, a different version of the local language she used and, in her bewildered state, found it hard to understand him.

He asked again, 'Why are you sleeping here alone? Are you hurt?'

Her mouth was so dry it was difficult to speak and she gulped a few times before managing to say, in a shaky voice, 'No, I'm not hurt except for scratches from wild cats and bushes, and my feet are sore. I'm very thirsty but I can't tell you why I am here, only that I'm running away.'

The farmer scratched his head, unsure of what she'd said, the dialect strange to him. Yet he could see how terrified she was.

'Can you follow me to the farm? I'll ask my wife to give you a drink. It's further down in the valley, about ten minutes' walk from here. I'll leave the dog to look after the sheep. Come on, take my hand.' He held it out to help Elena stand, and she noted it was calloused and strong.

The farmer gave a brief command to his dog then started down the hillside, Elena following slowly as her left leg was numb from where she'd slept on the hard ledge. She was also thirsty, her head ached and she felt muzzy, unable to find the energy to run away. She had noted the previous evening a solitary wisp of thin blue-grey smoke rising from a ramshackle farm in the distance and, as she approached it, she could see it had a ragged straw roof built over ivy-covered stone walls. A small dirty dog chased its tail in the dusty yard. It was a sight that had not changed for hundreds of years. The ramshackle buildings were strangely comforting and Elena sensed no threat. The farmer pushed open the door of the house and called inside.

'Anna, Anna, come quickly with a cup of water.'

The farmer's wife appeared and replied, 'Angelo, what's the hurry? Who's coming here in this lonely place?'

Elena had collapsed on the front step and leant her head against the door frame, too exhausted to react.

'When I took the sheep up the hill, I found this young girl sleeping alone in the empty villa there. I don't know her name or why she's here but she said she was thirsty and she seems very frightened.'

Anna fetched a cup of water and Elena gulped it down without taking a breath. She felt so tired, so traumatized, that she could not decide what to do anymore. Anna looked pityingly at her and held out her hand.

'Come inside and eat some bread and cheese. You can wash your hands and face too. When you feel sure of us, you can tell us why you are here. We won't hurt you. You're safe here as we are very isolated.'

Elena nodded and, understanding the meaning of her words, pulled herself up from the doorstep and followed Anna into the cool shady interior. The aroma of frying garlic and baked bread made her realise she was hungry, not having eaten anything other than wild fruit for days.

Anna gestured to Elena, 'Sit at the table and have some more water.'

'Si, grazie,' Elena replied hesitantly and, seeing the concerned faces of the farmer and his wife, slowly ate the bread and drank the water.

'I have run away. I don't know where to go as I have no family and my friends have deserted me. There are Germans in my village and I need somewhere to hide for a while.'

'You can sleep in the barn for now and later you can tell us more,' responded Angelo.

Elena followed him across the yard and into a ruined stone barn. He showed her an old wooden stepladder and pointed to the wood platform above.

'Hide in the straw. You'll be safe there.'

Elena climbed the stepladder, knelt down in the clean straw, and slowly laid her head down as the farmer walked out to tend his sheep. After a short while, she fell asleep, exhaustion overcoming her fear. That evening Anna called her to eat with them. Refreshed by her rest, Elena noted the inside of the cottage was clean but sparsely furnished and had just one room used for cooking and eating. There was a bed in a curtained alcove opposite the open fire, and sunlight drifted through holes in the thatched roof. A battered tin sink and a paraffin stove for cooking sat on one wall.

Elena sat at the scrubbed wooden kitchen table eating the plain sparse food served on tin plates. She realised she needed help and somewhere to hide for a while. Reassured by their kind smiles, she told Angelo and Anna a brief version of what had happened to her. They managed to understand each other with hand gestures and it seemed many of the words in both dialects were the same.

'My home village is many days walk from here but I was working in another village. The Germans occupied this village about two months ago. It was frightening how quickly they marched in and took command of everything, including the Mayor's office.'

Elena paused, tears flooding her face; she started shaking as she recalled the horror of the shootings. Anna patted her hand and handed her a scrap of cotton to wipe her eyes. Silence reigned for a moment as the tale had exhausted her and she needed to compose herself.

Then she said, her voice hoarse, 'Some villagers were discovered hiding a radio in a barn outside the village. The Germans lined them up against the church wall and shot them. They shot our priest and two children, but I was helped to escape. I cannot tell anymore …,' Elena whispered. She bowed her head to the table, guilt flooding in that she had escaped and a terrible sadness filling her for those who'd been shot. The farmer's wife rose and fetched a cup of water for her from the pump in the yard.

'I will talk with my husband and see if we can help. Rest here in the barn for a few hours,' she said.

Eating a vegetable stew later that day, Anna said, 'Okay, you can stay here for a few months and help us in the house and with the animals, if you feel safe.'

Elena almost cried with relief. '*Si. Grazie*. You are very kind.'

'No-one visits and we have no family nearby,' Anna stressed. 'We can't pay you but you can sleep in the barn and eat with us. You must stay out of sight inside the stone yard walls. Here are some old but clean working clothes of my son's that you can wear. He left the farm two years ago to fight in the war. They'll be more suitable for farm work and protect you against the winter weather.'

Anna handed Elena a patched cotton shirt, a stained brown leather jerkin, brown trousers and scuffed boots. She gave Elena a torn belt to hold up the trousers which were too large at the waist, cut her hair short and tucked it into a sweaty cloth cap.

Elena settled into the farm life, willingly helping in the fields and the house where needed. She enjoyed the tranquillity of the evenings when they rested outside after a hard day's work. The farm dogs barked occasionally when disturbed by rats or mice. The nights were silent, except for bats squeaking as they flitted between the house and the barn searching for prey. The blackness was total when she peered through the open barn doors, except when the moon cast its clear light over everything and shaped shadows of trees and buildings.

Elena sheltered at the remote farmhouse for the winter. She often had severe nightmares that woke her, her ears pounding with gunfire, her eyes swollen and smarting from the tears she'd shed over her lost life and friends. She felt a black sorrow deep in the pit of her stomach and in her mind, the endless guilt of the survivor.

Elena couldn't relate the full details of her escape to Anna and Angelo because she felt treacherous for leaving her friends and neighbours in Caterna. Some nights she woke drenched in sweat, or shivered uncontrollably as though she had a fever.

The peaceful winter days working with Angelo in the fields surrounding the farm developed a strength and resilience in her body. In early spring, she helped to pick the fava beans and spread them over the fields to dry. Angelo sold them as a staple diet for the poor who mashed them with olives. He also grew some wheat and hay which ripened by early April.

The simple homely tasks of helping Anna, learning to bake bread and to cook simple meals on the paraffin stove or on the open fire, provided a soothing and restorative effect on her wounded soul. She experienced comforting flashbacks of helping her grandparents cultivate their land outside Mitorna although she still had occasional vivid nightmares of them. Gradually the sun became warmer and the winter weather gave way to bright spring days. The peace of the countryside helped her close off the trauma of recent tragic events and the grief became more bearable. A steely determination to survive took over and Elena felt able to tell Anna about her escape and the horrific events that occurred in Caterna. Anna could see the naked despair deep in Elena's eyes and understood the hardships she had endured and would face in the future.

Journey to Naples 1943

By late spring, and with much regret, Elena decided to leave the farmer and his wife. The weather was more settled in April, and was warmer. Anna made her a replacement dress out of old curtain material and gave her a coat and old boots for walking. She set out at dawn, wearing her coat and boots, new dress and shawl, a bottle of water, and food in a rucksack Angelo had given her along with some coins for food. She headed west over the dry rocky Murge plateau towards Naples, as advised by Anna and Angelo. She needed to find work and somewhere to live but had no idea whether the journey would take weeks or months. She inhaled the scent of wild thyme and rosemary, looked around at the tiny wild flowers clustering in the shade and felt the first frisson of excitement and hope for the future.

The warmth of the sun increased as she trudged along dusty tracks. She took off the old coat and stopped to eat bread and olives in the shade of a thicket of prickly pear then walked for a few more hours before looking around for somewhere to rest for the night. As the setting sun cast a rosy glow over the stony ground, she put down her rucksack, sat on a flat outcrop of rocks under a large olive tree and looked over the terrain she had walked. She heard the lonely cry of a hunting bird and looked up at the distant dark speck in the sky as she spread the old coat on a flat piece of ground and laid out on the stone slab the remains of the food Anna had given her that morning.

As she ate she could see the track meandering through a grove of trees and disappearing over a hill to the west. She had seen no-one or any buildings that day, only a ramshackle goat shack which seemed deserted.

There had been no sign of the Germans and no news had reached the isolated farmhouse about the progress of the war. Unknowingly, as she walked and stumbled across the central arid plains of Italy, the Allied Forces had invaded Naples and were fighting to defeat the Germans.

Elena lay down, placed her knapsack as a pillow and wrapped herself in the old coat. A slight chill invaded the air once the sun had set, and behind the hill to the east a silver glow promised the moon would rise in the next hour and flood the countryside with light. She heard the flapping of wings as an owl flew into the olive tree and then over the hill, and shivered as she tried to find a comfortable place to lie. Although physically exhausted, she knew sleep would take a long time to come in these strange surroundings.

At dawn next morning, Elena picked up the rucksack, slung it on her shoulder, draped the old coat over the top and walked with her back to the rising sun. A tiny isolated village with white painted buildings sat over the hill and she decided to go there to buy food and fill her water bottle – Angelo had given her some lire for the work she'd done around the farm in the winter.

Trudging across the rocky, semi-arid ground dotted with olive groves that had battled to survive over hundreds of years, she approached the village beside small fields of wheat interspersed with cultivated strips of tomatoes, onions, beans, aubergines and capsicums. A hawk soared on the thermals in the deep blue sky and blossoms lay scattered on the earth from almond, quince trees and wild hawthorn. Their perfume mingled with the scent of wild buttercups and violets growing by the roadside, along with small flowers of vivid blue, white and yellow, red poppies standing over the coarse grass.

The reddish-brown earth surrounding the village was separated by dry stone walls, some in a state of disrepair. Tiny cultivated patches of melons trailed along the ground and she passed a small orchard of almond, fig and citrus trees.

Walking up to the main entrance to the village, Elena entered the piazza where stood the village pump. She filled her water bottle then looked around for a shop or a baker.

She noticed a few market stalls and bought freshly baked bread, vegetables and fruit, sensing the stall holders knew she was a stranger and were cautious, but were pleased to sell their produce when they saw her lire. She also bought a single puma in glazed pottery in the shape of a pine cone, the stall holder telling her it was a good luck symbol — she knew she needed luck to get her to Naples.

Elena stowed these items in her rucksack and, walking to the steps in front of the church, sat down to eat in the shade. A mangy dog roamed around, sniffed her feet then wandered into a side alley. A few children came running past chasing a ball. Otherwise no-one spoke to her. After ten minutes, she walked back to the gateway and continued along the dusty track.

Midday came and for an hour or so she sheltered from the heat in a ruined stone masseria — a fortified farmhouse with an interior courtyard and a protective exterior wall. She walked cautiously past the broken gate and into the ruined barn; lay down on the scattered hay and closed her eyes, waking after a few hours surrounded by scraggy chickens foraging in the hay. Hastily she packed her rucksack and set off again, noticing that the sun was much lower in the sky.

Her lonely journey continued across the Murge plateau in the centre of Puglia, a difficult place to walk over as the ground was rough with narrow ravines and little shade from trees. Occasionally, in early morning, she heard voices and the rattling of old carts going to market. She felt alone and was scared to be sleeping out but realised it was safer than inhabited places. She picked wild plums and olives, and other edible plants — nettles, herbs and dandelions all flourishing in the spring weather. She searched for wild mushrooms and berries, even snails hiding in the ditches to supplement her diet, giving her the energy to continue.

After a week of walking she desperately needed food and fresh water, and noticed a village in the distance. Drawing closer, she could hear water trickling under an old hump-backed stone bridge. An ancient campanile bell chimed midday and she waited until the echo of the bell died away. A wooden fingerpost sign on the track pointed left to the village and Elena followed it, the stony track barely wide enough for one person to walk between the crumbling dry stone walls. She tore a strip from the bottom of her cotton dress and fashioned a turban to protect her head against the searing heat of the sun.

She entered the village through a dilapidated archway and walked into the small piazza where she purchased food from a tiny shop with a beaded curtain hanging over the door; filled her water bottle at the village pump. The village seemed deserted except for a few old men sitting at a table outside a scruffy bar. They stared at her and nudged each other. Elena felt no threat but felt uncomfortable. She continued walking.

Over the following days, Elena crossed the wide limestone plateau that stretched as far as she could see. The area was wild, the arid stony ground supporting little but the grey-green mass of olive groves. Occasionally, low walls enclosed fertile red-brown soil, many uncultivated and invaded by tall weeds and grasses.

Almost hidden in the rocks were low hardy shrubs and spiky grasses; small cactus plants with prickly oval leaves grew in clusters in dips in the ground. Rocks were covered in lichen and bright green lizards flitted to and fro searching for insects. Ants ran across the ground busily searching for food. Elena was bitten when she inadvertently sat on a rock-like ants' nest. She followed animal tracks and indistinct paths used over centuries, battered by a hot dry wind, the trees leaning almost to the ground. She ate berries and nuts and drank stream water in cupped hands; sheltered under the broad leaves of wild fig or olive trees in the heat of the day. She became gaunt and listless but knew she must keep walking day after day to reach Naples.

After an endless four days, Elena left the limestone plateau with its odours of sun-beaten earth and dry grass, and walked through a more fertile area where cultivated orange and lemon groves flourished. She passed small villages built in local tufa stone surrounded by vegetable market gardens. Sometimes, when her hunger overcame her, she waited until dark and raided the gardens for food as she had no money left to buy anything. One evening in the distance, she saw a horse pulling an ancient plough and heard voices in a dialect she couldn't understand, and, at a tumbledown farm a fat couple sat outside on a bench soaking in the last of the sunlight. A small herd of goats clustered nearby, bleating mournfully.

She approached the farm through a gap in the broken boundary wall and noticed two grubby children dressed in rags playing with a mangy dog in a rough courtyard. The man leapt to his feet and brandished a stick, threatening her. He shouted '*Va via, puttana.*' Elena ran down the track, almost falling in her haste to leave.

It was mid-summer when she finally reached the outskirts of Naples, a wide expanse of shimmering azure-blue sea spreading out before her.

Elena stopped to stare, aware of the sun's hazy heat and a strong smell of burning on the hot wind. Evidence of the war surrounded her – crops burnt to stubble in the fields – many buildings destroyed. Two bent old women huddled outside the charred door of a stone hut. German bombers high overhead sought their next target, and out to sea a large ship burned ferociously with small explosions frequently occurring. She trudged on, bypassing the town of Nola at the foot of Monte Cicada and into the western outskirts of Naples.

Elena urgently needed to find shelter, somewhere to rest in safety, and she desperately needed food. When she saw a scruffy café by the roadside with a few dusty seats, she stopped and asked for bread and water from the man lounging in the doorway. He eyed Elena suspiciously, laughed at her unpleasantly and made a rude gesture.

'Aw, give her water – she looks exhausted,' said another dirty man seated at one table. 'Sit down by me,' he said, patting a spare chair. Elena did so and gratefully accepted a mug of water and a crust of stale bread.

The owner winked at his customer and said, 'Nice girl, huh? Alone, are you?' he asked Elena.

She nodded.

'Would you like to rest here?'

'Si, grazie,' replied Elena trustingly.

'Come inside then.'

The man stood in the doorway and Elena had to brush past him to enter. 'There's a bed. Lie down and rest,' he said.

As Elena lowered herself onto the dirty sheet, the owner roughly pushed her and tried to foist himself on her. Elena was physically strong after working on the farm in the winter, and the man was inebriated, fat and old. She heaved with all her strength and managed to push him off the bed onto the dirt floor. She leapt up and rushed out the door, abandoning her ragged backpack. The customer tried to trip her up but she avoided the outstretched leg and ran swiftly down the road, fright aiding her speed until she reached a crumbling stone wall behind which she could hide. Breathing heavily, she peered into the distance and could see no-one following her.

She had no idea the west coast of Italy, including Naples, had been badly bombed by the Allies and the Germans. From Salerno to Rome, villages and towns, farms and fishing harbours had been systematically destroyed, their inhabitants either killed or had escaped as refugees. Buildings around the port and seafront of Naples had been mined. The only thing that had kept Elena walking was the hope she could find safety in the city, but when she saw the state of the streets and buildings, she wondered how anyone could live there.

Her energy drained away as she walked past shattered glass shop windows, and smashed house windows, whether from bombing or looting she didn't know. Whole streets were wrecked and the smell of sewage and rotting rubbish emanated from deserted streets and narrow alleyways. Great piles of building rubble blocked the roads and, although many of the tenements were partially destroyed, people peering out of the leaning doorways and walls indicated they still lived in the wreckage.

The inhabitants were sparsely clothed in tattered black rags or blanket material. They gazed at her furtively with lacklustre eyes, the women, emaciated, grey and dirty, tugging torn shawls over their heads. There were no vehicles, only the occasional wooden cart pulled by a scruffy donkey or a man desperately conveying his possessions to somewhere safer. Four skeletal women crouched on rubble by the roadside nursing their infants and hopelessly staring at the bombed buildings surrounding them. Their clothes were torn and bloody, the children they clutched were lying as if dead, their tiny limbs protruding as if broken.

Not knowing the Neapolitan dialect fuelled Elena's fear.

As twilight gave way to darkness, she sought shelter; hid in the cellar of a blasted building. She trudged the next day further into the city suburbs, sheltered in a ruined church doorway for the night, the silence about her heavy and eerie as groups of soldiers lounging in doorways stared at her contemptuously. She took hope from the German soldiers who, having time to light a cigarette or pass around a bottle, clearly weren't expecting any immediate military action – patrolling the deserted, ruined streets was a formality. It seemed the only other living creatures were rats, feral cats and dogs. No children played in the streets. No women lounged in their doorways, gossiping with neighbours.

Elena's borrowed boots exacerbated her blisters, but she plodded on, determined to reach and find shelter near where people lived. Hunger and thirst plagued her, the dust from the roadway clogged in her throat and the sun beat mercilessly down on her head. Most buildings around her were in ruins, empty and roofless; a few people wandered about, searching with bowed heads for discarded bread and vegetables, even pulling up weeds which they pushed into their mouths with grim determination. She stumbled past burnt out tanks, wrecks of cars, broken furniture and rusted wheels.

In the distance thunder rumbled and swollen dark clouds blocked out the sun, shrouded the ruined buildings. Then large drops of rain dropped heavily, leaving brown stains as they hit the dusty road. And the wind increased. Suddenly rain burst out of the sky, transforming the street into a river. Elena's worn boots slid on the muddy surface, and she was soon soaked, her hair plastered to her head, her clothes sticking to her body.

She sought out shelter as lightning crackled in the black sky, its flash dazzling her. Crawling into a ruined church, she crouched on the ground, her arms hugging her body for warmth. As quickly as it arrived, the storm passed over and she pulled herself upright on the stone wall.

As she left the shelter, Elena noticed other figures creeping away from the church ruins. They were starving, dirty urchins, some clothed in rags, others in stolen oversized army shirts. They stopped and stared at her, blades reflecting the sunlight as they were pulled out of sleeves. A larger boy, about twelve years old, sauntered up to her, his eyes hard and cold. He held his blade out towards her, its angle set for a fast attack. He lifted his left hand to halt his gang members – scugnizzi – and screamed in a high voice, '*Stupido, puttana, dare pronto!*'

Grabbing Elena and reefing her into him, he held the knife at her throat; dragged her to the ground. His gang rough-handled her, searching her clothes for food or coins. She was in a wasteland of ruined buildings, jagged stones, rubble all around her, and no-one around to save her from this aggressive attack. Thinking quickly, she struggled to sit up, picked up a large stone and threw it at the gang.

'*Va, via.* She has nothing,' shouted the leader as his gang-mate clutched his brow, blood trickling from where the stone had struck. He pushed her again and the urchins ran off.

Elena clutched her ragged clothes around her, terrified they would see she was a girl. She scrambled away over the rubble until she found a deep hole in the ground. Once again, her life was in danger but recent experience had made her both cunning and cautious. She noticed a noisy convoy of armoured vehicles some distance away travelling slowly on the potholed road. Head down she scurried towards it, the noise made by loose stones as she ran covered by the engine noise. She scooted alongside it until a dark alleyway appeared – it was filled with noisome rubbish and water.

Leaning flat against a wall, breathing in the stench of sewerage and other putrid things, she waited until the truck had disappeared down the road then ran down the alley to a crossroads of ruined shops. She crouched in the back of a shop for hours, her tight muscles screaming with pain; hid there until daybreak then crept out and continued walking to the city centre, past more rows of empty houses and tall crumbling tenements. Around her, Naples was coming to life: vendors were selling stolen or grown produce – lemons, oranges or old clothes from wooden carts.

Gradually the streets broadened. She saw a few undamaged official buildings; saw German soldiers digging trenches and clearing lines of fire in front of them. An explosion of engine noise filled the air around her as tanks rattled and squealed from potholed side streets, their guns pointing into buildings, soldiers standing in the turrets training binoculars on windows.

Elena hurried on, hiding in the shadows and dodging stalls in a covered market-place. She was terrified, sick with hunger, and exhausted; she collapsed onto the cold stone steps of a church, bowed her head in her hands, no energy or will to continue. She hoped that someone might see her and offer her food and shelter. Tears welled up in her eyes and her shoulders shook as she leant against the cold stone wall sobbing with despair and hopelessness.

The market was set up on the platform of a ruined railway station. Metal archways held up a glass roof which was largely undamaged. The rail lines were rusted and overgrown with weeds, for a long time no trains running along the track. The crowded lively market continued around her for an hour or so as desperate mothers pushed and shoved to find food for the starving children clinging to their rags. Thieves stalked too, sinking their hands into pockets, moving fast in gangs or alone.

By late afternoon the stallholders started packing up and a middle-aged woman sitting on the edge of a wooden cart filled with worn clothes and spoiled fruit, glanced at Elena sitting on the stone steps. She wore a faded brown cotton dress with short sleeves that exposed muscular brown arms. Over her dress she wore a crumpled canvas apron while a cotton scarf was tied round her hair. Her face was brown with deep folds, poverty and tragedy having made their mark, but she had a kind smile. The woman walked over to Elena and touched her arm. Elena flinched and raised her head, tears streaming down her dirty face.

The woman said, "Look at you … you look exhausted and dirty. I can see your bones through your clothes. Where have you come from? Are you a refugee or have you been bombed out? You look so thin and grey, and you have blisters on your face.

'Are you alone? Do you live in Naples? I can give you some leftover fruit – it's worthless after a day in the sun.'

Elena gulped and looked down at her worn dusty boots, ashamed of her helplessness. She wrapped her arms around her chest as if to protect herself from further harm. After hesitating a moment, she nodded her head. '*Grazie*. I'm looking for somewhere safe to shelter tonight.'

Elena was unsure whether to trust the woman. She had travelled alone across Italy, never knowing where the next food or safe shelter would be, and terrified she would be handed over to the Germans. She knew from experience everyone was suspicious of strangers. Although exhausted, she knew the risks of walking through the ruined streets beneath a darkening sky. The woman held out her hand.

'My name is Chiara. I live in those caves in the hill over there. You can shelter with me tonight. It's basic but dry and safe. We keep hoping the Germans will soon be defeated by the Allied Forces and leave the city. It's not safe for you to be out on the streets now.'

Elena drew a deep breath then accepted Chiara's offer. Where else could she go? Just when life was so frightening and hopeless, she'd been offered food and much-needed shelter. '*Grazie*, that is kind of you,' she replied.

Chiara finished packing her stall onto the wooden handcart and beckoned Elena to follow. She plodded along with her bent head, looking only at the uneven ground. Then, when looking up, she realised with a shock they had reached a barren hillside hollowed with caves, outside of which played ragged children. Chiara pulled her cart to the end of a rocky ledge and ducked into a dark little cave, pulling aside a sack curtain hung at the entrance. Inside was a wood fire with a large clay pot on top. Chiara lit the fire and the aroma of herbs and vegetables scented the air. She put a match to a kerosene lamp that stood in the centre of a battered wooden table and beckoned Elena to enter. Elena's eyes took a while to adjust to the gloom then she saw a single room carved out of the rock.

At the back of the cave was a stone ledge with a blanket and pillow on it. Basic cooking utensils lay on another ledge. Chiara pointed to a small wooden stool; handed Elena an earthenware dish and ladled hot broth into the bowl. She perched on her rock bed and greedily spooned the soup into her mouth, using a crust of bread to mop up every morsel. Then she wiped her mouth with her hand when she had finished.

'I live here. My home was bombed a year ago killing my mother and father. I have no family in Naples as my sisters and brothers moved away before the war started. Many people were bombed out of their homes and had only a few basic possessions when they moved to the safety of these caves.'

Chiara took the two bowls and left them outside to be cleaned. She explained there was no piped water to the caves and the inhabitants collected their daily water from a nearby stream and waterfall. Chiara removed her cotton scarf, revealing her ragged short black hair shadowed with grey. The lamplight reflected on her dark eyes that were deep set in the folds of her face — eyes that held a mixture of curiosity and sadness. Her mouth was full but surrounded by deep lines. As Chiara took off her canvas apron and worn cardigan, Elena noticed in the lamplight that her body was spare and thin, years of an inadequate diet taking its toll. Despite her worn peasant clothes and scuffed boots, she spoke in an educated way, her accent not the language of the streets. Chiara used her hands generously to express her feelings and emphasised her words. 'Here's a spare blanket. You can lie on the floor.'

Chiara pulled the entrance curtain across and walked to her bed.

Elena lowered herself to the sandy floor and tucked the blanket around her. Physically and mentally exhausted, she lay on her back, listening to Chiara's light snores and felt so relieved she had somewhere dry and safe to rest for a while. The cave floor was hard but compared to other places she had slept over the past few weeks, she felt comfortable. When she adjusted her position to lie on her side and avoid a couple of jutting stones, she could look out of the cave entrance through a gap in the protective sack curtain. Darkness fell quickly and she saw the first stars appearing bright and clear in the navy sky. Slowly she drifted off to sleep.

Chiara woke her at daybreak. The rising sun cast its rays through the sack curtain making the cave interior glow. Elena folded her blanket and placed it on Chiara's ledge, brushed down her clothes, tied a cotton scarf over her dirty hair and pulled on her worn boots.

'Here's a cup of hot water with a few herbs and a crust of bread. I have brought water in a bowl from the stream so you can wash before you eat. You can borrow my comb to untangle your hair. Tonight we'll go to the stream so you can bathe and wash your hair. We'll go to the market now and look for old clothes for you. I hope to barter some vegetables for them.

'The cave community use the land belonging to a deserted villa a few minutes' walk away. Early in the war, the government allocated uncultivated land for growing vegetables and fruit in an attempt to reduce starvation amongst the people of Naples. The cave community has shared out the land between them and grow produce to eat or sell. There are a few olive and fruit trees on the land.

'But there is no meat so people keep chickens and a goat or two for the milk or trap rabbits. Potatoes, cabbage, tomatoes, parsnips and eggs aren't rationed but it's hard to get much of anything now as few farmers come into city markets.'

Chiara walked to the end of the caves and showed Elena the field where she grew vegetables and had some fruit trees. She straddled the neat rows and pulled lettuces, cabbages, onions and carrots; she dug out a bowl of potatoes and told Elena to pick olives and oranges from the trees. Chiara bundled up some wild herbs and garlic and packed them into a basket which she loaded with the other produce onto her small wooden cart. The two women pulled the cart, one on each handle, down the rocky slope to the lane where others were wending their way to the market, also carrying produce and bags of assorted articles to sell or exchange for food.

Chiara used her cart as a stall and manoeuvred it into position next to a young woman who had a small child tied to her back with cloth. Chiara introduced Elena to her.

'This is Sophia, and the child is Anna. Her husband is fighting somewhere and it's hard for Sophia to get food for her child so I help if I can. You can manage my stall while I barter for some clothes. Watch out for thieves and scugnizzi who pinch things as soon as your back is turned.'

Elena stationed herself behind Chiara's cart and sold the olives and lemons immediately as they were scarce. A bent old man sidled up to her with a begging bowl which he thrust out with dirty knobbly fingers and growled at her. Elena pushed the bowl away said, 'Va. Va presto.'

'*Quanto per le patate?*' a young girl asked her.

'*1 lire.*' Elena handed her the items which the girl placed in her basket and handed Elena the coin. '*Grazie.*'

Chiara returned with a faded cotton skirt and a grey blouse. 'It's the best I can find,' she said. The rest of Chiara's produce was sold by midday so they packed up the cart and bid goodbye to the other market people. Chiara walked with a slight limp over the cratered roads, the wooden cart bouncing noisily on the ridges. They walked past many ruined buildings, their floors exposed, with broken roof timbers projecting dangerously into the street. Some floors had washing strung on rope across the rooms, the owners squatting on the floor, and a woman was cooking on a paraffin stove. Skinny urchins in ragged dirty clothes ran squeaking and screaming, jumping barefoot over broken walls, chasing each other with no concern for danger.

'I'm very glad of your strength helping me push my cart on this part of the road,' puffed Chiara as they trudged up the rocky incline to the hillside. 'Few people walk up here through lack of energy so we live a fairly secure life away from looters. The rock provides a solid shelter against the bombs. Many people fled to the hills to avoid the Germans' mass deportation into forced labour in the camps in Northern Italy and Germany.'

The setting sun shone into the cave entrances, about twenty of which were occupied, some smaller than others. Many had women squatting outside stirring iron pots hung over wood fires, children clustered around them. Chiara noticed Elena sniffing the unusual smell of herbs mingling with burnt fat and singed skin.

'We catch rabbits to cook when we can and eat everything. Sophia there is stewing the last bit of skin with some herbs and bread crumbs to make soup. We dip balls of fat over and over again into hot water to make gruel.

'Some try to sell or barter shoes and such for essentials like bread and fish. Those with nothing to sell or barter are forced to beg, shame making them bow their heads, their children sitting listless at their feet. Some women earn food through prostitution. They avoid sitting by the ruined tenements where local police don't go but stand in market places and crossroads.'

Elena shook her head in dismay. Everyday living was primitive and there was no electricity; the few possessions of the cave dwellers were placed on natural rock shelves inside, although some families had tables and chairs. Small children were tethered to the rocks by strips of cloth to prevent them from falling over the cliff edge. Old people sat on rocks and lumps of wood, unable to comprehend the drastic changes in their lives.

Chiara explained that the cave dwellers helped each other when they could because they had all experienced the trauma of bombing. Young boys were encouraged to hunt for small animals like rabbits to supplement their diet. When darkness hid the devastated city, children cried with exhaustion as the cave dwellers silently drifted into their basic shelters, their only necessity trying to find something to eat the next day.

A few days later when returning from the market, Chiara stopped at a ruined tenement and called out, 'Maria, Maria, here's some food for you.'

A thin young woman with a worn face and roughly-cut, short hair peered over the edge of a broken floor. She gave a wobbly smile and held onto the small child clinging to her sack dress. 'Buongiorno, Chiara.'

'Here are a few vegetables and fruit that were spoiling in the hot sun. I scrounged half a loaf of stale bread for you too,' shouted Chiara.

'Grazie, grazie, Chiara. You are kind. My boys are always hungry. I'll make a soup with the bread and vegetables that will feed us for a few days,' replied Maria then she called her children to come and eat. Chiara placed the items in a battered straw basket that Maria hung over the rafters on a length of frayed string.

'*Ciao*, Maria. I will come again in a day or so. *Andare con Dio.*'

Chiara walked away, followed by Elena who glanced back at the ruined building that housed the small family. She could sense the danger and desperation that surrounded them. Several floors above, a wisp of smoke drifted from an iron pot hung on a beam, tended by a crouched old woman.

'Maria's husband was killed by a bomb last year when he was out searching for work. She lived in the countryside before she came to Naples and married Paolo. She was pregnant when she heard the news of his death. That same week, the tenement where they lived was bombed again and she tried to survive with her children in one room. She moved to this tenement about two months ago although she is desperately anxious all the time for the boys' safety, and worried about them mixing with scugnizzi. I save leftover vegetables when I can or scrounge a scrap of meat or a crust of bread to give them.'

Chiara and Elena left the bomb-damaged main street, and pushed the small wooden cart up the slight rugged incline to the caves. Elena glanced at Chiara, grateful that she had met someone who was caring.

'That's kind of you to help Maria and her family,' she said quietly.

'She was a school friend of my daughter, Lucia, who left Naples before the war and found work in Rome. Maria is a gentle person who cares deeply for her children. She has lost everything in this war yet still manages to keep her family fed and clothed. She saved very little from the bombing and helps out at the market when she can find someone to keep an eye on the children. Of course, there's no schooling for them.'

'When I can pick up a piece of material in the market, I make replacement clothes for the ones they've outgrown. Many young mothers have to prostitute themselves to the soldiers in order to support their families.'

'She is so thin and pale, she is probably starving herself to feed her children,' Elena said sadly.

'Like most people living in and around Naples now. You're very thin yourself. When you feel comfortable with me, perhaps you'd like to tell me how you came to be in Naples in such a ragged, desperate state. We cave dwellers barely have enough food for ourselves these days and all the children who live in the caves are barefoot and dressed in basic clothing which is shared between the families. You have noticed there are no men here – they have either been killed, are still fighting in the war, or have been captured by the Germans and transported to labour camps in Northern Italy or Germany.

'The whole of Naples is struggling ...' She shook her head. 'This war has gone on for four years now ... And the Germans ... they are brutal and shoot randomly on the streets. The small son of my neighbour was shot last week as he ran into a ruined shop to steal something to eat.' Chiara stopped talking, breathless from the exercise.

One evening a few weeks later, sitting beside a small wood fire at the cave's entrance while Chiara warmed a vegetable soup in a chipped terracotta pot, Elena decided to explain why she was in Naples.

'My village was invaded by German soldiers but a priest helped me escape. I walked across Italy from a small town in the west of Puglia. I have no family and wanted to reach Naples where I hoped to find work and shelter. I felt so frightened and alone but people helped me. It was a long exhausting trek over the Murge plateau and the ground was very rough most of the time. Few people live in the countryside now and those that remain are so poor, trying to eke an existence out of the arid land. I never thought I would get here as I walked through streets of damaged buildings and past hundreds of homeless people. I even managed to escape an attack by a gang of scugnizzi.

'I have no money and only the clothes I am wearing,' Elena stammered, trying to control her tears. She saw sympathy etched on Chiara's face and took several deep breaths as her words poured out, sharing her tragic story with someone who had also suffered in the war.

'You have no family to go to for support? There are many Italians who have suffered badly in this war. I sometimes wonder why it had to happen and when it will end,' Chiara said sadly.

An ancient bent woman stumbled up and stared at them, her white hair wild, her face badly marked by smallpox. She was gaunt with hunger and age, her hands misshapen claws as she reached out to Chiara's plate and grabbed a carrot, which she stuffed into her toothless mouth. Cackling with laughter, she leant into Elena, pointing a dirty finger. Elena shrank back in fear.

'Alicia, move away. You are scaring my niece who has come to live with me for a while.' Chiara gently pushed the distorted face away and stood to help the old woman to a cave further along the hillside.

'Pour soul. She lost her mind when her husband and four children were killed in an early bombing raid. Alicia was out shopping at a market and returned home to find the building destroyed and a pile of rubble. The searchers never found the bodies of her family. A neighbour now looks after her and feeds her. There are many similar tragedies that the people living here have experienced. That's why we support each other.'

Elena bit her lip and brushed away tears as she reflected that nearly every-one she met had painful experiences of loss and destruction.

'You can stay here with me for a while longer if you work on my market stall,' Chiara replied sympathetically.

Over the next few months, Elena helped Chiara. She felt safe living in Chiara's cave and enjoyed the community of the other cave dwellers and being with the market stallholders. Elena had no thought of the future and had deliberately shut out her memories of the past. She mourned her youth and the loss of her friends which had dimmed her natural zest for life. She had never had an easy life and must now deal with the constraints of being without family and a home.

Elena soon learned as she worked at the market that Chiara enjoyed haggling with customers in a friendly way but knew the value of her produce according to availability, demand and the season. She had several customers who regularly bought from her, some obviously friends, who greeted her with a smile and a kiss on the cheek, or a query about her family. Differentiating quickly between these people and those that insisted on a bargain regardless of the market price, Elena became competent and fast dealing with the customers, placing their purchases in a straw basket or string bag, mentally adding the prices in her head.

She adapted to the physical hardships of living in the cave through the winter months – Chiara found Elena an old man's cloth coat which they washed in the stream. Wearing thick stockings and a dress with some old boots Chiara obtained at the market, Elena kept warm. She made a straw pallet and knitted a woollen blanket to wrap around her. They made a tiny brick hearth with material gleaned from bombed buildings in the centre of the cave and, with the heavy sack curtain pulled across the entrance, Elena and Chiara were cosy inside. Some nights when the wind blew in from the sea and around the sack curtain, it was bitterly cold but they sat closer to the fire, creating an atmosphere of intimacy.

One miserable winter's night, the rain splashing down outside and the draughts drifting into the cave around the thick sack curtain, Chiara talked about living in Naples before the war. She sat comfortably on her bed, a blanket wrapped around her and Elena perched on a stool near the fire. They had grown close in the last few months and were drinking a cup of cheap wine to lessen the chill – Chiara now treated Elena like a daughter and Elena absorbed her motherly warmth.

'My father owned a small bookshop just off Via Spaccanapoli which bisects the historical city centre of Naples and is two kilometres long. The shop was in Via San Biagio dei Librai, where many Neapolitan bookshops are located. Outside the shop door, my father had placed two wooden bookcases with locked glass doors to display his best books, some very valuable, or special editions. My father had been educated at the University and spoke several languages – French and Spanish.' Chiara paused to sip some wine.

'Before the war, the street attracted many visitors. It was a picturesque street with tall three and four-storey stone buildings decorated with iron balconies and flowering plants. The street was narrow, and paved with large pitted granite stones. There were *Tabacchi, Trattoria and Merceria* between the bookshops, their fronts open to the street and canvas awnings providing shade from the sun. The church of Santa Chiara, my namesake saint, was about fifty metres from my father's bookshop and, as a family, we went there regularly for mass.'

Chiara rose and pulled the sack curtain tighter round the doorway, used a couple of heavy stones kept there to anchor it, then continued telling the story of her childhood.

'We were a happy family: my mother and father cared deeply for each other and for all of us. I had two older sisters and two older brothers and we lived in an apartment above the shop. We helped my father manage the bookshop and ran errands.

'New books arrived in rough wood crates and were stored at the back until they were unpacked. My father encouraged us to read any of the books in his shop and to learn French and Spanish. Then my father had to fight in World War I and was injured with gas in the trenches so, when he returned at the end of the war, he needed help lifting the crates of books and walking up and down the steep ladders to reach less popular books for customers. My mother and I continued working in the family shop as my sisters and brothers married and moved away.'

Chiara propped a pillow behind her head and laid down on her bed, lost in her memories. 'When this war started, we took most of the books off the shelves and packed them into crates, and moved them into the cellar, hoping they could be retrieved when the war ended. We had no idea how long the war would last, nor the scale of destruction by enemy bombs. We felt safe for the first year, sheltering in the cellar when the bombs dropped, but one night we heard hundreds of heavy aircraft flying low overhead. The ground shuddered as the bombs fell on the street. We cowered in the cellar praying the bookshop would be saved … but it wasn't. We heard the whistling as the bombs shot through the air and crashed into it, obliterating it completely. We managed to scramble out of the cellar and huddled together in the ruins of the street, shuddering in shock.' Chiara paused and bent her head, wiping the tears from her face.

'It was terrible. My mother was badly injured when some masonry fell on her leg and my father had great difficulty breathing because of the dust.

'Some neighbours helped us out of the rubble and we managed to reach the safety of the church of Santa Chiara. It had a deep stone crypt and we hoped to rest there, but the church had been bombed and crowds of families were trying to push their way into the crypt. We just sat down in the ruins. My father's face was blue with the effort of breathing and blood poured from my mother's leg. We were filthy, covered in dust, our clothes torn during the escape from the cellar. Everyone was stunned and mute with shock. After an endless time, we pushed into a tiny space in the crypt, a niche for a plaster Madonna statue.

'My father fell to the ground, panting heavily, and died that night of asphyxiation. My mother became feverish with an infection in her leg and died after a day. I was alone and had no other family. I sat in the gloom crying desperately for my dead parents and lost home. Someone shared a bottle of water with me and patted my back. I sat on the stone floor through that endless night, my knees pulled up and my head resting on my arms.

'When a dusty light shone through the open crypt door, I knew I had to help my parents so I walked to the nearest hospital. The emergency area was filled with injured and desperate people and I could find no-one to help me. I wandered outside and saw an ambulance unloading stretchers of wounded people and taking them inside the hospital. I hurried up to one ambulance man returning empty-handed to his vehicle and tugged on his sleeve, tears flooding my face.

"Please, please help me. My parents have been killed in the bombing and are still in the crypt of San Chiara with many other injured people. Can you bring my parents to the hospital and help the others?'

"I'll ask my boss if I can,' the ambulance driver told me. I hung onto his arm as he re-entered the hospital and interrupted a doctor sorting out the dead and wounded in his emergency room.

"*Sì, sì*,' the doctor replied, waving a blood-stained arm.

'I followed the driver to his ambulance and scrambled into the front seat to direct him to the church. I helped him to carry my parents to the vehicle and then assisted moving other injured people until the ambulance was full. We drove slowly through the ruined streets, avoiding bomb craters and dead bodies, burning buildings, smashed carts and bikes. I followed as the hospital staff took my parents to the morgue, said a brief prayer for them and kissed their faces. Then I wandered out of the hospital and sat on a broken tree stump in the street. Like you, Elena, I had no family, no home and didn't know where to go or what to do.'

'I sat there until darkness came, too traumatised with grief to find shelter and food. Then I saw a tiny corner café glowing with light across the road. It was blessedly whole and comforting when I walked inside. I found a few coins in my pocket and bought a coffee and bread. The food revived me and I looked around the room at the other customers. Many looked like me, covered in dust with tear-streaked faces or blood seeping from hastily patched wounds.'

Chiara paused, her emotions still raw with the trauma of the bombing and the searing tragedy of losing her parents. She took a few sips of the wine and shifted her position on the stone ledge, putting her hand to her back to ease the ache. This was the first time she had recounted her war experiences to anyone but she felt a deep connection with Elena who had also suffered such tragedy and loss.

Silence lingered a while as the two women relived their painful experiences and the gruelling attempts to start a new life in a war-torn country. The firelight flickered on the cave walls and Elena rose to put two small logs on the fire. She walked over to Chiara, held both her hands and kissed her cheek.

'Thank you for confiding in me. If you want to continue, I would be honoured to listen.'

Chiara unfolded her tightly held lips, lifted her shoulders to release her tension and smiled at Elena.

'I couldn't stay in the café all night so I asked the waiter if there was an air raid shelter nearby where I could sleep. He directed me down the road to an underground shelter that ran under the railway station. There was a dense blackness covering the streets except where rain puddles lay in the gutters. I felt my way along, touching the damp stone walls, stumbling at times over the rubble and broken paving caused by bombs. It was the most terrifying walk in my life as I sensed other people around but couldn't see them, and I didn't know if they were threatening and looting or bomb victims like me. Finally, I saw a kerosene lamp on the pavement lighting an entrance to a tunnel. A uniformed soldier beckoned to me and helped me into the tunnel. It was dimly lit by overhead lamps and a few candles in wall sconces, and was crowded with people. The smell that wafted over me was indescribable, a mixture of sweat, unwashed bodies and desperate fear. I crept inside and a woman moved slightly to leave me a space to sit down.

'I crouched in my tight spot for two days and nights, sobbing at times, dozing a little and shuddering with the fright and the terrible tragedy that had befallen me. People passed me as they walked in or out of the tunnel entrance, some clutched crying babies or tugged skeletal children by the hand. Occasionally someone slid in, a piece of bread or squashed fruit or even weeds held tightly to their chests. My stomach rumbled with hunger but I felt no inclination to eat, only taking an occasional cup of water given by a neighbour.

'I knew I had to get to my feet and walk out of the tunnel. I had to find some strength to continue living but had no idea where to start as getting any food on the streets was almost impossible. And it was dangerous for a lone woman out there amongst the ruined buildings, as looters and feral child gangs, scugnizzi, roamed the alleyways robbing with violence. I lifted my head and stared out the tunnel entrance, willing myself to move. A young woman struggled past, holding a howling baby, with two small children clutching one hand. They were dust covered and gaunt.

'I stood up and held out my hand to the children, deeply touched by the young woman's predicament. Can I help you? I am alone and bombed out of my home. Perhaps we could search together for something to eat. I can see you are as desperate as I am.'

The woman tried to push past me but the smallest child smiled tremulously and took my hand, looking up into my face with a heart-breaking plea for food. The woman stopped and shifted the crying baby to her other hip, staring at me suspiciously.

'I won't hurt you or the children. Please let me help.'

'Follow me closely and take one child. They are both tied to my waist with string so don't attempt to run away with her.' The woman looked frightened but was fiercely protective of her family. 'I am going to the market in the railway station where I beg for food. There may be some rotten fruit or ends of stale bread that I can give my kids.'

'I held the small girl's dirty hand and followed her mother closely, linked by the string like an umbilical cord. We trudged down the road and entered a marketplace, partly sheltered by iron girders overhead, some with glass intact. There were rough stalls selling worn clothing and shoes, their owners trading them for food. One stall was portioning out chunks of bread at extortionate prices and others held squashed and bruised tomatoes and potatoes.

'The market was crowded with people pushing and shoving to snatch something to eat. The young woman identified herself as Alicia and found a doorway to stand in and put down a battered tin plate. She handed me a tin can and asked me to fill it from the water pump nearby. Her desperation showed strongly on her face as a few crumbs of bread were dropped on the plate and the children scrabbled to shove it into their mouths. I gave the water to Alicia who rationed it to each child then dribbled some into the baby's mouth.

'We waited in that doorway for hours, sheltering from the heat of the sun. As the market stalls were emptied, a few owners walked past Alicia and dropped bits of fruit or bread onto her plate. She ate nothing but gave it all to her children. I kissed her and decided to leave. I wanted to ask the stall holders if they needed help and could suggest a safe place where I could sleep that night. A few the stallholders swore at me and called me 'puttana' but I carried on, hoping someone would be kind amidst all the horror and starvation around us. A priest in a dusty soutane was walking round the market, blessing people where he could and talking with others. He looked as thin and dirty as everyone else but I approached him and smiled to show I wasn't a threat.

'I have been bombed out of my home and my parents are dead. I am trying to find somewhere safe to sleep tonight and maybe something to eat. Can you help please?' The priest sternly looked me up and down, gauging my need and desperation.

'Come with me to my church where I am sheltering other homeless people and feeding them what I can.'

I nodded, too exhausted and grateful to word my thanks but I kissed his hand. I stayed in the church for several weeks, helping mothers with their children and collecting food from kindly stallholders. It was a rewarding experience and smothered the pain and trauma I had experienced when I saw emaciated and injured children, and desperate mothers. One stallholder selling piles of cast-off clothes said I could help him for a while and rest in the ruined building where he lived. That was the start of my recovery. I liked the rough and ready atmosphere of the market stallholders and after several months took over a vegetable stall on a handcart belonging to an old crippled man. I completely understood your despair and fear when I saw you crouched on the church steps.'

Bombing of Naples 1940-1943

Another evening while they huddled round the fire inside the cave, Chiara explained about the devastating impact of the German and Allied bombing on the city and its people. She had placed a lighted kerosene lantern on the table to cast a friendly glow over the cave walls. Sheets of rain hammered on the ground outside and blew the sack curtain inwards, causing the fire to smoke.

'It was before Christmas 1940, in November, when the British bombers attacked the port and the Stazione Centrale. We were told that they bombed at night to begin with to limit casualties. Throughout 1941 and 1942, the bombing continued, destroying the port, hitting the steel mills at Bagnoli, the munitions factory in Via Campegna, the explosives depot at Corso Malta and the aircraft engine factory at Pomigliano d'Arco. Neapolitans tried to get to the emergency shelters as residential and government buildings were hit by stray bombs and collapsed. The tenements were overcrowded and it was a nightmare to get out with small sleepy children and frail old people. We heard that one of the underground shelters in the Piazza Concordia had collapsed killing most of the people inside. It was terrible and we helped people where we could, but there were few medical facilities and no way to reach or contact hospitals.

By Christmas 1942, the Americans had bombed the port again and sunk three cruisers. We heard the explosions and saw clouds of black smoke and roaring flames spiral into the sky as vessels burned. In March 1943 the ship Caterina Costa was bombed while it was anchored in the port. We heard there were 600 people killed and 3,000 injured. On March 14 and 15 1943, the most severe bombing of the war by the

Germans left 300 Neapolitans dead and many injured, and few buildings were left intact. The heavy bombing continued and caused terrible destruction in the city, including hospitals and the Post Office. Hundreds of civilians were killed. Some of my neighbours had walked into the city when there seemed to be a lull in the bombing to search for lost relatives. They said that all the main streets had been destroyed, the roads were full of craters, ruined vehicles had been left abandoned and many buildings had collapsed. The Basilica of Santa Chiara, my namesake saint, had been severely damaged, the beautiful stained-glass windows shattered. Many hospitals were destroyed by US bombers, as well as the areas of Carmine and Capodimente.

'It was this daily massacre of civilians and destruction of whole streets including la Via Duomo and Via Tribundi that made me decide to move out of my apartment. I loaded what I could onto my handcart and headed to the hills with crowds of other locals where we found shelter in the caves. Whole families moved in, laying old people on the rock floor, placing their sparse belongings on stone ledges. It was very frightening, especially for the children. The caves are cold in winter but solidly protective against bombs, and at least there are enough caves for different families to live separately. The underground shelters in the city were horribly overcrowded, and noisy with babies crying and small children running around aimlessly. There was much drunkenness as people tried to drown their worries, and sickness was rife due to poor food and lack of medical aid. There was no toilet or washing facilities and cooking was difficult.

When the American B-24 Liberator bombers were destroying our city, we were so relieved we could shelter in the caves; the only defence we could see from the caves was a few guns placed on building rooftops.'

Chiara stopped to sip a mug of hot water and wipe away her tears: so many people had lost friends and relatives; they were all suffering and had no idea when the bombing and fighting would stop or when they could return to the city, even if they had no homes to return to.

Elena listened in silence, trying to understand the sheer terror of seeing a whole city demolished, night after night, by lethal swarms of bombs. The rain had stopped and a crowd of cave dwellers gathered at the cave entrance as Chiara told their story, many sobbing, and clutching their children protectively. There were no men and few youths. Some had been badly injured by bombs, including a child who had lost an arm. The survivors were gaunt and listless, their eyes blank; their clothes ragged and torn. Children were clothed in cut-down adult clothes with no shoes.

Chiara lifted her head and continued: 'At the start of the bombing, the government encouraged the inhabitants of Naples to shelter in the ancient tunnels under the city, these hollowed out in the soft volcanic rock by the Romans. In 1941, almost 250 miles of tunnels and waterways was cleared by Mussolini's government, wells sealed, stairways built, electricity and basic plumbing installed. Neapolitans lived in these tunnels throughout the continuous heavy British and US forces bombing.

'Many of the tunnels connected with natural cave systems, and had been used to bury plague victims in the seventeenth century, and by the Romans to store water in underground cisterns. Naples is built on tufo which is made of layer on layer of volcanic ash and rock from the eruptions of Mount Vesuvius. The Romans used it for building.'

Chiara's voice was eclipsed by the roar of German bombers overhead, pursued by American fighter planes. The cave dwellers hastily dispersed and rushed into their cave sanctuaries. The Germans, determined to delay the Allies as they approached from the south, wrecked the port of Naples and battered the city so badly there was nothing to benefit them. The Germans worked with brutal thoroughness as the citizens hid in fear as the city was destroyed around them. Smoke rose in clouds from burned business and hotels. The streets filled with mountains of rubble from dynamited buildings, wild fires and bomb crater holes. The Post Office was wrecked by a huge explosion, and there were frequent detonations of unexploded bombs hidden in booby traps.

Gangs of armed Neapolitans youths roamed the streets searching for guns on dead bodies. They stole tin hats and clothes from dead and wounded soldiers. Barefoot and starving, they smoked cigarette stubs found in the gutters, looted buildings and churches alike. They fought a guerrilla war as snipers, their knowledge of the back alleys and cellars invaluable. Many were injured and died as they fought the retreating Germans.

Allied Invasion of Italy Autumn 1943

In early September 1943, General Montgomery arrived from the port of Messina in Sicily and invaded Italy south of Salerno. His forces were supported by British battleships, *HMS Nelson, HMS Warspite, HMS Rodney* and *HMS Valiant*, and a fleet of cruisers, destroyers and gunboats. The fleet pounded the Germans until they withdrew to the north to a range of jagged mountains, where roads were narrow and winding, with many bridges, viaducts, culverts and tunnels. It was an easily defensible terrain for the Germans as the Allies fought through to reach Naples from Salerno and Sorrento. US and British troops fought the Germans for another nine days until they retreated from the beachhead between Salerno and Sorrento. Neapolitans could hear heavy clashes in the hills to the north and gunfire rattled like a storm, threatening but not visible.

Night after night the citizens of Naples were woken by the roar of four hundred Allied aircraft and bombs falling indiscriminately on housing and churches. The Basilica of Santa Chiara was severely damaged although the nearby church of Gesu Nuova was spared. Lurid flashes of anti-aircraft fire tore open the night sky, obliterating the stars. The citizens moved into cellars, tunnels, churches, anywhere to escape the continual danger. Shells screamed overhead and exploded in the streets. The ground shook and plaster fell from walls and ceilings of the remaining buildings. The final Allied bombing raids stopped and the 'all clear' sounded as Italy surrendered and the Armistice was signed on September 8 1943.

By now, the people of Naples had had enough and started to fight back against the Germans. On September 9 1943, clashes occurred between the remaining Germans and the citizens of Naples. On September 10, Neapolitan rebels fired on German military vehicles as they attempted to take over the Vittoria Gallery. Police officers opened fire as the Germans attacked their station in the city on September 11, forcing their surrender. Rebel barricades were erected in the streets and fierce fighting erupted all over the city. German command was forced to come to terms with the uprising as their forces needed to leave before the Allied forces took over the city, the Germans having to reach their defensive Gustav Line where their other military forces were based that could block the Allied troops from advancing.

On September 27, another uprising of Neapolitan rebels began in earnest. Barricades were erected and the fierce fighting caused a mass exodus of German civilians from Naples, some travelling in cars piled high with belongings, some pushing handcarts holding their possessions, others on foot clutching a case or sack of personal effects. The Neapolitans watched sullenly and in silence as the hated invaders moved out, dropping items in their haste.

A column of German military vehicles moved out of the city centre, torching government buildings and ransacking galleries where they could. Unexploded bombs were left where they fell. Time bombs were hidden in strategic places such as factories, offices and railway stations to terrorise those remaining. Military ships were scuttled in the harbour to hinder access for the Allied fleet.

By October 1, the advanced Allied units entered Naples, and the US 82nd Airborne Division occupied the city. The barrage of bombs stopped and Naples became a ferment of activity as Allied forces fought through the deserted streets towards the heart of the city. Explosions and gunfire continued day and night, the invasion ending suddenly, although sporadic gunfire continued to the south and east of the city. Smoke drifted across the devastated skyline.

Where they could, civilians scurried out from cellars, tunnels and basements into the sunlight, and neighbour embraced neighbour, congratulating themselves that they were still alive. They looked with disbelief through the metal beams that stretched across gaping, ruined buildings at the azure-blue Naples sky that had been obliterated for months by a curtain of bombs and dust.

On October 7, the major post office in Naples was destroyed by a delayed-action bomb, placed by the Germans before evacuating, killing and injuring many civilians and Allied soldiers.

The worst damage was in the port as the harbour was clogged with more than a hundred wrecked ships. Dockside cranes, piers and wharves had been dynamited by intensive German bombing over the previous weeks. US engineers marshalled the sunken vessels to form jetties so landing craft could be brought into the harbour a few days after the Germans left.

By early October 1943, Allied troops moved through the city in trucks and jeeps, the citizens cheering wildly, young girls blowing kisses to the men.

The remaining churches rang their bells, one after the other, in celebration of Naples being freed from the Germans.

The Germans retreated into the mountains behind Naples where local partisan brigades, based in forest camps, attacked them to protect isolated villages from killing and burning. Many of the guerrillas were anti-fascist and had helped downed or escaping Allied servicemen from being captured and either hung or despatched north as prisoners of war.

The Neapolitans who had survived the severe bombing attacks continued their search for the basics of life — shelter, food and clothing. They were skeleton thin and lice-ridden, their ill-nourished children covered in rat bites and rags, most of them barefoot, the smaller ones tagging behind. There was little food, only vegetables that could be grown in waste ground. Rabbits, rats and birds were trapped to supplement their diet.

Whole streets had been demolished including the stately buildings lining the Lungomare Partenope. The Excelsior

Hotel was still standing intact, as well as the Grand Hotel Parkers which had been requisitioned by the Germans.

Neapolitans worked alongside regiments of US engineers to clear city streets of rubble, assisted by bulldozers which lifted heavy building material. The engineers repaired the city sewers and aqueduct, and the transport infrastructure so supplies and ammunition arriving on ships could be carried into city by train. Within two weeks the Allies were unloading 3,500 tons of cargo a day. Food was delivered by trucks, and civilians queued for American food.

The Allies established military hospitals to treat the enormous number of wounded, both military and civilians. Many had died of typhus in the winter of 1943 and Allied forces used stretchers to remove the decaying bodies hidden under piles of stones and bricks.

Meanwhile the US Fifth Army moved on from Naples and headed to the east coast to capture the important airfield at Foggia from the Germans.

On December 2 1943 German bombers made a surprise raid on Bari harbour on the Adriatic Sea. A munitions ship secretly carrying mustard gas exploded and cause many casualties in the crew and dock civilians.

Eruption of Mount Vesuvius March 1944

Mount Vesuvius, one of the most dangerous volcanoes in the world, started erupting at the beginning of January 1944. Located nine kilometres east of Naples and a short distance from the sea, it destroyed the Roman cities of Pompeii, Herculaneum, Oplontis and Stabiae in AD 79.

US Fifth Army meteorologists based two miles from Mount Vesuvius noticed magma seeping from the edge and a plume of smoke rising from the summit. The smoke stopped on March 13 and Neapolitans emerged on the streets, accustomed to the minor eruptions and deep rumbling noises of their mountain. It was like living with a sleeping giant who occasionally became angry and emitted thunder-like crashes and spumes of burning lava.

On March 18, the caldera on the summit of Vesuvius ferociously erupted again and emitted a catastrophic flow of flashing red lava of molten rock, pulverised rock, ash and volcanic gases that developed into a front ten metres high. The thunderous noise of the continuous eruptions was deafening, and heavy clouds of ash and sulphuric fumes blocked out the sky and sun. Lava steamed down the mountain's flanks to the west and south west, uprooting flaming trees and bushes in its path, and carrying an avalanche of molten volcanic rock. It destroyed the villages of Massa di Somma, San Sebastiano al Vesuvio and Ottaviano, and part of San Giorgio a Cremano. The dome of the San Sebastiano church was swept away on the top of the lava and travelled some distance before being consumed.

The fiery lava advanced slowly and inexorably, systematically destroying everything in its path – churches, houses, monuments and farmland. Seemingly inexhaustible, the murderous flow crashed down roads, lanes and fields spreading over bomb craters and ditches, heedless in its fury of human life. The mountain behind roared its anger. The smell of sulphur filled the city and the hot air created a smoky haze that made it difficult to breathe and see. Huge clouds of sulphuric smoke continually billowed from the summit highlighted by static electricity.

In a futile attempt to ask God to stop the destruction, a group of courageous priests walked alone in front of the lava flow, carrying wooden effigies of saints. They seemed to be subsumed in their faith even though the elderly monks, choking on the poisonous air, collapsed in a heap on the burning ground.

No-one stood at the roadside to watch them passing. The fear of death or crippling injuries was pervasive and paralysed minds and bodies in the city of Naples. The ten-metre-high lava front dwarfed them like a burning flood tide. The sky was an opaque dark red; the suffocating heat settled like a heavy woollen blanket on the city. The horrific smell of burning flesh surrounded the priests as their sandaled feet and robes caught fire. They seemed to be in a holy hypnotic state, lifting their faces to the smoky dark sky, chanting Latin prayers and waving thuribles of incense. Their hands were raised to cast out blessings to the suffering populace. Nobody was near enough to receive them.

For days, Neapolitans watched through windows in fear and horror as huge fountains of burning lava erupted thousands of metres above the summit of Vesuvius and the black fiery force of the lava inched towards the city streets. Blue flames of gas and sheets of incandescent flames shot high into the sky and cascades of tephrite stones showered the city. A gigantic cloud of sulphuric ash spewed in the air and covered buildings in a deep blanket of burning debris and ash.

Chiara and Elena watched in horror with the other cave dwellers peering round their sack entrance coverings as the city was further destroyed in front of them. The sky was an eerie blood red, the atmosphere choked with toxic fumes, ash and burning embers. Street after street was demolished, the ruins glowing with fire. Fallen beams sparked and crackled. Buildings crumpled and crashed to the fiery ground. Church domes disintegrated into heaps of molten lead and glass.

Chiara and Elena watched the glass canopy of the rail station where their market was held tear apart as the metal frames melted and crashed to the ground. Ash obliterated vehicles and trees and they were deafened by the noise of destruction and the roar of Mount Vesuvius.

'I am so frightened for Maria and her children. They have no protection from the ash and burning stones in that tenement,' Chiara said to Elena wiping her tears. 'I pray for them. There are so many homeless people living on the streets and in the ruins of the city. There will be very little medical help for them.'

'I hope our friends in the station market got out before the glass roof collapsed. It's terrible to see Naples destroyed even more. We may be safe in the caves but so many friends and family still live in the city,' Elena shuddered with fear.

For a week, thick, gaseous, acid smoke obscured the city and the Bay of Naples. Ambulances and police vehicles could not travel through the blocked streets and medical services were tightly shut against the fumes and heat. People squatting in bombed tenements tried to find cover from the burning rain of embers and hot ash. The air raid shelters were crammed full of families and the sick.

At this time, one of the cave dwellers walked down to the station to see the bomb damage; she had picked up a local newspaper from the ground and handed it round the cave dwellers. The headlines stated that the 'Airfield of the USAAF 34th Bombardment Group located at Pompeii, a few kilometres from the base of the volcano, was covered in soot, ash and abrasive pumice. The tephra and hot ash damaged the fabric surfaces, engines, windscreens and gun turrets of nearly 80 B-25 Mitchell bombers. The scale of destruction hampered military transport and machinery from clearing the rubble and repairing the runways and hangars.

On the fertile plains outside Naples, peasants wept as their fields and crops were covered in poisonous ash one metre deep. Their livestock burned as they stood in the pastures, the thatched roofs and wooden structures of barns and sheds burst into flame and burnt to the ground.

The Bay of Naples and its port were obscured from view, although gigantic columns of flames from burning ships broke through the ash-laden atmosphere and highlighted the crane towers. Ghostly ships sank into the water, tiny stick figures trying frantically to douse the flaming decks or leaping into the sea in a desperate bid to save themselves before the vessels detonated and sank. The 19th century funicular cable car on Mount Vesuvius melted.

Tears, mingled with ash, poured down the cave dwellers cheeks as they watched the disaster, terrified for neighbours and family living in the city ruins. Basic meals were cooked and shared, and only the elderly was helped inside the caves to rest. Night and day looked the same with no sun rises or sunsets, only the poisonous blanketing cloud. Burning ash infiltrated the cave, covering everything, the flimsy blankets hung at the cave entrances swinging aside in the hot polluted air. Sleep became difficult as Mount Vesuvius thundered its fury and spewed its fiery magma in a murderous fountain over the city.

On March 26, a heavy snowstorm hit Naples, snow mixing with the deep ash covering, cementing on streets and roofs, further preventing access to shops and medical facilities.

By March 29, the eruption ceased and the lava flow reached its furthest point. After the endless nightmare days, the cave dwellers roused themselves to wash and dust off the ash coating them and their belongings. Mats and bedding, cloths and coats were shaken over the cliff edge and a continuous queue of people walked to the nearby waterfall and stream to cleanse and cool their bodies.

They heard that twenty-six people perished from the volcano's eruption, mostly from roofs collapsing under the weight of ash. Rail lines and streets were blocked for days, many obliterated. Italian crews used shovels and bulldozers to try and clear the tracks, their task gruesome as they dug out incinerated bodies caught in the deadly lava flow. Many tenements, already damaged by the continuous bombing, had crumbled into heaps of rubble, making the task of clearing streets almost impossible.

Despite the horrific impact of the volcanic eruption and the atrocities of war, Neapolitans tried to regain some form of normal life. A black market developed to supply basic necessities and food, but farmers sold their produce at very high prices. The aid from American sources was woefully inadequate and people were starving.

On a chilly winter's day at the end of March 1944, Chiara and Elena made their way into the devastated city to search for food and people they knew. Many fires still burned in the ruins; many buildings were now just crumbling walls with gaps where windows had been blown out or melted. Streets were coated with volcanic ash.

Chiara and Elena walked slowly down the hill towards the city, looking around at the devastation from the bombing and Vesuvius. Weeds and grass growing by the roadside were burnt to a crisp, and wooden wayside huts normally selling vegetables and fruit were piles of ash and detritus. As they neared the city outskirts they climbed over rubble, avoided bomb craters as they headed to the marketplace in the station.

Despite the terrible damage, the stall holders had optimistically gathered, greeting friends and sharing survival stories. Everyone helped to clear rubble and passageways. There was little produce to sell, but locals arrived desperate to find bread, flour and potatoes. One stall had a few shabby clothes and discarded American work shirts.

Thieves pushed and shoved, their fingers grasping items in pockets and bags. For Elena and Chiara, it was a time of thankfulness that they had survived unhurt, but great sadness when they saw gaps in the market stalls where friends had died. Most days the church bells tolled their sombre chimes for people to gather and mourn lost loved ones.

Elena had brought a few eggs from their hens to barter for bread. Their patch of land had suffered from the ash, the fruit burnt on the trees and only root vegetables had survived. Chiara used them to make vegetable broth which they ate but had saved two jars to sell. They exchanged a heel of dry bread for the eggs and a tiny portion of flour for pasta. They were emaciated with the lack of food and Chiara had developed a hacking cough from the smoke. Their cave offered little protection from the ash which lined their throats and clogged their noses. The two women sat down on the church steps to regain their energy before the uphill walk home. Chiara's market friend Michello joined them and shared a tiny square of goat's cheese whilst accepting a piece of bread.

'*Come va?* I see you survived in your cave. At least you had protection against the bombing. My place at the market is covered in stones and glass so I've been clearing it away. Andreas and Enrico have survived but have nowhere to live as their tenement was destroyed. They are squatting in a corner of the station now. Mario was killed with his family last week, and Pietro has been badly injured and is being cared for by the church.'

Michello raised his hands in the air, sadness and despair etching his face. He pulled his grey hair tiredly. 'What has Naples done to deserve this horror? Where is God's protection? We are all starving.'

He looked up at the polluted sky and shook his fists hopelessly. Chiara covered his thin, wrinkly hand in sympathy.

In order to buy food for their children, some women with no support, resorted to prostitution with the Allied Forces. Small children, armed with wooden boxes and brushes were sent out into the ruined streets as 'shoeshine' boys to obtain food or coins.

Ferocious gangs of homeless street children, the scugnizzi, lived in squalor, terrorising, starving and robbing anyone for food. They had staged an aggressive attack on the Germans on September 28 1943, angry at the passive city officials for accepting of the iron control by the Germans, riled by the devastating bombardment by the Allied Forces. They built barricades of stolen furniture and used guns thieved from the Germans to shoot the enemy.

As Chiara and Elena walked back to the caves through the streets they dodged and hid from these wild gangs, their members as ferocious as wolves. They passed gaunt, dirty women slumped hopelessly in ruined doorways, often with their children lying listlessly on the ground. They held out wrinkled hands, beseeching passers-by to give them food or coin. Few buildings stood to give protection, and pushing, stinking crowds poured from underground shelters. The churches were housing many homeless families but the conditions were primitive with no basic washing or toilet facilities. Sewers and gutters were clogged with ash, stones and detritus. The smell in the streets was overwhelming and putrid.

Elena and Chiara covered their faces with scarves but still the miasma of decaying and rotten flesh and rubbish penetrated through. They were relieved to reach the relatively clearer air in the hills and around the caves. It had been difficult for Chiara to walk over the heaps of stones and broken wood as her health had deteriorated in the last week due to the polluted air. Elena tucked her arm in Chiara's to steady her as they walked through the damaged city streets. At times they lapsed into silence overwhelmed by the horrible sights and the loss of their friends.

Life After the War and Volcanic Eruption 1944

Living in the cave through the long winter nights, reasonably safe from the destructive bombing and devastation by the volcano's lava flow, Elena talked with Chiara about her future. Chiara knew Elena was well educated and needed to find more interesting and better paid work than serving on a market stall.

With the bombing of the station, Chiara decided her days at the market were finished as she was getting older and unsteady on her feet. She was used to her cave home and didn't want to move to the city but the life was not suitable for Elena. She suggested Elena talk with the local priest.

'I've known the Padre a long time and he's a compassionate man who loves God and cares about the people in his parish. He is always optimistic and tries to find the best traits in people. His attitude to God is not based on fear and punishment but on kindness and prayer. He can advise you and help you to find better lodgings and work. I shall miss your company as we've rubbed along well in the past months but you need to earn money and find a proper home as a base for the future.'

Chiara smiled as she said this but Elena could see the sadness in her eyes and the vulnerability about managing in the caves as she became infirm.

'I'll see you often either at the market or the caves. I promise to care for you like a daughter as you get older. Maybe I can find a room or two and we can share a home again,' Elena said brightly. She took Chiara's arm and kissed her cheek. She was excited by the changes in her life and looked forward to the future and to burying the past and its traumas in a deep pit.

Elena visited the priest's house, located next to the church and the ruined market. The house and the church were damaged by a bomb blast and had patched, broken windows, leaking roofs and flaking paintwork. The cellars had been flooded too but the Padre said he had little time to worry about repairs – he was too busy assisting the locals. He was tall and thin and his soutane hung from bony shoulders. His face was long and bony on his scrawny neck but he welcomed Elena briskly with a smile and pointed to a wooden bench outside his church in the sunshine.

'Buongiorno, Padre Michello, do you have a few minutes to talk with me please? I need to find somewhere else to live.'

The Padre stroked his chin and pulled an ear as he thought about Elena's request. He said, 'I know a young married woman who has two small children to support as her husband is a German prisoner. We'll go and see Gina now. It's time I visited the apartment block to find out how the inhabitants are managing. It's two streets from here and fortunately was untouched by the bombing of the station and the market.'

The priest took Elena's arm and talked about Gina's situation as they walked. 'She's a lovely woman who's finding it hard to manage on her own. Her family live on the other side of Naples and were unable to visit her during the bombing. I worry about their safety as a gang of scugnizzi has moved into the ground floor of the apartment block. The street gang lives by trading stolen goods and dealing on the black market. Their leader is a troublemaker and aggressive.'

'Here we are. Gina lives on the third floor but we have to walk up the stairs as there's no electricity in the building.'

The Padre marched up the stained cement stairs with Elena behind him, and knocked on a battered wooden door that had a crack running down the central panel, its paint peeling.

'Who is it?' a voice called in response.

'Padre Michello, Gina dear.'

The door was unlocked and cautiously opened. Gina, dressed in a ragged cotton dress and barefooted, pushed her head through the narrow gap and beckoned the priest to enter. She slammed the door shut behind them. Two small children clung to her skirts and lifted their bowed heads as the priest introduced Elena. He explained the situation and suggested Gina could rent her bedroom to Elena and sleep with her children in the kitchen. Gina looked down and thought for a few minutes. 'I need company, and help looking after my children. If you can pay you can share our meals.'

Elena nodded and smiled. '*Grazie*. I hope to be working with Padre Michello and can pay for my room. Would you show it to me please?'

'I'll stay here and get a glass of water, my throat is dry with the dust and heat,' the priest said.

Gina walked up steep wooden winding stairs and showed Elena the attic room at the top. It had a small iron bedstead, a straw mattress covered in a frayed blanket and a wooden chair. Elena looked around and thought how good it would be sleep in a bed and have private space.

'*Molto grazie*, Gina. When can I move in? – Tomorrow?'

Gina nodded and smiled gratefully. She proudly introduced her children, placing a hand on each shoulder. 'This is my son, Pietro – he is six. My little girl is four. She is Angelina but we call her Angel. It's hard to find food for them but they make life worth living.'

The children looked shyly at Elena who smiled and held out her hand to them.

Their limbs were painfully thin and their faces grey with no childish bloom; their stomachs were bloated through lack of food. Gina herself was skeletal with a lined face and nervous manner. Her hair was long and dark and hung in clumps on her shoulders. As Elena left with the Padre, she noticed the kitchen was empty of food, not even a crust of bread or a few tomatoes by the sink. It was clean with damp rags fluttering in the window, and an aluminium pot and plates hung from nails on the wall. A split wooden table with three stools filled the tiny room.

Outside the apartment, Elena thanked the Padre and asked if he knew how she could earn money. 'In Puglia I worked for the local Mayor and the school teacher. Can you help me find similar work? I had schooling until I was 15 … I can read and write,' she asked hopefully.

'Let me think and ask around,' Padre Michello replied with a smile. 'I have many other duties at present helping people find food and shelter and to support those who have lost family members. Chiara told me in confidence a while back about your life and the tragedies you have experienced. It takes courage to move on from the trauma you have suffered. I understand that cave life is not suitable for a young woman for more than a short time but the city is a violent place with gangs of youths and street children robbing and fighting for their existence.

The nearest school is about ten minutes' walk from here through ruined streets.'

'*Molto grazie*,' Elena replied. She ran back to the cave and told Chiara about her new place to live and her request to the Padre for work.

'Can I borrow your handcart tomorrow to move my straw palette, blanket and clothes into Gina's apartment?'

Elena hauled her few belongings to Gina's tenement block. She could see Gina's children poking their heads out of the apartment door and then running down the steps to help, calling out to their mamma that Elena was there. The children were excited to see Elena again and wanted to show her their beds in the kitchen. Elena offered to share the cooking.

She wheeled the empty cart back up the rough track to the caves and bade Chiara an emotional farewell. 'See you at mass,' Elena said hugging Chiara tightly. 'I will never forget how you rescued me from the gutter and set me on my feet again. Look I am fatter than I was then, and stronger. I promise to see you often. *Andare con Dio.*'

After Sunday mass the following week, Padre Michello took Elena aside and made a suggestion for work.

'The Bishop of the diocese is setting up a programme to feed and house orphaned children. We intend to provide weekly meals after mass and I need all the help I can get to buy food and assist the children during the meal. The Bishop has asked for donations from local businesses.

'The church will provide funds and benches. We need practical help to repair damaged buildings and provide shelter for local people who have lost their homes. The bombed tenements housed many families before the war and are in a dangerous state. The Bishop has also contacted the Communal Institution for Assistance which has been set up in every commune, town and city to provide assistance for civilians who have been bombed out of their homes. The Red Cross are involved in the transportation of injured citizens to hospitals and to shelters as there is a shortage of ambulances. The Bishop said the *Genio Civile* are removing debris from bomb sites and reconstruction of ruined buildings.'

'The Allied Air Force based at Pomigliano has offered to donate money and send off duty servicemen to help with building repairs. I need assistance to organise this and of course there is always the paperwork required to manage the funds and the volunteers. Do you think you can help me? I can pay you a small weekly amount to cover your food and lodging. It will be a safe way for you to meet local people. There will be a commanding officer in charge of the servicemen to ensure they work hard and do not cause problems,' Padre Michello said seriously.

'Grazie, that sounds interesting and I can give Gina something for my room and food. Chiara says she is getting too old to continue with her market stall. She's asked me to work one day a week at her stall until she packs up in a month,' replied Elena.

'Good, that's such a relief because I was worrying how I could manage on my own with this extra work on top of my normal duties. They seem unending due to the tragedies of the war.'

Padre Michello's face lit up with a wide generous smile and his eyes twinkled. 'Can you start on Monday? I'll meet you at the church and we can look at the surrounding buildings to see if any can be repaired cheaply and easily. I know we'll have many children who need food and clothing, probably their mothers too. The Bishop thinks it will take time to find them as the children are living wild on the streets and scavenging for food.

'Then we'll need to find somewhere to cook food and serve meals. It will be sparse and plain but better for the children than searching in bins and gutters for morsels to eat. In their weakened state, they will catch diseases and often have to fight off starving dogs. I have asked for volunteer cooks. It will be a lot of hard work as many of the people who live around here have lost all their possessions in the bombing and were poor before the war started.'

'The Allied Air Force Base has offered to provide plates, cutlery and a few benches. I think your first job is to contact them and then make a list of food required each week.' Padre Michello's eyelids lowered and he rubbed his mouth anxiously, his nervousness about organising this huge project and managing the street children, especially the gangs of scugnizzi, obvious.

Elena said goodbye to the Padre and walked to the market where she relayed all she'd been told to Chiara, who nodded.

'You be very careful, Elena. There is so much aggression on the streets, so many children and fighting over food scraps and basic shelter. There are no rules as everyone is so desperate. The Allied Forces are trying their best, but the *polizia* are corrupt and brutal. Anyone who annoys them, kids and adults, are slung into jail.'

Elena nodded. 'I'll be very careful and I know the work will be challenging. The Padre needs to find a place and furniture and organise food deliveries each Sunday. He told me he wants injured tradesmen to repair some buildings so that homeless families can get shelter. He knows many women and children live in dirty unsafe places, and orphaned children have no hope of getting schooling. They are roaming the streets in search of food. He has asked me to help with the extra paperwork, and he wants to start next Monday morning. I told him that I needed to help you at the market one day a week until you give it up in a month. He agreed of course.'

Chiara listened carefully, nodding her agreement throughout. 'It is a good idea,' she said. 'It won't be hard to find the children but many will need discipline as they've lived wild on the streets during the war. They need to learn basic civility and honesty. The schools have shut down as there are few teachers and many buildings have been destroyed by bombs. The children have no future at present and they need to understand that thieving and bullying in order to survive is bad for them, their future and their country.'

Elena rose on Monday morning filled with excitement and looking forward to her new job. Living independently in her small room and taking on some worthwhile work had been her goal since leaving Caterna under such difficult circumstances. It had driven her on as she'd trudged across the hard, stony landscape of Puglia, experiencing the depths of loneliness and abandonment. If she worked hard and paid her way then she could have a reasonable future.

Padre Michello welcomed her on the doorstep of his house, his smile beaming. He kissed her briskly on the cheek, and she noticed that he smelt of incense and soap, although his robes and sandals were dusty.

'This is the room I thought you could use for your work. It's a cellar under my house and needs some cleaning. I have put in a table and a chair and provided pencils and a notebook for you to list the bills. The Bishop instructed me to use his system so I have given you an old page from his account book to copy. The Bishop told me to limit the number of children for the meals to forty. He insisted that they must live locally. We need to include the mothers and ask them to help. I have started a list of children to benefit.

'Now, there is one very important thing you must consider – learning the Neapolitan dialect. I've noticed you often have difficulty understanding people who come to the market. These street kids will be talking in a mixture of slang and swear words. At the start of each day I will give you lessons on how to talk with the children and advice on dealing with their attitudes and the aggression they have developed while surviving on the streets. You'll be shocked by their approach towards you and they will be dirty and smelly, clothed in rags and thin to their bones.

'However hard it is, we must be prepared to deal with them in a kind but disciplined manner, try to civilise and educate them to live in a normal world after the war. I will be with you so don't be afraid of them.'

Elena listened carefully, her head tilted to the side as she learnt about the challenges of her new job. She was used to having children around having lived next door to the town school in Caterna.

She had learnt to overcome her disgust, having worn dirty, smelly clothes day after day on her trek, and she had met many rough country people who lived on the dry and dusty land with little water to spare for washing and no money to buy fresh clothes. Although her grandparents had been poor, they had insisted on keeping clean as the public wells in Mitorna always had enough water.

'Grazie, Padre. I need to understand the street kids' language and attitudes and had no idea until I came to Naples that Italian could sound so different – there are many words and phrases I do not know. The farmers and herders I met on my way to Naples were almost incomprehensible to me. I talked by actions and gestures rather than words, which should help me with the street children. In Puglia where I lived we used local words that are never heard in Naples, the country people talk and move slowly. Here everyone talks so quickly and waves their arms, and flash their eyes in impatience if I misunderstand what they want to buy. The stallholders use swear words when their customers complain at the prices or quality of their goods,' Elena replied with a smile as the Padre continued planning.

'I'll write a notice about the Sunday free meals and post it on the church door. I need to ask for volunteers to help. There is an empty basement nearby in a bombed tenement which the Bishop said we can use. It needs to be cleared of rubbish but I am hoping the stall holders in the market will help me tomorrow when the market closes. I have spoken with the Bishop about furniture and he will arrange for some spare items from the church to be brought this week. We need to build several brick ovens so we can provide basic food like pasta and soup. I hope to get left over bread from somewhere.

'It's a huge task but the street children must be fed and cared for as they are the future of Naples. I intend for some of the older ones to be taught carpentry so they can help with the building repairs. The Bishop needs the project started immediately to get many people housed by next winter. I don't want to walk down the streets and see children dead of hunger lying in the gutters or mothers prostituting themselves to buy food for their families.'

The first Sunday meals were served, the street children pushed hard against a barricade built of discarded timber and bricks from the ruined buildings. The Padre had recruited two airmen to stand outside the barrier and move the children aside once they had their soup. They tumbled through the door to the basement, pushing, shoving and kicking in their desperation to get food. The big ones elbowed their way to the front, knocking over careless little children. Steam rose from large cooking pots placed on the brick ovens. An almost forgotten aroma of vegetables permeated the air and the mound of bread on the table was more than most had seen in their lifetime.

The street children were gaunt, bones sticking through their rags, their faces grey and wizened with deprivation. Many had sores on their exposed arms and legs, scraps of cloth tied round their feet and bodies.

Elena looked at them and felt a wrenching pity for the life they had and the hopelessness of their future. She stood at the barricade with the Padre taking the metal canisters of soup from the volunteer cooks and handing them to the children; she watched them clutch the canister and gulp down the liquid regardless of the heat that burnt their lips.

The shuffling and jostling, pushing and shoving swayed around them, peppered with curses from the older children anxious for another helping. Within an hour the supply of soup had gone but still the children queued for any fragments of bread left. Padre Michello pushed them gently outside the basement and told them,

'Come back another day. We have to find more food to make the soup and bread. We're closing now.'

His face was creased with sadness as he talked with the volunteers when the door was closed. 'I will ask the Allied air force base to donate more. The Bishop has underestimated the desperate need in this area as word has spread about free food. I'm worried about continuing with this work if there are not enough supplies available.'

'We could put pasta into the soup which is cheap and filling and use fewer vegetables, although the flour for pasta is often mixed with grit and is poor quality,' Elena suggested.

'I know a fisherman who lives nearby. He was wounded in the war but takes his boat out most mornings. Can you find someone to help him catch more fish to be put in the soup,' a young woman spoke up, wringing her hands nervously. She was thin as a rake with tangled dirty hair and torn clothes. A tiny child, equally dirty and starving clutched her skirt hem. He had the bloated stomach of a malnourished child.

'*Molte grazie*. I need to explain the problems to the Bishop. He is a kind man and disturbed by the situation,' Padre Michello said thoughtfully. 'He agreed we can give meals one day a week after mass. That gives us time to obtain food during the week. God moves in mysterious ways but at the moment, I will pray to him to concentrate a bit more on our problems,' the Padre said with a wry smile. '*Ciao and grazie*. Same time, same place next Sunday please.'

He ushered them out of the basement and locked the door. 'Will you walk back with me to your room, Elena? It will be safer I think.'

'*Si, grazie*. I am caring for Gina's children this afternoon. I take them for a walk and play ball on the waste land outside the market. Pietro is six and his sister is four. They wear Gina out.'

'Are you settled there, Elena? When the war is over, you'll need to find other work and somewhere better to live. You have to make the best of things like everyone does for now.'

'Yes, I agree but where shall I go as I have no family. It'll take years before the city is re-built and businesses operate properly. Many of the mothers I meet are waiting for news of their husbands, fathers and brothers who have been taken to German labour camps or are still fighting. Who knows what the future holds for any of us.'

'The Bishop said a British RAF officer will be coming next Sunday to help. His name is Flight Lieutenant Bill Whiteley. He visited me yesterday and said he can bring food parcels. He studied in Rome before the war and speaks excellent Italian. He was also a rugby player and has volunteered to teach the boys the game.'

'That's good to have extra help and food,' Elena replied.

Sunday dawned clear and bright and Elena was pleased to be working on the food distribution again. The week had flown by so fast she'd been so busy — she'd begged or bought old clothes at the market and planned tasks for the orphaned girls to cut up and make clothing or patches. It gave meaning to her life and helped her to push her traumas into the far reaches of her mind.

She walked to Padre Michello's house to accompany him to the tenement basement. The door was unlocked and three RAF officers were inside erecting trestle tables and benches. Plates of food were being put on the tables and several soup tureens were steaming on the brick ovens.

'*Buongiorno,*' one of the RAF officers said. He came forward and shook the Padre's hand. 'I'm Flight Lieutenant Bill Whiteley,' he said. 'We have a lull between flying missions, so have come to help. These guys are my bomber crew.'

'Grazie, Flight Lieutenant. This is Elena, my assistant.' The Padre turned and smiled at Elena. 'We started last week and were overwhelmed by the numbers of children needing food. The street kids are in a desperate state – starving, half-clothed and almost feral. They need to learn respect for others.'

'*Bene*. Can you explain the arrangements for feeding the children? Do you serve the little ones first? I was told that some of the boys might like to play ball games after they've eaten. We can help there … hope we're fit enough,' Bill said with a smile.

Elena and the Padre also smiled. 'You'll need lots of energy and firmness,' they said together.

'OK. What time do we start?'

'Now, but get the kids into a queue in front of the hatch and the barrier,' replied Padre Michello.

For the next two hours, the children jostled and shoved each other as they were handed soup in metal containers. Holding their food tightly, they pushed their way inside to the benches, fending off the grasping hands of children still queuing.

Elena was aware of a new energy Bill brought to the food distribution. She caught his eye several times as they marshalled the children into queues. He talked to the kids in the local dialect and managed to get a rare smile from one or two. As they ushered the last few out of the basement doors and closed them, Bill turned to Elena and smiled. 'That went well but we're short of food and there's still a queue.'

Elena looked up into Bill's dark brown eyes and saw the kindness and understanding in them. He wore a smart tailored uniform with an easy casualness, often tucking his hands into his trouser pockets. His light brown hair was regulation short and a cap stuck out of his jacket pocket. He held out his hand to Elena and she felt the strength and warmth in it when she shook hands. Bill turned away and called the other two airmen to herd the children over to the adjacent patch of waste ground, encouraging them to play a game of football.

Every Sunday after mass, Padre Michello, Elena and the volunteers to the basement food hall were greeted by swarms of street kids. The Allied airmen took the boys to the waste ground and played football with them when they could.

'I can stay behind some Sundays after the meals are finished and teach the girls to sew and patch their clothes,' Elena suggested to the Padre. 'We can encourage the girls to help with the cooking. What do you think?'

'That's a great idea but take it slowly until we understand these children better. Some will have come from good homes and ended up on the streets because they were bombed out of their homes or their parents died. Some may be too traumatised to talk about what has happened to them.'

Several Sundays later, the RAF crew drove up in a transport truck and offered to take some of the children for a ride and show them the sea. The boys crowded round the truck and clambered into the back, jostling to sit on the wooden side benches or on the floor.

Bill told them not to stand as it could be dangerous when the truck had to drive round crater holes or stop suddenly. 'We can look for the man with the ice cream cart.'

'Si, si,' they shouted excitedly.

'No promises. We'll take different children each month if the truck is available. Elena would you like to sit in the front and direct me, please? I'm not familiar with the layout of Naples and I need help to identify the craters and damaged buildings. We'll be about an hour,' Bill told the Padre.

The outing was a great success although disciplining the kids was tough. Bill didn't shout but severely told them to sit down in the back of the truck and behave. Surprisingly, parked amongst the ruins was a bicycle with a gelato cart attached to the back. The canopy on the cart had 'Rico's Gelato' stencilled on it. They shared the ices amidst the dust and dirt. Bill could see the children relaxing, even though their clothes were grubby rags and their wizened little faces were suspicious and unsmiling.

The following Sunday the Padre walked on ahead of Elena to the basement as Elena wanted to spend a few minutes talking with Chiara in the market as she had been ill for a few days. Elena could see that Chiara's limp was more pronounced and her face was shadowed with pain. 'Let me help you back to your cave and cook some food.' Elena was worried that her friend would have difficulty walking up the hill to her cave home.

Chiara shook her head. 'I'll be alright. I just need to lie down in the cool of the cave. Don't worry about me. I'll survive for a good while yet. I've closed my market stall for good now. It's too hard to get produce and serving customers is tiring and I have no energy left to walk home.'

Elena kissed her goodbye then ran over to the basement to help the Padre with the Sunday food distribution. As she drew nearer she could see a crowd of ragged children pushing and shoving someone to the ground then kicking him, screaming insults. The horror of the situation stopped Elena mid-stride as she glimpsed the bald head and dark soutane of the Padre. She looked around for help but there was no-one. Picking up a heavy stone from the ruined road, she threw it at the scugnizzi, then another, raining stones on the boys as fast as she could. The leader, skinny, tall and aggressive, strode over to her, beckoning his gang to follow, the Padre left lying in the gutter, blood pouring from his head. Elena stood her ground, her mouth hardening, her shoulders hunching, ready to run but she was reluctant to leave the Padre. The leader raised the wooden pole he'd been beating the priest with and thrust it at her face shouting, '*Va via, puttana.*'

Elena raised a large stone, ready to smash it into his face, needing to protect her friend. The leader, seeing the defiance and raw anger on her face, her posture, instinctively stepped back. Elena shoved the stone into his chest with one hand; swung a small bag of donated bread with her left hand. The bag burst open and bread scattered on the ground. The scugnizzi turned and scrabbled over the food.

Seeing her chance, Elena charged out of the aggressive ring; grabbed the Padre who was starting to sit up, staunching the blood with a piece of rag. His broken arm hung useless at his side, and tears of pain trickled down his face.

A sudden hit on the back of her head made her spin, and she stepped astride the Padre to protect him. Thinking rapidly, she screamed in gutter Italian, 'What the fuck are you beating an old man for, a man of God? He was giving food to street orphans like your pack of scugnizzi. You stinking pieces of sewer shit! Put your knives away!'

The leader, his face twitching and aggressive, raised the heavy baton to hit again; he screamed in Elena's face, 'We're starving. Some are ill. We are fighting to survive and avoid the police because they can throw us into jail with no hope of rescue.'

Still brandishing the wooden stick, he reached under his ragged shirt and whipped out a gleaming stiletto, held it to Elena's chest. 'Give us food or we'll damage you and the priest so badly you won't be able to walk.'

Suddenly his face crumpled with pain as his arms were wrenched behind his back. The hand holding the knife was crushed against the wall, the knife dropping to the ground with a clatter.

'Get down on the ground and stay down. Tell your mates to do the same!' Bill growled as he held onto the leader and instructed the airmen with him to disarm the gang members. 'If I see you and your wolves creeping around here again, I'll shoot you.'

Bill held his pistol at the leader's chest. 'Now get up and don't come back.'

The gang leapt to their feet and skulked away into the ruined alleyways.

'Help the Padre,' he instructed his airmen, 'and check if he needs to go to hospital.'

'Elena, Elena … my darling girl … did that bastard harm you?' Bill moved towards Elena, held out his arms and she slid into the safety of his embrace. She trembled even though the danger was over.

'No, he didn't hurt me but the Padre's head is bleeding and I think his arm is broken,' Elena replied shakily, looking around to ensure the scugnizzi had gone.

'I don't know how you can be protected from these gangs. The local police are too busy – many are looking after their own interests. We can't give you any military police as it won't be allowed. Maybe you should stop the food distribution for a while, especially as the Padre won't be fit enough to help for a few weeks.' Bill frowned and kissed the top of Elena's head; gently moved a few tendrils of hair from her eyes. His touch lingered as he traced the shape of her cheek and wiped away the tears falling down them.

'Put down the stone – you are safe now. I promise to come and help as often as I can between missions. Now, let me come with you to your room. My men will organise medical help for the Padre.'

Gina was home and Elena sat down in the kitchen while Bill explained what had happened. 'Please keep an eye on her and discourage her from working on the food distribution until the Padre is well enough to help.'

Bill kissed Elena on the cheek and returned to the airbase.

Gina offered Elena a glass of water and a damp rag to wipe away the tears and sweat on her face. She smiled sympathetically. She'd experienced the violence on the streets only a week earlier as she'd tried to buy bread in the next road. Standing in the queue she had seen youths punching an old man who was clutching his ration of bread to his chest. The baker unleashed his guard dog and it chased the youths away.

'Stay inside for a few days and rest. I'll find out how the Padre is tomorrow. Children, you must remain inside for a few days also. You can keep Elena company. She may have some stories to tell from her long walk across Italy.'

It was early summer before Padre Michello fully recovered from his injuries and asked Elena if she felt able to assist him again with the food distribution. The tenement basement had been closed for several weeks and needed cleaning before food could be brought in and prepared.

Bill sent several airmen to stand guard as he had promised and the children were not allowed inside. They were served through a strong metal barricade, loaned by the Allied forces, Elena and the Padre having discussed the safer way to distribute would be from behind protective barricades. The airmen marshalled the children into an orderly queue between the barricades and ensured each one moved away with their metal canister of soup.

The following week as Elena handed out the canisters she noticed a small boy clutching his sister and not eating. He seemed in shock and when asked a question could only nod while his sister spoke for him. The priest took them to one side and asked their names. 'Is your brother shy, injured or unable to talk?' he asked. 'What are your names?'

The girl looked up at the Padre and said carefully, 'My name is Olivia, my brother is Andrea. I am seven, Andrea is four. Our parents were killed in the bombing. The rescue people pulled us from under the building. My brother hasn't spoken since so I talk for him and look after him. We are always hungry and shelter where we can.'

'Do you have any family in Naples?' Padre Michello asked Olivia, his head shaking sadly.

'No. They moved before the bombings and I don't know where they went.'

The Padre looked at Elena. 'We'll help you.' Elena nodded, a tear touching her eye – she'd seen so much sadness and hopelessness in Naples. That evening she pondered the problem in her room, and after Sunday Mass discussed the children's predicament with the Padre and Bill and suggested how they could help.

'They need to feel secure with us. Perhaps we could take them into the basement while they eat and encourage Olivia to talk. It's so sad about these children I really want to help.' Elena's eyes shone with unshed tears and her face filled with compassion.

A few weeks later, Bill asked Elena if she would like to have a coffee with him after Mass. She hesitated, wary of trusting people, but Bill seemed decent, and she knew she needed to meet people.

'Si, grazie, I would like to, but I need to talk with my friend Chiara first,' she replied.

Elena walked back to her room, humming under her breath. She visited Chiara the next morning and told her about Bill's invitation. Chiara urged her to be careful and not too hasty in placing her trust.

'I enjoy his company and he is so handsome face, and he has a lovely deep voice,' Elena told Chiara, smiling shyly.

'Yes, but looks aren't everything,' Chiara cautioned. 'I wonder why an educated English airman would be interested in a young Italian girl. Have you asked him if he is married? Has he told you about his life in England before the war? Have you told him about your life? '

'Flight Lieutenant Whitely … Bill … has asked you to come as well to the café,' Elena replied.

'Oh, all right then,' Chiara said grudgingly.

With no piped water to the building where she and Gina lived, Elena washed at the public pump nearby. She combed her long black hair and sat outside to dry it in the warmth of the setting sun. On Sunday, the sun shone and a light breeze blew in from the sea. She put on a clean dress, rubbed the dust off her sandals and combed her hair. Without a mirror, Elena had no idea that she looked very pretty. Her long black hair was tied back with a bright ribbon, her face, bare legs and arms were tanned to a soft brown and her dark eyes smiled with anticipation.

After the street kids were fed, Elena walked with Bill to the café to meet Chiara. He pulled out two chairs for them and ordered drinks. Elena felt shy and awkward, aware that her English was basic. Bill was the smartest-looking man in the cafe in his uniform and Elena was conscious of her crumpled market-stall dress and scuffed sandals.

Chiara shifted uncomfortably on her chair and attempted a few words in English.

'How long you fly planes?' she asked. 'In England you have family? You return there after the war? How long you been in Naples?'

'Thank you for agreeing to meet me … and I understand your caution regarding Elena. I have been a bomber pilot for two years. I have parents, a sister and brother in England, but no wife,' Bill responded slowly and honestly. 'When the war is over, I want to improve my Italian and learn more about Italian culture.'

Chiara nodded thoughtfully. 'I think meeting at the café is good for now. I must care for Elena.'

'OK. How long have you lived in Naples, Elena?' Bill asked.

Elena shifted a little on her seat and thought of the tiny attic she called home. Bill waited patiently, sipping his coffee. 'I have lived in Naples for six months but before that I lived in the country.' Elena bowed her head and twisted her hands in her dress.

When Chiara asked Bill how long he'd been based near Naples, he said, 'I've been at the airbase for a year and before that I was in Sicily and North Africa. My squadron was involved in the North African desert fighting then we were transferred to Messina to support the Allied invasion of Italy and fight the Germans. We landed on the beach near Naples after the crews were killed.'

Elena looked up and met Bill's eyes. 'Was it very dangerous?'

'Yes, I had to make an emergency landing at Palermo after part of the plane's wing was shot off. Planes have been shot down in the raids and the crews killed.'

A few minutes of tense silence reigned. Then Bill looked up at the deep blue sky and at the pretty Italian girl sitting opposite. He said softly, 'I'd like to forget about the war for today and enjoy sitting in the peaceful sunshine with you, Elena, the prettiest girl in the cafe.

She blushed. During her eighteen years, no-one had given her compliments so she didn't know how to respond. Life had been too hard – a battle for survival during her childhood and adolescent years in Mitorna – the traumatic time in Caterna she had pushed far, far back into her mind.

'It's a beautiful day and I have the whole day off, so I thought I might go out on the motorbike. Can you suggest an interesting place to visit?' Bill asked.

Chiara bowed her head in thought then looked up and said, 'You could ride south to Sorrento which is on the bay of

Naples. It is a hilltop town. You should be safe to drive past Vesuvius which has stopped erupting now but be careful of German patrols.'

Chiara and Elena left then after agreeing that Elena would meet Bill at the café again. Elena looked backed as she walked away, and noted Bill was watching her, and she smiled inwardly.

Two weeks later, Bill arrived to help with the food distribution and asked Elena if she would have coffee with him again. Though still nervous about meeting Bill on her own, she took a deep breath and nodded, wondering, with their very different backgrounds, what could they have in common?

Bill sat at the same table, his smile welcoming her. She sat nervously, sipping her coffee, silence drifting between for a long while. Finally, Bill broke it, saying gently, 'Look, I understand your caution especially knowing what has happened to young girls spending time alone with military men during the war ...'

'Please forgive me but I speak only a little English and have to concentrate very hard to understand and think of a reply,' Elena said hesitantly.

He placed his hand gently over hers where it held the coffee cup; felt her warm soft skin tremble beneath his touch.

As she said goodbye and walked away, she could feel the warmth of his gaze on her back and turned round to wave to him. She longed to tell him about her life but she was not ready to share her tragedies with him. She hadn't even told Chiara the full story of why she had left Caterna after the German shooting and walked alone to Naples. The reluctance of her friend Marina and her family in Mitorna to protect her still hurt. Then, in Caterna, the betrayal of the Mayor who had become friendly with the occupying Germans was a horrible memory – she'd learnt of the grocer's betrayal by the Mayor while imprisoned in the Mayor's cellar.

Now she wanted to have fun and listen to Bill talk about his childhood, so different from hers. She felt comfortable with him even after this short time. She liked his sense of humour and the way his mouth curled up at the corners with amusement. She talked about Bill with Chiara and Gina. Chiara said she liked Bill and sensed his kindness and courtesy, and so, as the relationship continued Elena became less tense; she smiled more often and the nightmares became less frequent. Her face was more at peace and her eyes less shadowed.

Bill had come into her life when she was growing into womanhood and Chiara could see that Elena wanted to give him all the stored up, untapped love that was in her, the love that other girls had naturally given to their fathers and brothers.

Bill and Elena's courtship continued, their meetings arranged around Bill's flying roster and Elena's availability from work. Sometimes they snatched a brief kiss and a short meeting at the café. Other times they spent the day together, riding on Bill's motorbike to the sea where they kicked off their shoes and ran hand in hand into the water. It seemed as if the sun always shone and the autumn days were balmy with a fresh breeze from the sea. Sometimes they shared a picnic and sat, arms around each other, watching the sun set. Then reluctantly, as darkness fell, Bill would pull her up, kiss her gently and take her home to Gina on his motorbike. They were falling in love, giving gentle caresses and private smiles, and holding hands when they walked.

Bill's mother was a White Russian, he said. She'd escaped to Istanbul during the Russian Revolution. 'She arrived with nothing but the clothes she wore, travelling in a small boat across the Black Sea. She lived in Istanbul and suffered great hardship with other Russian emigres until she met and married my father. He was serving in the British military there. I grew up in Croydon, South London. When German bombing devastated many parts of London in 1942, I decided to enlist with the RAF, even though I was only seventeen and had to lie about my age. I was accepted and trained in England before becoming a pilot.'

A few weeks later, Elena sat silent at the cafe, preoccupied with her thoughts, her dark eyes sorrowful. The sunlight on her hair made its blackness gleam and emphasised her strong cheekbones. Bill watched her as her lips opened as if she were about to speak then stopped again.

'Elena Rossi,' Bill said quietly, 'what is it that troubles you so much?' He stretched out a hand to hers, as if he wanted to draw her closer to him.

Though from vastly different backgrounds, she felt secure with Bill and decided it was time to tell him her story, a story she was yet unready to explain to anyone else. She had been happier in the last few months since meeting Bill than ever in her life before.

Elena stood up and Bill saw a decision appear in her eyes and in the tension lines that creased the area around her mouth.

'Bill, I need your understanding. Can we walk to the beach and I will try to tell you about my life?'

They found a sheltered place and sat on some rocks. Elena chose a separate rock as she needed all her courage and resilience to talk about the terrible events of her childhood and teenage years. As Elena struggled to tell him her story, it was her sad tear-stained face that emphasised the horror of what she had experienced more than the words she used.

She bent her head as the grief swelled in her, a grief that was still intense and filled with despair. Her sobs were profound and shook her body.

'I believed that my life was filled with sorrow and everyone I loved would die or be killed and leave me alone. The kindness and friendship of Chiara and you has softened this despair and I have felt some peace and contentment in the last few months.' She stopped briefly and Bill could see the pain in her face.

He reached out to touch her; took her hands, wet with tears, and kissed her fingertips one by one; knelt in front of her and gently put his arms around her shaking shoulders. He held her until she stopped trembling and sobbing. Then he took out his handkerchief, softly patted the tears on her cheeks, and placed a soft kiss on her cheek.

Instinctively, feeling loved, she closed her eyes, pressed her face into his strong shoulder and felt comforted by his kindness and understanding. Lifting her young arms, she wrapped them about his neck, and planted a soft damp kiss there. All her past suffering seemed swept away – she had found a safe and impregnable place that nothing could threaten – she was safe at last from the unendurable tragedies she had experienced in her short life.

Bill embraced her. 'I might not be able to see you next week, things are getting busy on base. We must make the most of this precious time together. 'I love you, Elena. If it is your wish that we continue to spend time together, I promise I will protect you. I will let nothing hurt you like you've experienced before.'

Elena nodded, too overcome to reply. But she sensed hesitation in Bill's manner and shivered a little. Their relationship surprising, and special, and she wanted to capture it in her hands and wrap it up safe for the future.

'Come on, Elena, let's race back along the beach and I'll buy you an expresso at the café even if you win which I know you will.'

They ran along the water's edge splashing each other joyfully as they strove to reach the cafe first. The hot sun set in a cloudless sky and seagulls made their raucous calls as they searched for fish. They sat close together at their usual table, held hands and watched the rosy glow of the sun tint the sky and the sea. It seemed a good omen for their future and a symbol of the continuity of life. The café owner recognised them and smiled to see young love flourish amidst the war-torn city. Then they walked to Gina's home and with a passionate embrace and deep slow kiss parted in the cool evening breeze.

War in the Air 1943-4

Bill rode his motorbike back to the airfield at Pomigliano outside of Naples where his Bomber Group was attached to the USAAF.

He drove carefully over the cratered and rubble-filled road leading to the airfield, his conflicting thoughts focussing on his love for Elena and his utter determination to do all he could in the bombing raids to rid Italy of the German military. He was scheduled to do several more bombing raids in the next week mostly at night but one in the daytime. He needed all his concentration and honed flying skills to avoid tracer bullets, anti-aircraft fire and enemy planes flying up behind him. Now more than ever, he needed to survive so he could look forward to a future with Elena after the war ended.

He was on duty that night and attended a briefing with his commanding officer.

In 1943, the airfield, built between 1938 and 1939 by the Italians, was now under American control after concerted attacks by the USAAF on mainland Italy. The RAF knew Italy was poorly prepared for an Allied attack because it had made no preparations for either anti-aircraft defences or protection of civilians in densely populated cities like Naples. Allied leaders had decided to use their collective military might in the Mediterranean to launch an invasion of Italy, the objectives of which were to force the Italians out of the war. In 1943 the Allies made a series of beach landings in Sicily as a forerunner to the planned attack on German forces in the major southern Italian ports of Bari, Brindisi and Taranto.

Then he rode back to his billet, leaping through the main door in a hurry to change into his flying gear. As he pulled on his trousers and jacket, his mates teased Bill about his romance with the beautiful Italian girl.

'Does she make good pasta as well as having beautiful black hair?' Tony cried, winking at the other airmen.

'Does she cling onto your arm and gaze boldly into your eyes while smiling at you enticingly?' jested Bob, his co-pilot.

'You're all jealous that the most beautiful girl in Naples is enjoying my wit and handsome face,' quipped Bill, accustomed to these suggestive comments, and there was no point explaining that Elena was not a typical friendly Italian girl angling for an English boyfriend to give her cigarettes and clothes.

Suddenly, the siren blared. Airmen quickly scrambled out to the runways, gathered impatiently for the usual safety talk by their squadron leader.

'Don't go mad chasing enemy aircraft or taking unnecessary risks. Keep calm. Focus on maintaining formation so you arrive together at the target as planned. We can't afford to lose any of you or our planes at this critical stage. Good luck.'

The bombers were assembled in take-off order allowing for their wingspan. The squadron was, as usual, accompanied by USAAF heavy bombers.

Bill pulled on his gloves and noticed the cold night was heavy with cloud, which was good for bombing raids. Each pilot had their flight plan – their destination, the railway centre and airfield complex near Foggia, an important city and rail hub in south eastern Italy – similar to other targets of industrial buildings, rail yards, bridges, tunnels and tracks. They all airmen knew their objective: secure the Mediterranean for Allied shipping and divert German forces from Northern France where the Allies were planning to land in Normandy. Communication and supply lines had to be damaged to hamper the Germans fighting south of the Gustav line. Bombing in southern Italy would also defeat the Axis in Africa because the southern ports, including Naples, shipped supplies to Libya.

He had sent a note to Padre Michello for delivery to Elena describing his feelings for her.

Bill's engineer stood by his plane as his crew of seven jogged across the runway, the rear gunner climbing in first to get through to his gun turret at the back of the aircraft.

'She's in good shape, Bill. Just go careful with that joystick as it's a little stiff now it's been repaired. Good luck, boys.' Alfred shut the aircraft door behind them and stepped back as the engines roared to life.

Bill went through his routine checks and turned the aircraft into the wind, increasing the throttle as they bumped across the concrete runway, the vibration of the Rolls Royce Merlin V12 engine coursing through his body along with the adrenalin rush of take-off. The joystick responded to his hands, and he nodded at his co-pilot and watched the angle of the wings as they soared into the night sky.

The other bombers took off and assembled into formation as they set off for Foggia. Bill listened to the exchange of pilots on his radio transmitter, mentally checking the process for releasing the bombs. At 20,000 feet and a speed of 280 mph, Bill leant back in his seat and checked the other bombers in his squadron were in place. This was the moment when greatest surge of adrenalin kicked in – excitement and determination swelling to destroy the target.

After about an hour's flying, Bill saw the lights of a large city ahead of him, non-compliance with the Republic's blackout regulations largely due to apathy, fear and resentment of the Nazi regime. Bill checked his weather instruments; informed his squadron they would approach Foggia from the east.

'Bandits behind,' Bert, his co-pilot, shouted as he spotted a several fighter planes closing in on them. As the bomber squadron dipped lower, anti-aircraft fire spattered around them, some hitting the aircraft's wings. Bill saw a huge conflagration in the city ahead of them and the aircraft flew through a dense cloud of black oily smoke before circling to drop their bombs on the airfield complex and rail centre. He started to call, 'Bombs away!' when the plane shuddered violently. Bert yelled: 'We're hit! The tail's alight! *Phil! Phil! …* … Aahh … Phil's gone … he's gone!'

Bill's brain raced through options; he dropped his bombs on the target then ascended into cloud knowing with his mission completed, he had to get his crew safely back to the Naples airfield. German fighter planes circled around the squadron, mingling with the US fighter escorts. More German aircraft fire battered the plane, and Bill smelt burning fuel.

'We're on fire,' Bert yelled again. 'Engine Two is burning.'

They had to land somewhere fast. Bill caught a glimpse of water ahead of him and, judging it to be the Adriatic, opened the throttle and gained speed.

The speed fanned the flames, igniting more of the interior. Five minutes to the sea, a long five minutes. He pushed forward, put the place in a dive towards the ocean – they had to land immediately before they were engulfed in flames. He could see no vessel lights so hoped the plane would miss fishing or military ships; controlled the descent so he could pull the nose up before hitting the water. The only problem was, he didn't know how rough the sea was nor the height of the waves.

'Mayday, Mayday,' he called into the radio. Flames and smoke where billowing out of the rear of the aircraft and they only a few seconds before they would spread and engulfed the cabin. Bill ordered his crew to Crash Stations and to Brace.

He instructed Bert to open the escape hatch above the cockpit and those in the centre section of the bomber. He prayed his crew remembered their role in a ditching procedure: how to launch the dinghy; the survival equipment it contained, and the correct manner to leave the aircraft. He hoped it was enough to save them and signalled to the airman in the centre section to release through the escape hatch the flock of homing pigeons with details of their position attached to their legs.

Bill maintained height as long as he could until the altimeter neared zero. Then he lowered speed, approached the water cross wind, and splashed down on the sea, the bomber's tail down. The impact was heavy, the aircraft jolting from side to side as waves battered it and surged up over the canopy. The strong smell of fuel filled his nostrils, and Bill saw it streaming out of the aircraft.

He'd already instructed his crew to don their inflatable life vests, to not pull the inflation cords until they were through the hatches. With water rushing in, filling tight spaces, the airmen climbed over pieces of equipment to exit the cabin; they struggled to push the dinghy out while the aircraft floated precariously on rough water. The crew climbed onto the wing; struggled to get the dinghy right side up, then pulled the inflation cords.

Bill and Bert climbed out through the hatch above them and leapt into the sea beside the dinghy. In the glimmer of pre-dawn light the crew grabbed and hauled them into the craft then manned the oars and paddled away from the bomber. It's slow sinking below the waves quenched the fires.

The dinghy was crammed with men, Tim and Bob bleeding from wounds as they knocked against the fuselage during the ditching. They all checked the pockets for the escape ration packs which included high energy foods such as chewing gum, chocolate and boiled sweets, tablets to combat tiredness and for water purification. The survival kit included water, matches, a simple fishing line, waterproof compass, sewing kit and shaving items. It also contained a flare gun, flares, and several tins of drinking water.

Bill outlined the rules for sharing the rations which seemed totally inadequate for six men for forty-eight hours. Knowing the chocolate would melt in the heat, he packed the bars into the emergency map cover and, attaching the ties to the dinghy straps, hung the packet over the side into the sea.

Bill raised his hand. 'Each of you is allowed one square of chocolate in the morning and one at night, each person can take a few sips of water three times a day. That means the rations can last for four to five days. We will start this routine today. We just have to wait and be patient as we're so closely packed in this dinghy. If anyone notices a leak, we have rubber patches for repairs. Bert, can you pass first aid kit to Tim and Bob so they can staunch the bleeding. If anyone starts to feel seasick lean over the side of the dinghy, for hygiene's sake!'

On Day One, a watery sun slowly rose from the horizon and the airmen could see the roughness of the waves surrounding them. The plane had gone but trails of fuel oil drifted across the wave tops. The dinghy tilted up and down, up and down, as it bobbed on the sea, the crew thrown from side to side despite them pushing their feet together in the centre. A sudden squall washed over them, soaking their clothes and filling the bottom of the craft. They used their hands to bail the water out.

Bill removed the compass and the waterproof emergency map and tried to gain an approximate direction by using the position of the sun and the compass. There was no indication on the map which way the ocean currents ran. His thoughts flipped between re-living the flying procedures and his inability to fly the bomber back to safety. Endless questions bombarded his mind. Could he have arranged for his crew to extinguish the fire while still flying? Should he have continued with the cargo of bombs on board and attempted to return to Naples? The burden of guilt sat heavily on his shoulders as he contemplated the possibility of rescue. Had his SOS call been received? Where were the homing pigeons?

The crew slumped together in silence, nudging each other involuntarily as the waves tilted the dinghy, each man lost in his own thoughts, wondering whether they would be rescued and see their families again. Every airman's nightmare was to be cast afloat, drifting in an unknown direction to an unknown destination. Apart from the dangers of leaks in the dinghy and storm damage, the most worrying problems were dehydration and exposure to sun and wind.

On Day Two, the sun rose in a blaze of red; the sky was a brilliant blue and the heat beat down, making them sweat in their heavy uniforms. Cramp started in their legs as they were unable to move easily without upsetting the dinghy. As the day wore on, some dozed, their heads drooping on their chests, others gazed blindly out to sea desperately hoping to catch sight of a vessel or land. In each of their thoughts was the possibility they could drift for days and eventually run out of water and survival rations. Ocean-going seabirds dived into the water searching for fish or floated around them for a short while. The faint sound of aircraft engines encouraged them to search the sky but heavy clouds now obscured the sun and the planes remained out of sight.

At night a bitter, sharp cold chilled the exposed parts of their bodies that had been sunburnt by the strong sun. Their feet became cold as their boots and socks were sodden with water, and the silence was eerie, only the slapping of waves against the side of the dinghy came in the absolute blackness. While some of the men drifted to sleep lulled by the rocking of the dinghy, Bill stayed awake, his brain turning over the events that had led to their current predicament. He tried to stem the fear creeping into his mind, bringing with it the guilt and helplessness of the survivor.

He stirred as the sun rose on Day Three and searched the ocean for anything that would mean rescue and safety – land, aircraft, fishing vessels. But nothing appeared, just the rolling waves reaching into the horizon and meeting the brilliant blue sky. Another scorching hot day, he registered in his mind. That meant more dehydration as their heavily-clothed bodies absorbed the heat and sweating started again.

Bill desperately hoped the airbase had received his SOS calls and the homing pigeons, and that planes would be searching for them. He knew how difficult that would be, trying to locate a tiny dinghy in thousands of square miles of ocean.

'Do we have fishing hooks in the emergency pack?' Bill asked.

'No, we don't have hooks, only lines,' replied Bert, shaking his head. 'Anyway, we don't have anything to use as bait.'

As the men sat in silence a faint engine noise drifted on the air and they searched the sky desperately. It was a bomber, high up in the west, probably returning from a mission over Italy. Bert lunged for the flare gun and loaded a cartridge, knelt and pulled the trigger. The gun jerked in his hand and the red flare streaked up into the sky, sparks splattering them with brilliant particles of light. He loaded another and shot that off too. The crew all looked up, willing the aircraft to see the flares, but it kept going and the flares sputtered out. The sight of the bomber and its height made them realise how far they had drifted from land and that the chances of an early rescue were remote.

Another sweltering day, the sips of water just wetting their mouths but not replacing the copious sweat. The men slouched against each other as the sun dipped below the watery horizon. Bill had ascertained that, with every hour, they would drift further east towards German-occupied Yugoslavia. The crew's condition was seriously declining and they were intensely hungry and thirsty, the rationed chocolate no longer available to give them energy. Bill rationed the water to a few sips per man every evening but their lips were blistered and their tongues swollen.

With another night of biting cold, their morale diminished further. Bill knew that if they weren't found that day, the search could be called off, their only hope then was to drift to land somewhere. Tim was so ill with sea-sickness he was constantly leaning over the side of the dinghy, only bile left to bring up. He lay with his head back retching continuously, exhausted and faint. He was in such poor shape he could no longer talk or keep his eyes open.

Edwin had said nothing for several days and then suddenly screamed: 'We're all going to die!' Wild-eyed, he waved his arms about, knocking his companions uncontrollably. He couldn't stop shivering and tears fell down his face.

Bill leant forward and slapped his cheek hard to halt the hysteria. Then Edwin abruptly went silent and pulled his legs to his chest, shaking his head.

By the fifth day, the crew were badly sunburned, their lips cracked and bleeding, their hands swollen and blistered. Harsh sunlight glared off the sea causing blindness and headaches. They had no protection from the weather.

Billowing dark clouds formed on the horizon and blocked the sun. Then rain came lashing down out of a leaden sky. The men tilted their faces, opened their mouths to gulp down the life-saving liquid. They held out their hands to collect rain to wipe over their burning faces. The rain soothed them, soothed their faces and hands and soaked their clothing.

'Get out the water cans! Hold them out to be filled,' Bill ordered, and they looked around the dinghy for rubber bottles; emptied out the packets of emergency supplies in an effort to collect the water. All too soon though the storm passed over and the sun emerged with its burning heat. The rain water had temporarily filled their stomachs and revived Tom and Edwin a little but they were all ravenous, thinking solely of food and their favourite meals.

They tried to catch sea birds as they hovered overhead or occasionally landed on the side of the dinghy, but had no success. Finally Bert managed to pull a large seabird down and knock it senseless with his water tin. Bill reached up and grabbed another nearly capsizing the dinghy. Encouraged, Tom reached out and just caught a wing as the bird hovered over his head. They tried to pull the feathers out and reach the flesh with pen knives but couldn't get through the thick layer of fat.

'We can use the fat as bait and try to catch fish,' Bill suggested. He hung two lines over the dinghy and waited until he felt a tug on the line. A large flat fish covered in pink scales hung on one, the other line had one similar. Pulling the two fish apart, Bill handed each man a piece of the raw fish. Tim turned his head away and refused to eat but the others bit down on the skin, flesh and bones, uncaring that it was flavourless. With the rain water and the fish morsels in their stomach, the men cheered a little and sat up straighter in the dinghy.

Another day passed and the minor sense of well-being that the fish and rain water had given them dissipated. The sea was calm and the sun continued to shine in a cloudless sky. There was no land in sight nor sound of aircraft and the men subsided into a vacuum of silence and despair.

Bill realised he had to keep his crews' minds alert and suggested they talked about their families or favourite occupation. They mumbled stories of their wives and children, parents and homes during the day but it was hard to understand the indistinct and sometimes incoherent mutterings.

Night fell and the wind became stronger and stronger, rocking the dinghy as the swell increased. The men rolled from side to side against each other as it was impossible to brace themselves with feet and arms. Lightning flashed across the sky followed swiftly by ear-shattering crashes of thunder. Rain fell in torrents filling the bottom of the dinghy and drenching the men. Their clothes and hair were stiff with salt.

It was an awful night and none of them slept. As the dinghy rocked viciously, there was a moan and a shift between the men. No-one took any notice as they were intent on hanging on and saving themselves. Edwin shifted himself nearer to the edge of the dinghy and, when the next wave tilted the boat down to the sea, he pushed himself out and fell face first into the icy sea. His last thoughts were of relief that he no longer had to endure sitting in the dinghy waiting hopelessly for rescue. He knew he had no future after the war as the letter he'd read before he'd boarded the bomber was from his mother telling him that his beloved wife had died in childbirth with their new-born son. He welcomed the dark cold sea around him, opening his mouth and gulping in water, feeling the weight of his heavy uniform drag him down and the unconsciousness of hypothermia drown his thought.

On Day Seven, there was no dawn only faint shafts of milky light edging between the dark billowing clouds that seemed to enclose the little dinghy in a wet suffocating blanket. The men shifted and dozed; cramp and exhaustion reduced the blood flow, their body temperatures dropping as hypothermia started to take hold.

'Someone's missing,' cried Bert, trying to sit up. 'It's Edwin. He must have been washed out of the dinghy in the night, that's why we had more room.'

'He received a letter before we left the airbase and was extremely upset, shaking and sobbing,' replied Tom, sadly shaking his head.

The day passed with only a gradual illumination of a brooding sky. The wind caught them sharply and they could see a huge storm coming. The sea started to heave under the dinghy, sending the men up to a dizzying height and then sliding down into the churning water.

They clung on desperately, unable to bail the water out, and huddling together for protection. After what seemed like hours of drenching misery, the storm passed over but dehydration, starvation and exposure took its toll.

Bill worried about their sanity, aware that people hallucinated, argued with themselves, flung themselves hopelessly overboard in an effort to reach imaginary ships. He realised that, although they all faced the same hardship, their different reactions to it would shape their fates, and resignation was paralyzing and self-fulfilling. It impacted on the will to survive. They had all lost weight, their eyes had sunk into their sockets, their skin hung from their bodies and faces. He was determined the men wouldn't resort to cannibalism.

Dredging up an enormous effort to inspire his men to hope for rescue and to temporarily displace their fear, Bill made one last attempt. 'Come on, men, stir yourselves! Bert, tell me about your very first memory …'

Then 'Tim, tell us about the last holiday you had – what did you do? Where are you going next?' He needed them to see a future even though it was obvious they were dying slowly and painfully. He asked them to remember jokes and urged them to sing songs to keep their minds alert and create something to live for. The men mumbled through blistered swollen lips, nothing making any sense except that Bill sensed a feeling of desperate unity as they shared their lives and dreams as they drifted endlessly on a calm, flat ocean that went nowhere.

Rescue Summer 1944

With the sea so flat, Bill half-heartedly scanned the horizon, as he had been for days, then he blinked through the glare coming off the water, and stared harder. Wiping his eyes, he tried to focus better; rubbed his eyes again, harder. Unbelievably on the horizon was a faint mark – it seemed to be coming closer.

A ship! A small ship …

Fumbling frantically, he groped for the waterproof package, ripped it open and pulled out the remaining flare gun. Scrabbling with stiff fingers, he clumsily loaded the cartridge, aimed skyward and pulled the trigger. The flare burst over the water, and he quickly fired a second.

The men stirred, then knelt in the dinghy, balancing precariously as they waved their arms to attract attention. Their hearts pounded with excitement for the ship was definitely drawing closer. From its shape, it appeared to be a fishing vessel, and Bill peered over the slight swell to identify a flag on the mast. An excruciating thirty minutes passed before the men were sure the fishing boat crew had seen them, the boat adjusting its course to head straight for them. An Italian flag flapped in the rising breeze and the seamen lined the deck rails shouting at the airmen.

'*Inglese, Inglese?*' one yelled when the boat was a few metres of the dinghy, its bow wash causing waves that rocked the dinghy.

'*Si! Si!* Help us …' Bill called back.

A rope was hurled at the dinghy and snaked over the airmen. Bert grabbed it and tied it around his waist. The seaman heaved and dragged Bert up out of the dinghy and over the side of the fishing boat. Another rope was thrown over to the dinghy and Tom reached up and attached it to his jacket. Soon it was only Bill left on the dinghy waiting for the rope to be flung again and within minutes it hit his head and he had tied it around himself. He was dragged out of the dinghy, across the waves and up the side of the fishing boat. He noticed its hull was peeling and dirty as he scrambled up the side and was heaved over the rail onto the deck where he lay face down in the swilling fishy water, exhausted and incredibly relieved.

The airmen lifted themselves off the deck onto their knees and tried to stand up holding the rail. They were weak and their legs so feeble from inactivity that it took several attempts before they were upright. The captain walked over and fired a question in Italian at them.

Bill answered hoarsely. 'Si, we are English and have been adrift for over a week after my plane was shot down and caught fire. We had to bail out, ditch the aircraft in the sea. My crew are exhausted, starving and dehydrated as we ran out of food and water days ago.'

'OK, we share food and water with you. We fish near Croatia and land you there at dawn. But you stay out of sight. And you look out when you get off the boat. Germans are everywhere.'

The crew thirstily drank the water given them, then stumbled through the hatch and down the ladder into the ship's cabin. They lay on benches, too exhausted to take off their salt-encrusted clothes. Lying down full length was bliss, allowing the men to stretch cramped limbs and rest their heads on their arms. It was hot and, though the cabin reeked of fuel and fish, it felt like paradise. Soon, snores and grunts emitted from below as the fishing boat headed for harbour and safety.

'Get up and get out!' the captain roused them sharply as he opened the hatch and let in the morning sun. 'I don't want any trouble. Come … you go quickly … up that cliff. Above is a goat track. You walk across the fields … keep your backs to the sun. I radio local Croatian partisans to help you. Good luck.'

'*Molto grazie*,' Bill said and shook the captain's hand. The airmen scrambled over the side of the boat, swam until they could stand, then waded through the cold water to the sandy beach then stumbled to the steep cliffs. Huddling together, they watched as the vessel backed out to sea and powered away. Bill realised the captain's fear of being seen with English airmen in a German-occupied country. He guided the men to an overhanging rock that provided some shelter from the sun and prying eyes.

'We will rest here until nightfall,' he said, 'then we'll start the trek to Naples.'

Despite his exhaustion, Bill couldn't relax as thoughts whirled around in his head. It was going to be tough getting back to Naples and the risk of being captured by the Germans, or betrayed by locals, was high. As he finally drifted into a light doze, he remembered Elena telling him about her escape and the nightmare trek from Puglia to Naples.

Night came too quickly for the exhausted crew but Bill chivvied them to search the cliff-face for the path the boat captain had pointed out to them. The moon shone through the light cloud cover and they discovered the cliff path at the far end of the cove and struggled up the rocky slope, trying to climb quietly in the loose scree. Reaching the top, each man crawled over and lay flat; scanned the land in all directions. The complete silence unsettled them, amplified the low sound of their laboured breathing, barely muffled by the short turf. Taking a bearing from the moon, Bill signalled his crew to crawl away from the edge and gather in a windswept clump of trees to their left, their limbs stiff from by inactivity and further hampered by salt-encrusted clothes.

The fishing boat captain had told them to head towards a stone tower, which acted as a landmark for incoming boats. There they would meet two local fishermen who would guide them past the nearby village and brief them of any German activity in the area. Painfully, the crew approached the crumbling tower, crawling on their bellies to stay hidden in undergrowth shadows.

Bill tapped quietly on the cracked wooden door. For several terrifying minutes no response came, then a raspy voice called quietly in Italian. Bill replied with a single name and they were beckoned into the tower base; slid through the partly opened door into an airless darkness that smelt of seawater and bird droppings.

A faint torchlight scanned their faces, but the fishermen remained hidden in the dense blackness. The crew were told to sit on the earth floor and rest while Bill was briefed in Italian. Then the single torchlight extinguished. Bill whispered instructions to his crew: 'Move quietly. And follow the partisans. Stay together.'

The crew stumbled along in a crouching single file over rough ground in the darkness, their tired bodies moving automatically. At times, a single hand waved them to lie flat until their rescuers had determined if it was safe to move on. One time they could hear marching soldiers and harsh voices passing on a nearby lane.

A faint glimmer of dawn appeared on the horizon as they reached a steep hill hollowed out with natural caves. Pushing aside an old olive tree, the partisans led the crew inside a deep cave, the floor sandy underfoot, the rocky walls of a narrow chasm damp as they stumbled deeper into the darkness. Finally, they arrived at a large space dimly lit by dishes of burning oil. Even through the smoky air, the crew noted several figures seated around a wood fire, the pan balanced precariously on top crackling and spitting.

The rebel's leader gestured for the crew to sit on the floor while a terracotta flagon of water was passed around. They were handed slices of oily bread with shreds of tomato piled on them.

In the dense black silence of the cavern, the airmen stretched out on the sandy floor and fell into a troubled doze, interspersed by a spluttering cough from Bert and light snoring from Tom. Bill sat with his back propped against the rock wall, his head nodding gently. For the first time in weeks, they felt safe, their thirst and hunger temporarily allayed. After a few hours they were roughly shaken awake and guided out of the cavern into the fresh air where a faint light glimmered to the west as the sun sank below the hills. The partisan leader pointed to the south and muttered a few directions to Bill.

Stiff and sore, the exhausted men trudged across the rough terrain, linked by a hand on the shoulder of the man in front, their eyes gradually adjusting to the grainy dark. A large owl flapped past them and a vixen screeched from a hedgerow to their left.

They reached a tiny hamlet and crawled behind a ruined stone wall. Bill put his hands to his mouth and hooted convincing, as instructed, and a battered blue door in a burnt cottage opened a crack and a hand beckoned them in. Sliding over the ground one by one, the men reached the door and were pulled inside a stone-floored kitchen. A rough wood table held bread, cheese and onions, and a jug of well water. The partisan signalled the crew to sit on the floor to eat and drink. In the dim light of a kerosene lamp, the crew gazed at each other in amazement, and ate hungrily.

The partisan then indicated that they should throw their badges of rank and identification into the fire which he then stoked, then doused with water.

'Follow,' he said as he opened the door and beckoned the crew. The silence and dark outside were intense as they crept behind the partisan to an earth bunker in the hills. 'Hide until sunset,' he mumbled in poor Italian, and mimed German soldiers shooting guns at them. The crew spent the night there, twitching at every sound, unable to doze for fear of capture. They were deep in German territory and knew the partisan had risked the lives of his friends and family by helping them.

It was still dark when a shadowy figure appeared at the entrance to the bunker; he pushed aside the animal hide covering the bunker entrance, and stepped inside; lit the brushwood in the metal wall bracket with a match. In the dim light, the crew saw an old farmer wearing a flat cap, dark overalls and heavy boots. They stood and brushed dust from their trousers as the farmer shone the torch over each face. '*Inglese*. Follow,' he said.

Once again in single file, the crew were taken along muddy roads, up steep mountain trails and through thick forests, avoiding any settlements and major roads where German soldiers searched for escapees to gun down. The stars-studded sky held no moon to illuminate their surroundings or highlight their location to their enemies as they waded through bitterly cold mountain streams and slid quietly past a herd of wild goats. As the dawn light emphasised the contours of the land, a phalanx of German fighters strafed them randomly even though the crew were shadowed by a copse of trees and the farmer had flattened himself in a ditch. The men were bone weary, their throats parched with thirst, their bodies weak from hunger. Yet they forced their legs to move and followed the farmer to a group of houses bordering a farm track.

Silently he handed them over to two more partisans, the women wearing loose cotton trousers and smocks, their hair stuffed under caps. Only the lightness of their voices indicated their femininity. The women guided them to an empty isolated farmhouse hidden in a deep valley a few miles further south. The men were told to rest there in the daylight hours and remain out of sight. They gathered straw to lie on and used the water from a large battered enamel jug to drink and wipe their faces of sweat and mud. Within minutes of resting on the ground, heavy breathing and snores surrounded them, their exhausted bodies finally giving in.

The airmen had spoken little during the last few days, aware of the grave danger they were in and totally dependent on the partisan underground network. Their faces and uniforms were so encrusted with mud it was difficult to identify each person, and thick matted beards covered the lower parts of their faces. Their boots were no longer waterproof, the soles flapping apart from the uppers as they walked over the rocky ground. In the darkness, Tom had walked into a tree and a low branch had sliced open his cheek, the blood trickling down his face congealing on his jacket collar. They all now limped, and their uniforms became tattered.

Bill found it difficult to relinquish control over the safety of his crew, yet he was so exhausted he could barely think how they were going to get back to Italy. He realised the chance they could be rescued or handed over to the Germans was 50/50. His warm memories of Elena had sunk under the weight of hunger, thirst and danger. As he lay on the dirty straw, Elena's cheeky warm smile drifted into his head and he longed to hold her in his arms and kiss her face.

With no means of communicating with their partisan rescuers by language, the British airmen used hand gestures, but did so sparingly for fear of misinterpretation. They had no idea where they were but Bill guessed the fishing boat captain had taken them to Tito's Yugoslavia. The partisans could therefore be Croatian, Bosnian or from Slovenia. They knew the country was controlled by Germans and that their rescuers were risking their lives and those of their family.

The crew all needed medical attention: their feet were blistered, limbs bleeding from falls and tree branches. Despite the food given by the partisans, they were faint with hunger, their faces hollow and grey with fatigue. Tim's uniform hung on his skeletal frame as he had been seasick and unable to eat and now could only swallow light food as he had lost a few teeth. Tom and Bob had been injured when they'd escaped the burning aircraft and their wounds were going septic. Bill realised that only he and his co-pilot, Bert, could walk unaided.

Unbeknown to them, hundreds of downed Allied pilots in Yugoslavia were being aided by communist partisans. US Air Force commanders actively encouraged the partisans to cooperate in their rescue from German occupied Yugoslavia. Mostly they were flown out by US C47 transport planes, using primitive air strips made by Croatian and Bosnian partisans, and returned to American airbases in Italy. Many of these partisans lost their lives, families and homes when discovered by the German invaders. In the north west around Zadar heavy fighting broke out between the different groups, the communist partisans, Serbian Chetniks and the Germans.

By late spring 1944, US Commanders had formed a unit of medical airmen and officers, in cooperation with the British, to expedite the rescue of Allied airmen downed in the Balkans. They realised the minimal chance of rescuing aircrews missing in action even though it was thought those surviving the loss of their aircraft were rescued by local partisans. News had been received that many Allied airmen had been captured and imprisoned in closely guarded camps.

The enforced reprieve for the airmen in the isolated farm renewed their energy and re-kindled their optimism. They had to trust the local partisans to move them safely from their temporary refuge and find some way of leaving Yugoslavia. The two female guides returned after nightfall and gestured the men to follow them again. They stumbled through the dark with aching bones and hunched shoulders across ploughed fields, sheltering behind hedges and stone walls where possible. They bypassed a smouldering ruined barn, the women ignoring the mutilated bodies of two adults and a small child. They flung themselves in a wet roadside ditch as a group of German fighters swooped along the country road as they crossed it. The spatter of bullets on the road added to the men's terror, their innate bravery stripped away by their physical condition and absolute reliance on the local partisans for their safety and rescue. Bill could no longer think of encouraging words for his crew, his energy and physical strength totally depleted. He could only pat the shoulders of his men as they rose from the ditch, crossed the pockmarked road, and slid behind a crumbling stone wall.

In silence the rebels beckoned them to follow through a thick wood of oak trees and on past a tiny village burnt to the ground, the smell of decaying bodies reaching them on the light breeze. The walk seemed endless and pointless. Tim was being held up by Bert, Tom hobbled along slowly and Bill limped in their wake. The women stopped briefly by a small stream allowing the men to take sips of cool water before pulling them to their feet and marching ahead at a faster pace.

A pair of owls swooped past them, screeching loudly and a harsh vixen's cry hung in the dense air.

A sliver of light appeared through the trees as the partisans crouched in front of a thicket, parted the branches to show a shallow niche in rocks overhung by olive trees roots. The men were helped inside and the women pushed and plaited the branches to cover the cave.

'Stay' they hissed and mimed the sun setting.

The cave was damp and smelt of rabbit dung with very little space for the men to sit but they were thankful for the respite and wriggled together to support each other. The pungent smell of unwashed bodies and urine, the cramp of hunger and aching limbs prevented the men from sleeping; they could only drop their heads on their chests. Tim whispered a prayer and the others joined him, their dry mud-encrusted lips scarcely forming coherent words. Bill felt a wave of thankfulness that they were still alive, and pride for the stamina of his crew.

It seemed a long time before dusk crept through the trees and the sun's last rays glinted on flying insects and dust. The cry of a hunting owl reached them and they sensed the branches being gently pulled aside with a slight crackling noise. Muscles tensed and heads raised in fear. Men shifted together; prepared to flee, desperately hoping the enemy hadn't found them. A female hand with a brass wedding ring pushed through the branches and beckoned them to come out. Crouching and crawling, the men assembled outside the cave; rose shakily to their feet and limped in single file after the female partisan.

She led them through a pass in a low mountain range until they reached a vast flat space. Incredibly there was a small dirt airstrip at the far side and a few shadows moved towards the British crew. They were lighting brushwood torches at one end of the airstrip as a heavy aircraft descended with a bump and taxied to the end of the runway. A door opened in the side of the plane and an American officer, briefly silhouetted as he jumped to the ground, hissed, 'Quickly, get in. The longer we stay on the ground the greater the danger.'

Bill's crew stumbled across the rough field and fell into the open door without a word. The door shut on Bill as he entered last. Then the aircraft engine roared and the plane lifted slowly from the ground. It gained height, circled over the mountains and headed to the sea and Italy. They were safe at last and in a few hours would reach the Bari airfield to get medical treatment before continuing on to Pomigliano.

Naples Winter 1944

After Elena had talked to Bill about her life, she felt closer to him and knew he felt the same closeness. She thought about him most of the time, remembering his arms about her and soft kisses on her mouth. Chiara commented on the change in Elena, her frequent laughter and happy smiles. She was glad for her and hoped for a secure future for them both. Chiara and Gina both cautioned Elena not to expect too much from Bill during the war.

Chiara warned that fighting men had to change their attitudes in war and suffocate their emotions so they were able to fight and stay alive. 'Bill said he fought with our enemies, the British and Americans, until a year ago, bombing and killing Italians when they were allies of the Germans. I remember my father couldn't talk about his time in the First World War because it was so horrendous, the sights of mangled and dying soldiers forever haunting him. Bill is not fighting in trench warfare but seeing his crew struggling to get out of burning aircraft and counting the squadron's dead and wounded is heart-breaking. You see a normally peaceful man struggling to contain his emotions when he's with you, Elena, but he is terribly aware there might be no future for your relationship.'

'We don't want to see you deeply hurt again because you have loved and lost someone special,' Gina added. 'I find it so hard to picture my husband's face and remember his passionate embraces and kisses. Like other woman living in Naples now, finding food and keeping shelter for my children consumes all my energy and waking thoughts.'

Elena listened to the advice from her friends but at night continued to dream of travelling with Bill to England, getting married and finding a home to have a family. She looked forward with trepidation to meeting Bill's parents who would no doubt have found a more suitable partner for their son than an Italian orphan peasant girl.

She busied herself with her church work and the food distribution and knew that Bill's flying roster often meant he couldn't meet her after Sunday Mass every week but when he didn't come for two weeks, she became anxious. She missed him more than she could have imagined and tried to stay positive. Gina noticed Elena's listlessness with her children; noticed she seemed weary after the church food distribution days.

Finally, when after another week passed with no word or sight of Bill, she asked the Padre if he'd heard any news. He held out his hand to her and led her back into the church after they had finished giving food to the children.

'I'm sad to say I have bad news for you, Elena. The RAF commander at the Allied Air Base told me Bill and his crew had been ordered to carry out a mission. His plane has not returned to the base and they have had no news of what happened or where he and his crew are. I am deeply sorry, Elena. I will pray every day for his safe return as I know you are so fond of him. Go home now and pray for him.'

Elena leant against the cold stone wall and couldn't move – too stunned by the news. As the Padre walked away, tears coursed down her cheeks. She shook with terror and her old feelings of insecurity and loneliness flooded her. She needed to find a quiet place to hide from the world, like a wounded animal. Running to Gina's house, she quickly climbed the stairs to her room and shut the door behind her. She shook so hard she couldn't stop the tears flooding in a rainstorm down her face, dampening her dress. She collapsed on the bed, her arms squashed protectively around her body, conscious only of the searing sorrow she felt. She was alone and unprotected again, with no future.

She lay a long time, unaware of the sinking sun, of dusk falling in patterns of light around her, or the birds and insects chirping their evening song. She felt weighted by immense sorrow and a feeling of abandonment overcame her. She ignored Gina's knock on the door, wishing only to sink into oblivion.

Even though exhausted, she slept little that night, and stayed in her room for the next several days, ignoring Gina's concerned pleas to talk with her, or to eat. She had no resilience left to face the future without Bill, and sobbed and cried, and thumped the bed in despair until she heard Chiara's anxious voice outside the door.

'Elena, Elena, let us help you. You aren't alone. We're your friends and care for you. Please open the door.'

Elena slid off her bed and stumbled to the door; opened it to see both Chiara and Gina standing there. Chiara's arms opened to comfort her. Elena leant into her motherly embrace, her tears wetting Chiara's blouse. She gently pushed Elena away to look into her face, to softly wipe Elena's tears; she noted the red swollen eyes and blotched cheeks, the pain etched on Elena's face.

'Come back into your room and tell me what's happened.' Chiara nodded at Gina and gently steered Elena back into the bedroom and sat by her on the bed. Gina softly closed the door respecting their privacy and gently coaxed her children back down the stairs. Chiara put her arm around the distraught girl and held her close. They sat in silence for a long while, Chiara embracing Elena while she patiently waited for the girl to stop sobbing and speak.

'Oh Chiara, what am I going to do now? They told me Bill didn't return from a bombing run, and they don't know where he is or if he will ever come back. He didn't tell me before he left and I am so frightened he will be killed and won't return. What am I to do – I care for him so much – I want to be with him.' Elena's words were interspersed with heavy sobs.

Chiara held Elena against her soft bosom, trying to comfort the girl in her deep misery.

'I think Bill didn't tell you because he wanted to save you from worrying about him. He has flown many missions before and returned safely, I am sure he will do everything in his power to come back to you. It is clear he loves you very much. I will ask someone to go to the airbase tomorrow and find out what is happening.'

Elena pulled away from Chiara's embrace and, looking up, said, 'Will you do that? Please, oh please I need to know.'

'I'll ask Gina to bring some food and water to you. You try to sleep a little, and remember the wonderful times you've shared with your Bill.'

Elena slept briefly that night, her curtains pulled back so she could see the night sky and pray for Bill's safety. She stayed in her room sunk in misery until she heard Chiara's voice and a knock at her door the next morning. She leapt off the bed, opened the door, eager for good news but all she saw on Chiara's face was sorrow and knew her world had been shattered for ever. She fled back to bed and flung herself face down, and sobbed out her breaking heart.

Chiara entered the room, shut the door and sat on the bed, her hand gently stroking the girl's shaking body. 'Elena, Elena, the news is that Bill's plane has not returned to the airbase but the commanding officer has no information to report Bill missing. It's a waiting game. Until the base can confirm the location of his plane, you have to rely on your strength and resilience to bear the situation patiently.'

After a few more days of grieving in her room, Gina and the Padre coaxed Elena out. Being with the street children on Sundays and playing with Gina's children helped fill the empty days. As each sorrowful day passed, her hopes waned and she dwelt more on the memories of the happy times she'd spent with Bill. She drifted through the days mechanically, slept little and cried a lot in her room. Every day seemed dull and monotonous, without purpose. Her grief swelled inside her and she had never felt such intense despair. Another miserable month passed with no news of Bill, and Chiara told Elena she must start looking for full-time work in the area.

'The Mayor's office posts up lists of all types of jobs. You've had a decent education, and like children, so apply for teaching or clerical work,' Chiara said briskly. 'You cannot continue to feel sorry for yourself when there are thousands of women in this city who have lost husbands and sons. You need to pay Gina for your room and food as it's not fair to depend on her.'

Elena nodded and hugged Chiara, agreeing with her advice. She met with the Mayor and discussed the work required; he arranged for her to meet a few people and she was offered clerical and teaching work at the local school. Many of the former teachers had left before the war or had not returned due to death or injury.

Elena had always enjoyed working with young children in Caterna and she patiently encouraged them in their learning and organised playground games. The school had been partially bombed but several areas were repaired as temporary classrooms. She pinned the childish drawings on the walls of her room and tried to imagine a future without Bill. Slowly the paralysing sorrow eased and she woke each day with some anticipation of enjoyment in her work. She met with and visited some of the mothers and shared war experiences with them, many of them tragic due to the death of loved family members or neighbours.

Every morning Elena walked to the school through narrow dirty streets between tall buildings, many without roofs, sunlight pushing between the gaps where bombs had destroyed an apartment block. She quickly realised how lucky she was to have a job and somewhere to live as she passed thin scraggy women leaning in the doorways, small children crawling in the filth at their feet, their faces devoid of hope and bony with hunger. They eyed her with hatred and envy for her clothing and long hair. Many women were toothless, their lips sunk between their nose and chin, their hair thin and straggly through lack of food. Few had the energy to return Elena's weak smile as they clutched a few rags around them to maintain some decency. Elena could see no attempt had been made to keep themselves or their children clean and an overwhelming odour of sewage and rotting rubbish drifted around them.

Elena started bringing bread to distribute, but the women snatched the bread, pushing and shoving in their desperation to survive. Several times Elena was knocked to the ground, and received no gratitude or pleasantry. The children crawled at her feet, unable to stand on ricket-effected legs. They clawed at her ankles, scratched her legs as they tried to prop themselves up. Elena's heart filled with sympathy for their plight but feared their feeble ferocity.

One morning Elena was greeted by a smile and a pat on the back by a withered, bent old woman. 'You are kind to help these families but their men are dead or fighting and they can only support themselves by thieving or prostitution. They are angry and bitter and see you as a threat. You always walk down the same streets, don't you?' she said.

'Yes, because it's the most direct route,' Elena replied.

'Take another route some days so the locals aren't around to ill-treat you,' the old woman advised.

Elena continued to help with the Padre's Sunday food distribution although sourcing decent food had become more difficult and time consuming. The market in the bombed train station started up again, the stall holders piling stones and bricks and laying planks of wood on top as makeshift tables. Their wares were sparse – bruised and limp vegetables and fruit or discarded clothing. Castoff army shirts were popular for mothers to cut down for their children.

Elena, Gina and Chiara shared what food they could find and patched their clothes with torn army shirts. Due to increasing infirmity, Chiara moved from her cave-home and shared Elena's room. She became frail and skeletal, her eyes dull and her face lined with deep creases. She had no teeth so could only eat liquid food and her eyesight deteriorated. Elena cherished her old friend and saviour, and cooked weak soups, encouraged her to sleep in the single bed whilst Elena slept on the floor on old rugs.

After two weeks of increasing pain and debilitation, Chiara died quietly one morning. Elena, tears pouring down her cheeks, told Gina over breakfast, "Chiara has been my support my whole time in Naples. She could always find food of some sort and she became my dearest friend and mentor."

It was a sad time for them all and Elena doubted she would hear about Bill's demise as the Allied Forces were fully occupied in defeating the Germans in the mountains south of Rome. Fierce battles were fought at Monte Cassini and many small mountain villages were destroyed, their inhabitants either killed or fleeing for their lives.

Gina told her some Neapolitans earned money by selling pieces of lead stolen from ruined church roofs. They were frying weeds and insects in oil and gathering lemons and oranges from gutters. Occasionally dogs or cats were thrown into stews, the obnoxious smell deterring most people. Blankets supplied by the Allied reconstruction funds were often sold to buy food.

She'd heard that crime was rife as people were unemployed and many had no proper housing. The centuries-old Camorra organised crime network had developed as a Mafia-type syndicate in Naples and the surrounding region of Campania. Their business included prostitution, illegal gambling, corruption and murder. She knew many Neapolitans who'd became victims in order to survive and feed their families. Widowed mothers especially succumbed to prostitution.

Many of the orphaned street urchins became shoeshine boys (*sciuscia*) to earn money for food. They sat in ruined buildings or on the steps of churches at cross roads or main streets offering their services to Allied forces personnel, local gangsters or citizens with money to spare. It was a risky and competitive business as patrolling police could impound their cloths and polish and insist they moved somewhere else.

Slowly the streets of central Naples were being cleared of bomb-damaged buildings as the Italian government started to provide funds for the renovation of important and historical city landmarks like the central Piazza del Plebiscito and famous churches. Dust filled the air and the noise of bulldozers and buildings being detonated replaced the deadening sound of enemy bombs falling. Neapolitans started congregating in the streets and basic cafes opened up for business.

Elena had little spare time and energy to mourn Bill as Chiara became bedridden and needed feeding and washing. The school work was difficult as many of the children being educated were orphans and homeless, and disciplining them was almost impossible. She continued to help the Padre with his Sunday food distribution and had heard about another priest doing the same thing. They were sitting on a stone bench in front of the church discussing how they could meet and work together with the priest.

'He is Father Mario Borelli and he's trying to help the scugnizzi. He dresses in rags and sleeps on the streets with them, joining in begging at the railway terminal in Central Naples. They search through rubbish for scraps of food which they heat over fires in tin cans. He knows they are tough, cunning thieves who beg for food or work with criminal gangs but Father Borelli wants to understand and help them,' Elena told the Padre. 'He's looking for a place where the scugnizzi can live safely during the winter and has started to repair the abandoned ruins of Saint Gennaro. I think we should meet him and join our efforts. What do you think, Padre?'

'I think that more people should try to help these unfortunate kids so I will contact my bishop and we'll arrange to join forces. I'll talk to you next Sunday about what the Bishop says we can do.'

The Padre continued sitting with Elena in the sun on the bench as they discussed the information she had heard so far about Father Borelli. A shadow blocked the weak winter sun and the Padre looked up with curiosity then delight.

'I think there's someone here who you very much want to see,' he said smiling and nudging Elena's arm.

The Padre stood up and put out his hand. '*Buongiorno.*'

Elena looked up into the sun at the tall figure in uniform standing in front of her. It was Bill, alive and healthy and with an enormous grin on his face. He lifted Elena from the bench into his arms. So overjoyed she could not speak, the happy tears streaming down her face showed her relief that her dearly beloved man had returned safe and sound. Bill kissed her face and nose and chin; he wiped away the tears and clutched her tightly to him. The Padre disappeared and they sat close together on the stone bench, totally absorbed in each other. Protected within the circle of Bill's embrace, Elena looked up at his face and traced her fingers over the subtle contours, noting the fresh lines of hardship.

Bill leant nearer and kissed her lips again, Elena returning it with growing ardour. They needed no words to express their feelings just a physical closeness so tight their bodies were melded into one. They remained like that for some time, disregarding the passers-by and the noise of the streets, lost in their own world of love.

'Elena ...'

'Bill ......'

They started talking at the same time, eager to discover each other again, their hands linked and Elena still had tears of happiness flowing down her face. Bill shivered a little, sensing her depths of concern, and brushed away the moisture in his eyes.

'This place is too public. Where can we go to be alone?' Bill asked gently.

'I have the keys to the schoolroom where I work ... we can go there. It's only a short walk.' They walked arm in arm down the narrow streets, their hands held loosely when they had to jump over a gutter.

'Here it is. The school is closed on Sundays so we can be alone,' Elena said softly. She shut the door behind them and moved into Bill's protective embrace, unable to believe that her man had returned. They sat on the school benches for a long time, sharing the moments of their lives when they had been apart, good and bad, frightening and despairing. Many experiences Bill couldn't explain to Elena as they were too fresh and painful in his mind. Elena skimmed over the work she was doing at the school and the church and the sad deterioration of Chiara's health. Then she burst into sobs again.

'It has been such a terrible few months. I couldn't get any real information about your mission. They wouldn't tell me where you were, only that they had lost radio contact with your plane. It felt like a nightmare that we might not meet again. I couldn't bear it because I thought you had left me and I would never see you again,' Elena choked as she bent her head and wiped her tears. She sheltered in Bill's shoulder, desperate for his solace and understanding.

'It was impossible to contact our airbase for weeks. When the bomber was severely damaged, we had to bail out over the Adriatic Sea. We launched the life raft, but noticed it was only equipped with basic supplies for a few days. We had no idea where we were or the direction the currents would take us, and we had no radio with us. We drifted for days until an Italian fishing boat rescued us and landed us on the Yugoslavian coast. The Croatian resistance helped us avoid the German forces. Finally, we reached a small airfield and managed to get to Bari.' Bill bowed his head. 'I lost several of my crew. That's all I can tell you today, Elena. It's just too fresh in my mind and too hard to talk about.'

He leaned over and gently re-arranged a tendril of Elena's hair that had drifted onto her cheek. His touch lingered as he traced the shape of her cheekbones and the outline of her mouth, trembling with a mixture of sorrow and joy. 'Oh but I've missed you. I saw you in my dreams and my waking moments and desperately hoped I would survive to see you again.' He lifted her hands and kissed the tip of each finger, then her eyes, nose and finally her mouth.

Elena pressed into Bill more firmly and whispered into his chest about her doubts for the future. 'So much has happened to both of us that we have changed and I feel confused about our future together. I love you and want to be with you so much but I know you must take up your air force responsibilities and I am sharing a room with Gina and her children, and busy caring for Chiara. Where and how can our love continue while Naples is so devastated, and food is almost impossible to obtain ...' Elena sat up and stared out of the classroom window, her despair evident on her face.

'I don't have any answers right now but I want and need you to be my wife. That is the one thing that kept me alive and sane during the plane crash and rescue. I had to return to you, to hold you in my arms and kiss you. Please, please don't say this is over because our lives will be so difficult. We can work things out and meet as often as possible for a few months. Then we will have more idea of how to make our future together.' Bill's eyes were moist as he pleaded, as he took Elena's hands again and lovingly kissed the palms. 'I may not be able to meet you for a week or so until I know my next duty roster but I will keep the Padre informed and tell him when we can meet again.'

Elena nodded and touched his mouth gently. 'OK,' she said softly. 'I will stay and lock up the school while you leave separately. I hope we meet again soon. I love you.'

The Reunion – Spring 1945

Elena walked across the soft sand to the wavelets gently lapping at the shore and felt joyously happy. Her steps quickened and she began to run a little, her smile like warm sunshine as she hastened to the rendezvous with Bill by the rocks. She wore a pale dress printed with wild flowers, and a straw hat over her flowing dark hair. A tall young man appeared from behind the rocks, laughing. He moved quickly towards her holding out his arms.

'Bill, oh, Bill,' she called, running towards him as he ran to her. He caught her; embraced her; lifted her up in his strong arms. The strength and warmth of him and the security of his love filled her with joy. His lips were on hers and she flung her arms around his neck; nestled her head in his chest. 'You are safe! You haven't forgotten me.'

'Never will I leave you again, my dearest girl. I thought of you every waking moment. You are always there like a bright ray of sunshine in my life,' Bill said tenderly. He had forgotten how young she was, and felt only that he must comfort and protect her. Like a miracle, the sun shone brightly on the lovers. The sea whispered a soothing melody and seagulls gentled their harsh calls. Little waves lapped around their feet but they were unaware of it, exhilarated by their joy and love.

Bill gently lifted Elena's head from his shoulder, kissed her tears and gazed into her dark eyes, glimpsing the love in them. Her arms wrapped around his neck and all the suffering and terror she had experienced in her short life was swept away, leaving a profound and satisfying passion and an intense feeling of security that Bill gave her. He kissed her again more passionately, then gently pulled away from their tight embrace, led her to the rock to watch the sunset.

The sky reflected the brilliant colours of the sea, green, azure, indigo as the sun slowly sank in the cloudless sky. A balmy breeze wafted the scent of salt and wildflowers growing in the cliffs above them. They were peacefully content in their reunion. Elena felt the sun pass from her face, over her closed eyes and his mouth on hers, gentle and loving, his hands holding her to him. She felt the softness of his lips and the stubble of his jaw. She inhaled the masculine warmth of his body and reached out and placed her hands gently on his neck.

He held her for a very long time and only drew away when he heard the faint sound of feet crunching over the sand. He looked around and saw a young girl with a dog enjoying the romantic moment. Elena blushed and hid her face in Bill's shoulder.

'Now, my love, we can make our plans for a future together. I can't lose you again. I know we haven't been together much in the last few months, but will you marry me, Elena?' Bill asked. 'I know you will miss Italy but you will soon get used to living in England and we can have many loving years together. The sadness that has tormented you for so long will, I hope, gradually fade as we make a contented life.'

Elena remained silent a moment, thinking about the consequences of her response. She wanted to be his wife and knew the exact moment when she had fallen in love with him — it was the first evening they had walked along the beach before his plane crash. Bill's kindness and patience were comforting and she knew he loved her deeply. She drew a deep breath; made a decision and said, 'Yes, Bill, I will marry you, and I do want to spend the rest of my life with you. Planning for our future will make me forget any homesickness for Italy. I believe that, although we may disagree about small things, we will always be able to laugh together as we are lovers and friends.'

Bill asked, 'Would you like to come with me to the officers' club one evening for a meal? I want to introduce you to my best mate. We fly in the same squadron.'

'Yes,' replied Elena, 'but I need to find something nice to wear. I only have two dresses which I bought at the market and they are only flowered cotton.'

'Perhaps Saturday evening would be a good time for you? I can meet you at the market and we can ride on my motorbike to the airbase. I'll return you to Gina's room after.'

'Yes, thank you,' replied Elena. They walked arm in arm to the road where Elena had parked her bike and they parted with a passionate kiss.

Saturday evening was a great success and Elena wore her favourite cotton flowered dress with a red sash she had made. She borrowed some lipstick from Gina and her dried hair was held in place with two slides. She enjoyed meeting Bill's friend, Sam. She liked his friendly manner when Bill introduced her.

'Elena has agreed to marry me when I am demobbed and come to England to live,' Bill said proudly, his arm around Elena's shoulder.

'Lucky man,' said Sam. He gave her a peck on the cheek and excused himself to the bar.

'Will you meet me at the First Star Hotel tomorrow evening?' Bill asked tentatively. 'I am so in love with you and I want to show you how much.'

The next evening Elena walked to the Hotel to calm her nerves, but they dissipated when she saw Bill waiting outside Reception, a huge grin on his face.

'I have booked a special room for tonight,' he said.

He led her to the lift, shielding her from the Receptionist and other patrons.

'We are on the top floor, with views over the bay. I thought we could have breakfast here in the morning, sitting on the balcony.'

'That sounds lovely,' Elena replied shyly.

Bill ushered her out of the lift and down the corridor to a door on the right which he opened with his key. The door opened onto a narrow but light and airy room with a quilt-covered cushion-strewn bed in the centre. The French doors led out to a small Juliet balcony and stunning views over the bay.

He turned to her after softly closing the door. Then she was in his arms, her head on his chest as Bill lent down and kissed her on her mouth. Elena tensed at first then relaxed into the warmth of his embrace. She felt the length of his body, hard and muscular and desire raced through here in a tingling wave.

'I ordered a bottle of wine and some slices of pizza. We can eat now or later. You choose.'

Elena knew Bill understood she felt nervous and was trying to put her at her ease. She walked to the French doors and stood looking out at the bay. Bill moved behind her and put his arms around her and she leaned back into his embrace, her cheek against his then she turned around and kissed him on his nose, each ear and finally on his mouth. They clung together for a while until Bill suggested they sit and have a glass of wine. The wine was clear gold and smelt of sun-warmed grapes and herbs.

As Elena sipped hers, she felt her back and shoulders relax and her breathing slowed. A glow of love for Bill that he had so carefully planned for this momentous occasion overcame her. She could see the desire in his eyes mingled with his love for her. She reached out and held his hand, her smile wide.

'Shall we eat the pizza after?' Elena asked. Then taking another gulp of wine, she stood up and pulled Bill into her embrace. Their arms entwined, their lips pressed in desire, their hearts beat fast. Bill drew her to the bed and she lay on the soft cushions, lifting her arms to Bill in invitation. He lay down beside her, drew her head down and softly touched her lips with his. Her dark hair tumbled around the cushions and her face was so innocent and open it made his heart beat faster. As his desire rose, Bill kissed the hollow at the base of her throat, gently caressed her breasts and rose on his elbow to kiss her mouth again.

Slowly and gently he undid the buttons of her soft shirt and slid it from her shoulders; he placed it on the bed. She shivered with anticipation and knew he was gazing at her. She stood and stepped out of her blue cotton skirt; stood barefoot on the warm floorboards in her cotton bra and underwear; shivered as his hands ran over her body.

His eyes swept over her tanned shapely figure. 'You're so beautiful,' he whispered. 'So beautiful.'

He pulled her back to the bed; quickly took off his shirt, trousers and underwear. She gently moved her hands over his warm flesh, caressing the contoured muscles of his chest, shoulders, stomach. He had surprisingly little body hair and his upper body was lightly tanned.

She bent her head and kissed him, suddenly overwhelmed with love for this strong, tall man who loved her as much she loved him. She'd never had a lover or seen a naked man before, and felt nervous, but not frightened. She wanted a union between them more than anything in the world.

He held himself on one elbow, his eyes shining with desire, and kissed her deeply. She closed her eyes as his hand caressed her belly and moved down to her thighs and to the place between her legs. She felt a strong mixture of emotion and embarrassment. She wanted him to continue yet she was a little scared of what would follow next.

She held him tightly as he lifted himself over her and arched her body to meet his. After their loving union, they lay for a moment, the steady pounding of their hearts beating as one, their breathing mingling together in the hot dusty air. She knew without doubt she had found the man she wanted to spend the rest of her life with.

Bill eventually drifted off to sleep, but Elena couldn't, fearing she would wake and find she'd been dreaming. She could not believe, in her inexperience, that physical love could be so entwined with her emotional feelings for Bill. Her fingers curled into his hair; her hands stroked his chest. She thought how the future would be meaningless and cold without him. She knew his love for her would be constant and unconditional.

In the small hours of the morning, Bill turned to her, awoken by her touch. He tilted her face to him, lightly kissed her mouth and caressed her long hair spread over the pillow.

They made love again, this time more slowly, gently. It was still too warm in the room for them to lie entwined but they held hands tightly as they lay on their backs. The window was open, the shutters latched against the lights of the town. A fresh gentle breeze laden with salty air wafted over their naked bodies. They drifted back to sleep, their hands and arms interlocked.

The rising sun gradually lit the room with a golden glow as Bill raised himself on his arm and gazed down at Elena. He was thoughtful as he looked lovingly at Elena's black hair spread on the pillow, at the way she was gazing at him now through half-closed sleepy eyes, at the curve of her thigh and breast.

'Elena, I will ask you again … will you marry me?' he whispered. She looked up at him, her dark eyes widening. A gentle smile tugged at the corner of her lips. She didn't hesitate.

'Yes, Bill, I will. I did not think it possible that I could care for anyone so much,' Elena whispered in his ear. 'I know I will have to learn the ways of your country and your language. Your life has been so different from mine.'

She felt it was a miracle that this handsome, brave airman should love her enough to propose to her in the middle of a brutal war that seemed to have no end.

Sailing for Southampton – Summer 1945

Elena made her way to the bustling, noisy dockside at Naples, accompanied by Gina carrying a suitcase. She reflected sadly that Chiara wasn't at the quayside to wave her goodbye.

Battered trucks and horse-drawn carts carrying heavy loads were drawn up on the cobbled quayside. The evidence of severe bombing raids was apparent everywhere: ruined warehouses roofless; uneven cobbles with crater holes defacing the surface. The stench of unwashed bodies and the strong waft of horse manure mingled with the tang of salt and sea. Gulls swooped and screamed as they searched for food. Pickpockets sidled around looking for victims. The raucous shouts and swearing of sailors and hawkers filled the air.

The cargo and passenger ship towered over the crumbling warehouses, blocking the sunlight; it tilted back and forth with the incoming tide, straining against the tethered ropes. Boxes and chests containing personal belongings were carried up the two gangways and loaded into the hold. Huge wooden crates containing livestock and machinery were lifted from the quayside and lowered into the gaping hold in the centre of the ship. It was taking much needed provisions and engineering materiel to England.

Bill and Elena had been married a week before in the RAF chapel on the base. Now the airbase was closing and they were leaving the devastation of Naples and hoping for a new peaceful life in the English countryside. Bill was searching for work but finding it difficult with all the ex-servicemen returning.

At dawn, Gina and Elena had travelled by cart to the port of Naples. Gina's neighbours had gathered around them as they left, wishing Elena a happy future, many wiping the tears on their faces. They waved until Gina and Elena disappeared over the hill and clattered along the broken roads to the quay. The carter helped them down and handed Elena her few belongings packed in a cardboard case. Gina and Elena struggled through crowds of excited Italian families, obviously from all parts if Italy judging by their dialects, to reach the ship moored at the quayside. Two gangways spanned the gap between ship and shore, one for First-Class passengers, the other for families and working folk. An officer checked tickets and ushered people onto the appropriate gangway, telling them to hasten as the ship was due to leave at midday.

Women struggled to pull small children up the gangway while their menfolk carried bundles of belongings in hessian sacks and cloth parcels. The chaos was a little disconcerting to Elena as she showed the officer her ticket, gave Gina a last emotional hug and trudged up the gangway carrying her case and satchel. She had chosen the least faded and worn of her dresses to wear and had thrown a colourful shawl around her shoulders. She was conscious that Bill would meet her at Southampton and wanted to look her best for him though her long dark hair was being tugged and blown by the fresh sea breeze.

Elena found her berth in the lower section of the ship, sharing with three other women. Leaving her case in the cabin, she went back on deck to wave goodbye to Gina. As smoke from the funnels streamed into the blue sky, as the propellers churned the dirty water filled with rubbish and the ship's siren announced its departure, tears streamed from Elena's eyes. She blew multiple kisses to Gina who seemed a small lonely figure on the quayside, surrounded by other Italian families watching their relations leave for a better life. The ship drew away from the dock and headed through the harbour entrance.

Elena found a place to sit on a wooden bench in the hazy sunshine, an old woman sitting next to her offering her a slice of salami and a ripe tomato from a piece of newspaper. The other passengers opened their food and shared bread, fruit and cheese. Some were surreptitiously wiping their eyes and not eating, others were staring sadly back to shore. Some were lively and chatting about their experiences in the war and the bombing of Naples. Children raced around in excitement, unaware of their parents' concerns and sadness.

Elena sat quietly and listened to their stories, aware that these were the grateful survivors of a long and terrible war. She gazed at the blue sea and the flock of raucous seagulls following the ship and thought, 'I may never return here or see Gina again,' and was saddened and anxious about her future in a different land, knowing no-one except Bill and with little understanding of English.

Gradually she relaxed, lulled by the warm sun, the rhythm of the ship's engines and the soothing mumble of Italian. Although aware of the unexploded mines in the sea which the ship must avoid, she felt safe. She thought of Bill and was comforted by his love; knew it would be exciting to live in a foreign land but felt able to cope with the challenge as long as Bill shared it with her.

'*Buongiorno*. Are you Elena Rossi?'

Shaken from her dreaming by a female voice that sounded familiar, she raised her head and looked up at the speaker, a petite, dark-haired young woman with a small child clinging to her leg. She recognised Marina, her childhood friend from Mitorna who had sadly turned her away from the village after Elena's escape from the Germans in Caterna.

'Si,' Elena replied cautiously. She waited for Marina to continue talking or to turn away as she had before.

'Elena, I am so sorry about our last meeting in the village. I had no choice but to ask you to leave. My family were frightened that if they let you inside their home, the whole family and the village would be killed by the Germans. They knew that people had been shot by them or captured for their labour camps,' Marina explained, and wiped away tears of remorse and sadness. 'We were only twenty kilometres from Caterna, not far for the Germans to travel in trucks and armoured cars. For two years, everyone stayed within the village, only lighting fires at night and trying to muffle noise so that any approaching Germans would think the village was unoccupied. We locked the two tower gates in the walls and people brought their rubbish and broken furniture to pile outside to pretend it was deserted. Children played indoors, the market was closed down, shops and cafes only opened on demand. It was a terrifying, suffocating time for us all. Although we saw a convoy of military vehicles in the distance, they never invaded Mitorna. We were lucky but I have never forgotten my unkindness to you when you needed my kindness the most. You know in Italy it is always *'prima la famiglia.'*

Elena sat immobile, stunned by her memories. She opened her mouth to respond but could only say, '*Buongiorno. Capisco.* I understand. Is this your child and are you married now?'

'*Sì.* I married Marco. He was wounded in the fighting and returned home. He lost a leg. My daughter is called Sophia; she is three. Marco is on board as we decided to leave Mitorna and emigrate to Australia, hoping for a better and safer life for Sophia. The villagers collected their savings to help us and two other families to emigrate. We go to England first then take a ship to Fremantle in Western Australia. We are told there is a large Italian community who will help us.'

Elena nodded and tried to smile. 'I don't want to discuss the past with you. I can try to understand your actions but I desperately needed help and had nowhere else to go. I had no family and was escaping from death. I don't want to meet you again, or Marco, although I wish you well in the future. I have married an English pilot who was based in Naples during the war and I am travelling to England to meet him. We plan to settle down wherever Bill can find work.'

'I understand,' replied Marina. 'If you change your mind in the future, you can write to the Italian Club in Fremantle. I must go now and find something for Sophia to eat. Can I tell Marco about our meeting?'

'*Sì,* but only when we have all left the ship. I need to look forward to the future and my new life. It is too painful to be reminded of the past. *Arrivederci.*'

Elena rose from the bench and walked away, down the steps to her cabin. She needed time to think about this chance meeting on-board ship. Luckily, the women who shared her cabin were outside on deck catching their last glimpse of Italy. Elena lay face-down on her bunk and sobbed, her tears flooding into the pillow. Once again, her tragic past had caught up with her, and her future with Bill seemed almost a mirage in comparison. She stayed in the cabin until dark when the other occupants came in to sleep. She muttered a reply to their good nights and hoped they would think she was crying because she was leaving Italy.

During the voyage to England, Elena stayed in the cabin when it was empty or sat on deck in a secluded area out of the cool wind. The ship took four days to sail through the Mediterranean, around Gibraltar and into the rough Atlantic sea. Crossing the Bay of Biscay, the ship rocked and tilted alarmingly and many passengers were sick. Elena was not affected by seasickness and enjoyed feeling she was in limbo on the ocean, between two lives.

The weather changed significantly as the ship sailed north. The sunny skies of Italy and France were left behind and squalls of rain lashed the deck. Passengers remained in their cabins or the common areas. It was hard for parents to keep small children occupied and many suffered from seasickness. Elena was relieved that she didn't meet either Marina, Marco or their daughter again.

She took out her wedding photo in the cabin and gazed at her and Bill's smiling faces, with Gina standing in the background. She knew she would never forget the kindness and companionship of the Neapolitans who were generous to her despite the poverty of their lives.

On the last night aboard ship, Elena packed her few possessions in the cardboard suitcase. Her stomach was upset and her fingernails bitten down as she grew more nervous about meeting Bill. She bathed in the communal facilities, washing the salt out of her hair, which she tied back with a green ribbon, a present from Gina. She lay awake in her bunk, shifting and turning all night until the woman in the bunk below told her to keep still.

Finally, the ship's engines slowed and the vessel manoeuvred itself into position at Southampton dockside. Elena said goodbye to her cabin companions, picked up her case and made her way up to the deck. Sunlight briefly flickered through the thick grey clouds and a misty rain drifted across the land. The sea was choppy, whipped by the wind and the seamen had difficulty mooring the boat to the dock. Elena hugged her old coat around her to keep out the cold and tried not to shiver in case Bill thought she was nervous. She gazed at the crowds of people lining the dock, many waving as they spied their family or friends. She couldn't see Bill, and her heart sank to her shoes as she thought he might have forgotten to meet her or had changed his mind about being with her.

She pressed back as many families and children bunched onto the gangways, pushing and shoving in their eagerness to reach family members. Elena was knocked into the rail and her foot trodden on by a boisterous group of children; she nearly lost her case overboard as she clutched at the rail. The rain misted her hair and face, flecked her coat with tiny droplets.

Her mind raced: 'What have I done coming here to this strange place where I have difficulty speaking the language? How will I manage the different customs and attitudes? I know nothing about the English lifestyle or food. This place looks so drab and gloomy, and forbidding.' Once again in her life, she felt abandoned, desperately lonely and vulnerable. She stayed at the rail for a long time, reluctant to launch herself into the dockside crowds and search for Bill. She bowed her head and a few tears mingled with the rain on her face.

She raised her head as a ray of sunshine filtered across her face and saw Bill leaping up the gangway towards her. He reached the deck, opened his arms and grinned widely. Elena dropped her case and ran into his strong arms; nestled her head on his shoulder in the exact place that fitted so well.

Filled with so much joy and happiness, she could not speak; could only return Bill's kiss with such passion that his arms tightened around her until she was breathless. He tilted her face to his, wiped her tears and continued kissing her, amid whoops and clapping from sailors nearby.

'Come on, sweetheart. Let's leave these crowds and find somewhere private where we can talk and love and start our lives.' Bill loosened his embrace, picked up her case and, tugging her arm in his, helped her down the gangway. He ushered her through Customs as quickly as the queues allowed then they waited for a bus to take them to a nearby hotel. It was the first time Elena would sign her name as Mrs Whiteley – she was no longer Elena Rossi. A glow of warmth drifted through her body and she turned to Bill standing protectively beside her and smiled with joy and happiness.

The hotel was in the centre of Southampton with a view of the docks from the window of their third-floor room. It was simply furnished and comfortable with a small gas fire for cold nights. Bill put down her suitcase and drew Elena over to the bed where they sat snuggled together for warmth. He put his arm around her shoulders and kissed her neck and face again and again, murmuring softly about his love for her and soothing her worries about their new life. After a long while, they decided to find something to eat, the receptionist directing them to a workman's café nearby where they were served vegetable soup followed by fresh fish with bread and butter. The waitress winked at them and asked if they were a honeymoon couple. Bill and Elena nodded as they sat shoulder to shoulder gazing at each other while eating. They finished their meal and left, running through the misty rain to their hotel, laughing.

Their reunion in the hotel bed was joyful and loving. Elena's nervousness was overwhelmed by Bill's sensitive caresses, soft kisses and words of everlasting love. The bed was narrow and lumpy and the traffic outside noisy but the two lovers held each other close, moving together as they consummated their marriage, Elena crying softly in ecstasy and Bill clutching her tightly with ardour. Elena's head lay on

Bill's arm as they separated and lay side by side, warm and relaxed, whispering soft endearments. She had never felt so loved and secure. It was like a dream, a miracle that she and Bill had met, survived the war and married. Neither of them slept that night despite being travel-weary as they needed to savour every precious moment together.

They had toast and eggs for breakfast at the same workmen's café, braving the nudges and winks of the waitress and cook as they kissed between mouthfuls.

'Elena, I've booked two seats on the train leaving Southampton tomorrow morning at 10 o'clock. It goes direct to Bristol Temple Meads but I've been told there may be delays due to line damage or priority of troop and freight trains. I thought we could have a few days of our honeymoon in Bristol as there is so much to see especially the famous suspension bridge. I've got a job as an engineer at Filton airfield just outside the city and have rented a small flat in an old house nearby. It has some furniture but we can buy more to suit us. There's a small garden that everyone shares and vegetable patches allocated to each tenant. It's going to be hard for you and you will be alone when I'm at work but we will find someone to teach you English and help you to settle in.' Bill kissed the tip of Elena's nose and brought their clasped hands to his mouth to kiss her knuckles. He whispered in his ear, "I will protect you with my life."

Elena quietly absorbed the words, translating them into Italian in her head where the meaning was unclear. She'd already noticed the order of words in English was often different to a sentence in Italian and that some phrases seemed impossible to understand. Why did the waitress say that *it was raining cats and dogs* when they arrived at the café? Why would the hotel receptionist refer to the shared bathroom as a WC?

Bill said, 'I understand your concern and will help you improve your English when I'm not working, or we're not making love.' He circled his arm around her shoulders and Elena laid her head against his chest, listening to the throbbing of his heart and felt the strength of his body protecting her.

'Elena, I love you so much. I know we'll have a wonderful life together. I look forward to eating great Italian meals, singing to the radio and maybe dancing together if we can find a hall nearby. The hotel receptionist suggested a few places to visit, including Bargate, the gateway to the old medieval town and the Dolphin Hotel where the famous lady writer Jane Austen stayed.

Bill thanked her and took Elena's hand as they walked outside to wait for a bus. Elena felt bemused by the sudden change in her surroundings and cautiously stepped up to the bus holding Bill's hand. 'We'll sit downstairs at the front so you can see better,' Bill whispered as he led the way. The bus conductor told them where to alight to see the historical buildings and directed them to a tiny corner café for lunch. The sun shone intermittently through the clouds and the streets shone from recent rain. They took the bus back to the hotel before dark and were glad to be alone in their room.

'Tomorrow, we'll take a bus to the train station. I hope you'll enjoy the ride because the railway goes through lovely countryside where there's not much bomb damage. We'll arrive at Bristol Temple Meads by tea-time and we can walk to the hotel where we'll stay for two nights. I'll take you shopping tomorrow to buy you new clothes and shoes and of course a new suitcase to carry them in.' Bill smiled at Elena and hugged her tightly as they sat on the bed in their room. 'I've bought a large old wardrobe for us and we need to fill it mostly with your clothes.'

Elena's stomach churned with a mixture of joy and pleasure at being with Bill but with some trepidation on how she would fit in as his wife. At the café she had seen how carefully Bill had cut up his food with a knife and fork and ate, pausing between mouthfuls. As a child living in Puglia, meals were mainly pasta and vegetables – they seldom had meat – which they ate quickly with a spoon. Well water was the only drink and bread with meals was rare. Her grandparents had eaten at a rough wooden table, sitting on handmade stools so taking a meal in a café with a cloth on the table and a cushion on the seat seemed an expensive way to do things. When the waitress asked her if she wanted rhubarb and custard for pudding, Elena had no idea what I was, so declined.

There were so many cultural differences: the man walking on the outside of the pavement, letting her go first boarding the bus, and choosing food from a written list. Sharing an indoor bathroom with Bill and other hotel guests was a dubious pleasure.

Water was scarce in Puglian villages so villagers washed rarely, using a bowl filled from the village pump and hard home-made soap. Elena used the hotel bath alone and dried herself on soft cotton towels, which she thought was enjoyable but time consuming. She rinsed out her underwear in the bath water and placed it on the line strung over the bath to dry, not at all embarrassed for other people to see her clothes – there was little privacy in sharing a small two-bedroomed cottage with her grandparents and pegging out washed clothes on a metal frame hanging from the window onto the village street. Elena wondered how and where she would wash Bill's clothes, and how the English cooked their meals, especially roasting large chunks of meat to be sliced and shared. She slept little that night, even though their lovemaking had relaxed her, as she worried about her new life and how she would fit in being the wife of an English airman and engineer. She decided to talk with Bill during the train ride to Bristol so she could be better prepared.

Elena and Bill packed their clothes in the hotel room the next morning and walked to the workman's café for breakfast. Then they took a bus to the train station. The station was packed with people rushing between ticket offices and platforms. Elena noticed that men usually wore flat caps and heavy boots with dark trousers and jackets, varying in quality from tailored wool suits to gabardine trousers and shirts. The women, old and young, often wore head scarves tied under the chin, long skirts and thick faded coats made of different materials. They had flat lace-up dark shoes and carried handbags of different sizes. The common facial expression was one of anxiety and hunger. These were the ordinary people who had suffered food shortages during the war, sometimes resulting in starvation as mothers gave food to their children rather than eating it themselves. Some passengers carried their possessions in suitcases or cloth bags.

Smoke from the engines filled the concourse and the noise became deafening as the train drew into the station and stopped. Flung open doors banged against the carriage. Passengers surged forward while others waiting for family or friends stood back on the platform. Elena felt stifled by the fumes, the closeness of people and the overpowering odour of unwashed bodies.

She was bewildered by the language and the shouting of porters and railway officials, by the loudspeakers announcing train arrivals and departures on a crackly announcing system. She clung to Bill's arm and held her suitcase under her other arm, frightened it would be snatched or knocked from her. Bill marched briskly towards the train doors and opened one for Elena.

'This compartment will suit us fine,' he said as he helped Elena onto a bench seat and placed her suitcase on the metal rack above. 'Right,' he said. 'That was hard going as everyone pushed forward when the train stopped. Now we can relax and enjoy the journey and hope we aren't delayed.' He smiled at Elena and tucked her arm into his, mouthing the words, 'I love you.'

Elena smiled nervously and clenched her free hand in her lap. Several people, clutching luggage and food parcels, joined them in the compartment. Bill had bought some egg sandwiches at the café where they had breakfast, and had also bought a bottle of a red fizzy drink called *Tizer* and two plastic cups. Elena looked out the dirty window, through the heavy smoke at the travellers still crowding the platform, and shifted position as the train jolted forward. Although she was comforted by Bill's presence, she trembled, her thoughts jumbled, her nerves ragged. All her worries from last night reoccurred and she wanted to find a quiet corner to be alone and safe from the unknown perils of the future.

The train passed along the backs of dirty three and four storey houses, warehouses and used a railway crossing over a main street before arriving in the country. Elena noticed how green and fresh the trees and fields looked interspersed by low hedges. Healthy cows and white woolly sheep grazed in the small fields. The peacefulness of the scene seemed vastly different to the bombed city buildings of Naples and the arid lands of southern Italy. Farmers ploughed brown fertile fields using oxen or mules often followed by flocks of seagulls. Farm dogs barked at the train and children waved.

As the train picked up speed, the small villages appeared indistinct against the dark grey clouds threatening rain. The train rushed through tunnels and the passengers pulled the windows shut so black smoke and smuts from the engine were kept out. They stopped at several small stations with wooden platforms where people left or joined the train. Station guards waved flags and blew their whistles to alert passengers of departure.

Elena was absorbed by the scenery, the villages and the people, so different to Puglia. She excitedly pointed things out to Bill and asked the names in English. Bill had bought a small writing pad and wrote the words in Italian and English for her. 'This is a good place to start learning the language … we have plenty of time and no distractions,'; he smiled. He hugged her closer as he leant to look out of the window. Once he brushed her hair aside and kissed her neck to the embarrassment of the other passengers. 'We are on our honeymoon,' Bill explained and kissed Elena on her forehead.

The train was delayed for thirty minutes outside a large town but the journey was pleasant and passed very quickly. Elena was so interested in learning English and looking at the countryside she forgot to ask Bill about the things that had worried her in the night. They ate their sandwiches and shared the Tizer at midday when the other passengers ate their lunch.

A smart young woman sitting next to Elena and travelling on her own asked Elena where she came from. She was interested to hear it was Italy and mentioned that her brother had been fighting at Monte Cassino during the war with the Allied forces. 'Luckily he survived but many of his mates did not. When he came home, he suffered from shell-shock for a while but I encouraged him to talk. He praised the Italian resistance movement who sheltered and provided food for the Allied soldiers at great danger to their lives. I have enjoyed talking to you but I must get off the train here. Enjoy your honeymoon.' The train slowed down and stopped at a small station.

Elena smiled at Bill and then sat in silence looking out of the window, trying to remember some of the English words while Bill opened his newspaper and read for a while. Eventually the train chugged through the bombed city suburbs and slowed as it arrived at Bristol Temple Meads station. Several trains at the platforms belched out black smoke and passengers, and people rushed to and fro, many anxious or excited. Porters helped by carrying luggage or small children. A second train, loaded with soldiers returning from the war zones, arrived at another platform. They were greeted by crying or smiling women holding children. Bill had difficulty opening the carriage door due to the press of people but pushed his way through, tugging Elena by the hand. 'Stay with me,' he mouthed at her, the words indistinct in the chaos.

He headed towards the exit, showing his tickets to the officer at the gate and led Elena outside onto the pavement which was also crowded with people. Bill turned left and walked a few paces until they came to an ornate brick building with a set of stone steps leading to two wooden, glass-paned doors. The doorman ushered them through to hotel reception and Bill signed for their room before leading Elena to a lift.

'Phew. That was hard work,' he sighed. 'I had no idea so many people were travelling now as the trains were quieter during the war, probably because of the danger of bombs and derailment. This is our room – it's the best they have. I asked for a large comfortable bed and a view of the city. We can have dinner later when we've unpacked and freshened up.

Now I need to give you a big hug and kiss you to show you how much I love you.'

Elena moved into Bill's embrace and held him tightly, raising her face for his kisses. She loved to be alone with him and tell him how she loved him, how he had changed her life and given her security and happiness. She looked forward to going to their first home together, cooking for him and cherishing him.

England – Summer 1945

Elena woke early as the rising sun flowed through the thin hotel curtains and the sounds of city life filled the air. She had slept well, lying close to Bill in the comfortable hotel divan and felt full of energy to start her new life. She carefully slipped out of bed and padded in bare feet across the painted wooden floorboards to the large window overlooking the street where she pulled the curtain aside and sat on a cushioned cane chair in the warm sunshine. She wore the blue silk nightgown and wrap Bill had bought her the day before from a lingerie shop on Park Street, an expensive area near Bristol centre. They had then taken a bus to the Downs and wandered along the pathways overlooking the Avon Gorge and the Suspension Bridge.

It was magical to Elena - a chance for a wonderful new life with a loving husband in a safe country, and at that moment the horrific memories of her past life fled to the farthest corner of her mind and she vowed to be a good wife for Bill, to have his children and experience all she could of English life. Glancing across to the bed, she noticed Bill was awake and watching her. He held out his arms and she went to him; snuggled into his warm embrace. He kissed her on her face and neck, shoulder and hair before lingering on her lips. She closed her eyes and tears of joy drifted down her cheek.

'Come on. Let's hurry so we can catch the bus from the train station. I'll carry your new suitcase. It would be nice if you wear that new suit we bought yesterday because you look beautiful in it,' Bill said softly. He pushed her gently out of bed and, standing next to her, looked out the window. She turned and kissed him again then walked away to the wardrobe for her clothes. Elena caressed the soft texture of the silk blouse and light wool skirt as she put them on. Then she pulled the tailored jacket around her and slipped her feet into the first pair of new leather footwear she had ever worn. She felt like a princess as she applied some lipstick and brushed her long dark hair which had been neatly trimmed by a hairdresser the day before. Bill donned his good suit, shirt and tie then, picking up Elena's case, opened the door and they descended the stairs to the street. Together they walked hand in hand to the bustling train station to wait for a bus to Filton.

The bus drove north through the city streets towards the Severn River, passing through country lanes bordered by flowering hedges and pastel coloured wild flowers. The journey took an hour, people getting on and off along the way. They passed a wide airfield where a range of civil and military planes parked on the tarmac. Bill pointed out the large building where he would be working and explained that Filton had been an RAF base during the war but had closed a year ago to allow for the expansion of the civil aviation business.

They alighted at West Ashton, a village near Filton, and Bill pointed across the green to an old, four-storey Victorian house surrounded by tall trees. 'That's where we'll live. It's in the centre of the village so there are plenty of shops, a post office and a chemist. The other tenants in the house are friendly and want to meet you so you won't be lonely during the day. I have spoken with the local school teacher and she is happy to teach you English. I know it will be a overwhelming at first.' Bill squeezed Elena's arm and bent to kiss her on the lips. 'Come on, let's get settled into our new home. I painted the kitchen walls yellow to remind you of Italian sunshine on dull grey days. I have more presents for you upstairs.'

Elena walked slowly across the village green looking at the old stone cottages with thatched roofs and garden filled with flowering plants. She noticed the ancient stone church with its tall steeple. When the bells started chiming, she felt a tremor of fear, remembering the church bells of Puglia and Naples ringing to give warning of invasion or a bombing raid. She felt the soft grass under her feet as Bill pulled her out of her reverie and she smiled with gratitude and love for this miracle of a new safe future.

Bill pulled a large key from his jacket pocket and walked up the paved pathway to the ornate front door of the Victorian house. The small front garden had a few tired-looking bushes, and a clipped hedge bordered the road. Inside, coloured patterned tiles covered floor of the cavernous hall, and dark brown walls were divided at waist height by a wooden railing painted dark green. A door stood on each side, firmly closed, and a wide, dusty, red carpeted staircase ascended to upper floors, its carpeted treads held in place by brass rods. A hall table on the right of the front door held mail in a brass dish and was flanked by a tall, large leaved plant in a china pot.

'Our rooms are at the top in the converted attic so they are larger than normal. The windows overlook the village green and the beautiful chestnut tree in the middle. Come on. I'm looking forward to being in our new home together.'

Bill pounded up the stairs two at a time, while Elena mounted slowly, taking it all in. She was not used to stairs inside a house and enjoyed looking below, holding tightly onto the carved wooden balustrade. A door opened and a young woman with a small child on her hip peered out and waved to them. Elena said hello and waved back.

Bill opened the door to their rooms with a flourish then lifted her, carried her over the threshold, grinning. 'This is an old English custom for newlyweds,' he said as he put her down on the floor and kissed her. 'I hope you like your new home and that you feel safe and comfortable here. This is the sitting room … and the kitchen is over there in the alcove. The bedroom is through this door here. We have our own toilet by the kitchen but the shared bathroom is on the next floor down. A gas geyser provides hot water for the bath — such a luxury.'

He tugged Elena into the bedroom, dropped her case on the bed and showed her the view from the window in the sloping roof. 'This is the wardrobe for you to fill with clothes. There is a spare blanket in the drawer and I bought the bedding last week so we have clean sheets and an eiderdown … patterned with yellow flowers like sunflowers,' Bill said excitedly.

'And this is the kitchen with its sink, oven and table and chairs. I searched for a bottle of wine in the village shop but could only find beer. We can eat at the village pub tonight and shop for food tomorrow.' Bill finally stopped talking and drew Elena over to the worn, cloth-covered settee and wrapped his arms around her. She leaned back into his arms and sighed with deep relief. She would be happy here.

The next morning was bright and sunny as they walked across the green to the village shop to buy groceries. It was filled from top to bottom with tins piled on wooden shelves, baskets and lamps hanging from the ceiling and dried goods in bins on the floor. Elena had never seen so much food in one place, and wandered around inspecting the price labels and looking in vegetable baskets. The rosy-faced woman behind the counter studied them briefly before nodding. She was short and plump with dark hair tied back in a bun.

'Good morning, Mrs Franks,' Bill greeted her cheerfully. 'This is my new wife – she is from Italy. Do you have spaghetti so she can cook our first Italian meal together? We arrived yesterday and are living in the big old house opposite.'

'Good morning, Mr Whitely … Mrs Whitely. That makes three new families that have moved in recently. The other two men work at the Filton airfield. Do you work there, Mr Whitely?' Mrs Franks asked whilst spooning white flour into brown paper bags and weighing them.

'Yes, I do.'

'That is good,' she added, nodding. 'I wish you well there. This is a friendly village but smaller than it used to be – sadly some of our young men were killed in the war – so families coming in to work at the airbase will help us grow again.'

'Tell me, does the village have a hall were locals can meet and chat? It would be good for Elena to meet other people while I'm at work. She will be having English lessons with Miss Brown, the school teacher.'

Bill smiled at Elena and beckoned her over to the counter. 'What do we need to buy to make the best spaghetti dinner?' Bill asked in Italian so Elena could understand and not feel nervous. He picked up two large brown onions, some tomatoes and greens. 'Shall we start with these?'

Elena nodded and pointed to the loaf of bread on the counter. 'Can I buy this please, Mrs Franks?' she asked slowly forming the sentence in her mind before speaking. 'I want some milk and jam and tea. This is a nice shop. We have not so many foods in Naples,' she continued.

'So, you come from Naples. Is that in Italy? I heard it was badly bombed and lots of people killed.' She looked up at Bill. 'We don't have any other foreigners in this village,' she said slightly acerbically and sucked in her cheeks.

She continued to chatter away to them while collecting the goods Bill wished to buy. 'Well, well. I'm sure you'll like it here. We're ordinary folk with no foibles or airs and graces. Mind, we keep gossip to ourselves as it don't do no good to shout your problems to the wind for everyone to hear.' She emphasised her instructions by tapping the counter with her right hand. 'Here you are — your things all packed into this bag. You need to buy a string bag for your vegetables, Mrs Whitely?'

Elena nodded and said goodbye as Bill picked up the bag of shopping and pushed open the shop door. 'Don't mind Mrs Franks' comments. She's a kind person but you'll find everywhere that the English are parochial and suspicious of people who come from other places, even as near as Bristol. But I'm here to hug and protect you so don't worry. They'll soon get used to seeing you around especially if you smile at them and talk to them. Being open and friendly seems to work wherever one lives.' Bill smiled down at her and patted her shoulder gently.

Elena vowed to learn English as quickly as possible and be friendly when meeting the locals. She had encountered a lot of suspicion when trekking across Italy to Naples as people rarely left their villages, except for going to market, and the war had magnified peoples' distrust of anyone from outside their locale. She understood Mrs Franks being cautious as during the early part of the war, the Italians had been fighting with the Germans against the Allied forces. She had Bill's support and her native inclination to socialise. As they walked into the house and shut the door, Elena impulsively flung her arms around Bill's neck, disregarding the shopping bags that he was carrying. He laughed and bent down to kiss her cheek before climbing the stairs to their rooms.

Elena helped him unpack their goods then made them a cup of expresso. They sat at their kitchen table and discussed the small improvements they could make.

'I need to buy some bright material to make curtains and cushions. I can cut them out on the kitchen table and sew them by hand,' Elena said excitedly. 'Can we go shopping one day please?'

Bill laughed and walked round the table to hug her. 'Yes, of course. Now, before we eat lunch, let's walk to the school and meet Miss Stayt, the school teacher, while the children are having their lunch break and playing outside. We can ask her advice about buying material and … …' Bill paused and hugged Elena again, 'maybe a sewing machine to keep you busy while I'm at work.' He winked at her and leant over and kissed both cheeks, in the Italian way. He donned his jacket, opened the door and hurried down the stairs, calling to Elena. 'Come on. We are starting our new life together today.'

They walked across the village green to the small stone school as the bell tolled for lunchbreak. Children poured out into the playground, boys on the left and girls on the right. They noisily gathered in groups, the girls laughing as they did cartwheels and somersaults, the boys kicking a couple of balls about. Miss Stayt came out to supervise them and Bill opened the schoolyard gate and greeted her.

'Hello Miss Stayt. I have brought Elena, my wife, to meet you. I asked last week if you would teach Elena English so she can talk more freely with the locals. Are you still be able to?'

'Hello, Elena. It will be a pleasure to teach you. I can spare an hour twice a week in the evenings if that suits. We can meet here in the classroom then I can write the words on the blackboard. I can loan you some simple children's books and we can read through them together to help with your vocabulary. They have pictures to go with the words. I learnt Italian at school that way. Shall we start next Tuesday?'

Elena looked at Bill and held out her hand to shake Miss Stayt's. She nodded, then said hesitantly, 'I would like to start next week. I think the first words I must learn are the English names for flour and eggs and other basic food so that when I go shopping I buy the right things. I think Mrs Franks is suspicious of me when I point at things and don't understand how much I am buying.'

'Mrs Franks is suspicious of anyone whose family haven't lived in this village for centuries. She's cautious with me because I studied teaching in Bristol so my accent is slightly different and I am seen as a 'townie.' Miss Stayt smiled as she shook Elena's hand. 'That's great. I will look for some starter books for next Tuesday. Now I must control these kids and stop that fight between two boys over there.'

Bill left for work the next day and Elena stood in the sunshine and waved from the door of the house. She walked back up the stairs and washed up the breakfast things and made their bed. She washed a few underclothes and wandered downstairs and out to the back garden to peg them on the shared clothes line. She hadn't met any of the other tenants but had heard a baby crying and a young child laughing. It was a bright sunny morning so she decided to walk around the village and look at the few shops. Maybe she would meet a few villagers.

Next to the grocery shop was a newsagent and post office agency. Elena pushed the door open, a bell tinkling as she closed it. She looked around. Like the grocery shop there were rows of wooden shelves behind the counter and racks for magazines and newspapers. The smartly dressed older woman behind the counter looked up from the book she was writing in.

'Good morning. Can I help you?' she asked and smiled at Elena. 'You must be Bill's wife. He came here often to post letters to you.' She unlatched the flap on the counter and walked out to greet her.

'Welcome to the village. My name is Mrs Wells. I'm a foreigner here too – I was born in Gloucestershire, about ten miles away, so my accent is different to the locals. People from Bristol have a different accent again. Is it the same in Italy where you lived? Bill told me you are Italian and a refugee from Naples.'

'Hello,' Elena replied, grateful to meet a friendly person. 'Yes. I was born in the south of Italy and escaped to Naples where I met Bill. Now I try to learn better English. Miss Stayt give me lessons. Do you have simple newspaper that I can understand – using a dictionary of course?' Elena smiled at Mrs Wells and paid for the newspaper.

'I can deliver the paper each day or perhaps you prefer to come and collect it?'

'I think I will walk each day so will come to the shop to buy. Thank you. I bought an English-Italian dictionary in Bristol so now I go home and practise my English.' Elena walked out of the Post Office with the paper tucked under her arm and continued exploring the village. The sun was shining brightly in a pale blue sky dotted with white clouds; it was warm with a fresh breeze. Elena walked past the butcher and the hardware store to the edge of the village green and the small, pale stone church. She pushed open the heavy carved wooden door and slipped inside, smelling the familiar perfume of lit candles. She pulled a soft scarf from her pocket and tied it round her head before walking towards the altar. She knelt down in a wooden pew and bowed her head in prayer, remembering the friends she had left behind in Naples and those who had died. The peace of the church comforted her as she prayed. The bright sunlight created coloured patterns on the old stone floor and softened the stone pillars. Behind the altar a stained-glass window depicting Jesus and a lamb was highlighted by the sun. Two shadowy alcove chapels sat on either side of the altar, and ten wooden choir pews and an ornately carved wooden pulpit sat to the left. It looked plain to Elena, so accustomed to Catholic churches with painted walls and frescos, and faded oil paintings of the Crucifixion. She wandered back down the central aisle to the door and outside into the bright village green, where a huge old chestnut tree spread its branches filled with small chattering birds. She sat on a worn wooden bench to listen to the birds and breathe in the fresh air and silence, so dramatically different to the battered ruins and constant noise of Naples.

Elena wandered around the small well-kept churchyard where the graves were mostly plain marble slabs carved with names and dedications, decorated with fresh and artificial bunches of flowers. She noticed the dark green trees planted at intervals lining the walkways and thought they seemed like Italian poplar trees.

She walked back to the house and up the broad stairs that creaked despite the thin carpet covering. The doors to the other flats were shut and there was no sound of people talking or radios. As she unlocked her flat door, a wave of loneliness and homesickness for the noisy boisterous Italian way of life washed over her, but she quickly realised that so much of that had been destroyed by the bombing and fighting on Italian soil. She went into the tiny kitchen and cleared up the breakfast things then checked the food cupboards. She could make a minestrone soup if she bought vegetables from the grocery shop. It was time she started her vegetable patch.

Elena put on her hat and cardigan, slipped her feet into her new red leather shoes and meandered to the grocery shop, mentally bracing herself for the disparaging looks of Mrs Franks. Last night with Bill's help she had made a list of items she wanted to buy and had practised saying the words in her mind.

She almost bumped into an old man with a stick and said sorry to him. 'I suppose you be the pilot's new wife?' he said, peering at her face. 'You look dark and foreign to me but that'll change as you get little sunshine here to keep the tan.' Smacking his lips in satisfaction, he trudged away without introducing himself and went into an old rundown cottage near the church via a garden massed with weeds as high as his head in places. She smiled and stood looking at the rest of the pretty and neat village. Roses bloomed in the gardens and the grass was sprinkled with tiny star-like white flowers interspersed with blue and orange dots. The village green had a soft thick grass of a luscious green, sparkling with the morning dew on the cobwebs. It was a 'good to be alive' day as she looked up at the pastel blue sky, clear of clouds and fighting planes. Birds flew between branches in the old chestnut tree, their melodic song filling the tranquil air, uninterrupted by sounds of war and people screaming.

Elena shook her sad memories away, lifted her face to the sun and walked on to the grocery shop. The bell tinkled as she opened the door and she pushed it shut behind her as instructed. Mrs Franks was talking to another customer and shovelling oats from a wooden barrel into a paper sack. They both looked up at her; scanned her from head to toe, then Mrs Franks sniffed and carried on talking to her lady customer. Elena waited patiently searching for the items she needed to buy. She reached out to touch the vegetables spread out on a wooden tray to check their freshness.

'Don't touch, missy. My regulars won't buy mauled goods.' Mrs Franks glared at Elena then muttered a few words under her breath to her customer who turned and smiled at Elena before picking up the paper sack and walking over to the counter to pay. Elena stood at the end of the counter and waited patiently to be served while the two women gossiped endlessly about their husbands and neighbours. Finally, as her customer left, Mrs Franks turned to Elena and brusquely asked what she wanted.

Elena gave her the list and continued waiting, unable to respond to the shopkeeper's unpleasantness. She paid, took her two paper sacks and quickly left, afraid Mrs Franks would notice her watery eyes and the few tears spilling to her cheeks. Humiliated by both the encounters, she hurried to safety in her flat. She had experienced aggression, been shouted and screamed at, been pushed aside but never spoken to so nastily in a shop by local people.

Elena started her English lessons with Miss Stayt and enjoyed going twice a week to the school after the children finished their classes. A few of the mothers said hello to her and smiled as they took their children's hands and walked them home for tea. After a few weeks, one of the mothers introduced herself as Jo.

'We're all meeting for tea and cakes at my home for my birthday. Will you come?' Jo said.

Elena hesitated but needed to meet more people, other than just shopkeepers. She nodded thank you and shook Jo's hand. They walked across the green with the children running off their excess energy, pushing and shoving as they went through the gate of an old cottage with a red painted door.

'Come in please,' Jo said to Elena, 'and meet the other mums. Sit anywhere. Would you like tea or coffee, only instant I'm afraid? I made the chocolate cake yesterday so help yourself to a slice and a plate at the table.'

Elena found a corner seat, smiling at the other women as she sidled past them. Children yelled and shouted out in the back garden, the girls taking turns on a tree swing, the boys kicking a football. They were all about six or seven years old, healthy with plenty of fresh air, free school milk and a diet of home-grown vegetables and tinned meat. Elena couldn't help comparing them with the street kids of Naples, clothed in rags, shoeless and starved by years of neglect, existing on scraps of food.

Jo handed Elena a cup of coffee. She was very pretty with shoulder-length blonde hair, blue eyes and a warm smile. 'Ladies, this is Elena who I met at the school – she is learning English with Miss Stayt. She has married a British pilot, Bill, and comes from Italy. Please make her welcome but don't teach her any bad language!'

Jo's comment was met with smiles and greetings, and Elena felt comforted by these friendly local mothers and longed for a child herself. She took a slice of delicious chocolate cake and relaxed. Jo sat near Elena and asked her about Italy. 'I would like to take a holiday there but I heard it was badly bombed during the war.'

Elena nodded and replied a little stiltedly, 'I lived in Naples during war ... grew up in small village in the south east. I left village ... when seventeen ... travelled to Naples where I met Bill. We married in Naples ... at his airbase ... six months ... ago. He work at Filton ... I learn to be a good English wife,' she said with a smile. 'I cook good spaghetti but not roast beef.'

'Welcome to West Ashton,' the young woman sitting opposite in the circle of chairs leaned forward and said, brushing her thick, dark. curly hair from her face. 'I am new to the village and my husband works at Filton too. I have two small children so don't work of course.'

The next hour passed swiftly as the women chatted amongst themselves and several asked Elena about the bombing in Italy. They started to leave and carried their cups and plates to the tiny kitchen at the back of the living room, and called to their children. Elena walked to the door and thanked Jo for the invitation. 'I will make some Italian cakes ... and invite you for tea. Miss Stayt said afternoon tea is English custom. I liked the chocolate cake, Jo. Thank you.'

Elena walked across the green feeling more settled than she had for many years. She walked up the stairs and started preparing dinner for Bill. It had been difficult to buy spaghetti but Bill had asked at his work and was told to go into Filton where there was a shop run by former Italian prisoners-of-war and they sold all kinds of 'foreign food!'

England – Winter and Spring 1945-6

Elena sat on the comfortable old settee and put her hand on her stomach. She was almost sure she was pregnant and had decided to tell Bill that night and arrange to see a doctor. She knew he would be pleased and happy, and anxious that she looked after herself and ate properly. She mused about taking a bus to Bristol and buying baby things; about making some of the clothes herself; about knitting tiny socks and vests. The baby would fill their small flat with joyfulness and make them a real family.

A few weeks later when their doctor had confirmed the pregnancy, Elena was walking home from the surgery when she noticed Jo sitting on a bench watching her children playing ball on the village green.

'Hello, Jo,' she called as she walked. 'Can I sit with you?'

'Yes, of course.' Jo smiled and moved her shopping bag to the ground. 'How are you settling in? I think it must be hard to move from a different country and way of life to a small English village as there's so much to learn of the culture and how people live.'

'I am happy here – it is safe – no bombs, no ruined buildings – people can buy food in the shop and walk around safe. Their children are well-fed and healthy.'

'I heard Naples was bombed heavily and its people were starving. Is that true?' Jo asked with a frown. 'It must be terrible not to have food for your children or a safe place to live.'

Elena sat silent for a moment watching Jo's two boys race around the peaceful village green and other mothers ushering their children to the playground before settling on wooden seats nearby. The children were warmly dressed, full of boisterous energy and enjoying life outside during a rare few hours of late winter sunshine. The recent snow still lay in ditches and on hedges surrounding the green but the trees were sprouting bright green foliage. A multitude of small colourful birds nesting in the trees chirped and chattered, and sang their pleasure at the warm spring weather. Clumps of yellow daffodils waved in the soft breeze and crocuses mingled with tiny white daisies on the grass.

Elena shivered a little even though she wore the thick woollen coat Bill had bought her. She tried to explain the situation to Jo, stumbling at times with her knowledge of English, searching her mind for the unfamiliar nouns and verbs.

'Jo, I will try to tell you … but still need some … help with the English. It was very frightening living in Naples … many people lost their homes to the bombs and tried to live in the ruins. I lived in a cave in the hills … outside the city … with an old lady who rescued me when I first got to Naples. It was cold and basic in the cave … but safe from the bombs. Many children living on the streets existed by thieving … and organised gangs roamed about terrorising the locals. We could not buy meat and there were long queues for bread and vegetables. Every night we were bombed … by either the Germans or the Allies until the Germans surrendered … and the Americans poured into the city in their tanks and jeeps, handing out food parcels and blankets. People were trampled underfoot … rushing to get the food. I helped the priest of a local church … give food to street kids and he found somewhere I could live nearby. I shared with a widow and her children. I met Bill when the Airforce Base sent food and airmen to help the priest. I feel so lucky to have met him … feel so lucky to escape to England.'

Elena sniffed and wiped a tear away on her glove then turned to smile at Jo as her friend grasped her hand in sympathy.

'I can't possibly understand what your life was like in Naples. We had a lot of bombing around Bristol, mostly on the Avon docks, to destroy the shipping. Several churches are in ruins as well as many streets in the city centre. Food was rationed but we could still eat home-grown vegetables, and the men caught rabbits. The countryside around here is fertile and we pick wild fruit and leaves, keep chickens and grown mushrooms. There was no invasion by the Germans with tanks and ground forces because the RAF fought them in the air and Churchill defied them continually.'

'I have to push my wartime experiences into the past now … and enjoy what I have been given here by the grace of God,' Elena replied fervently. 'I am a long way from the village where I was born and grew up as a child … and have no family in Italy but I have Bill and … and … I am pregnant so we have our own family together.' Elena gently patted her belly and smiled with happiness.

'Oh, Elena, congratulations! I'll help you with your English and the way of living in a small country village. I expect you've met with some resentment as the British fought the Italians when they were allied with the Germans. There is a prisoner-of-war camp a few miles away and the captured Italians have been made to work on local farms but the villagers have had to accept them as they plant and pick vegetables and crops. Many of them are friendly and cheery and pleased to stop fighting and return to the land.

'A few of the young girls have been meeting them at the village pub as they do not seem aggressive. They are strictly monitored, of course, to protect the people who live around here. Now I must collect my boys and take them home to feed them and make dinner for Martin. I hope to see you soon. Take care.' Jo stood, patted Elena on the shoulder and walked across to the playground, calling to her sons to come home.

Elena's son was born safely and easily in the spring of 1946 and was named Andrea by Elena, and called Andrew by Bill and their friends. He was a plump, contented baby and grew into a lovable mischievous boy. They moved to a larger ground floor flat in the old Victorian house so Andrea could run out and play safely in the garden. Bill spoilt him and Elena adored him. Bill was so proud of his son that he walked him in his pushchair to the shops at the weekend, showing him off.

'You are spoiling him,' Elena chided him with a smile. 'I know Andrea is a beautiful and loving child but he also needs discipline,' she added, picking up the baby and tickling him to hear his infectious chuckle. 'I wish we could have more children, a big noisy Italian family, but God is not permitting it even though I pray to him every night and light a candle in the church.'

It was her one big sorrow that clouded the happy years with Bill. Sometimes, when it rained all day long, the heavy grey clouds hanging like a blanket over the village without a single bright moment of sunshine, Elena felt miserable; longed with homesickness for the endless blue skies of Italy and the warmth of the sun and neighbours. She longed to take off the thick woollen clothes of winter and run out in a thin cotton dress and bare feet into a garden filled with warmth and colour. She wanted to open all the windows and allow soft breezes to take away the dampness of the old Victorian house and the continual smells of gas heaters and wet washing. Although she was making friends in the village, she missed the open-hearted vivacity of Italians, the enticing smells of garlic and pasta cooking in big earthenware pots and children running and laughing in the village.

Elena learnt to keep her depressed feelings to herself and not burden Bill with them when he came home from work, tired and fed up at times. Bill seemed to understood that when a huge bowl of steaming pasta was set on the kitchen table for dinner, sprinkled with lumpy cheddar cheese and the windows were wide open despite the cold, that she missed living in Italy even though her last few years there had been filled with danger and unhappiness. At these times, Elena sat in the kitchen near the warmth of the gas fire and made cushions or a small tablecloth, pedalling her Singer sewing machine furiously to drive away her sad feelings.

She told herself sharply over and over that she was fortunate to have survived uninjured from the bombed ruins of Naples; that her life was filled with security and love; that she was blessed by having Andrea. Traumatic memories still crept in around the edges of her mind; dark pictures of living in the cave with Chiara; giving food to skeletal street children who behaved like animals in order to survive; the terror during the ferocious bombing raids and the eruption of Mount Vesuvius as it poured its devastating fury over Naples. Some days, when she was shut in all day and snow fell in thick clumps outside, making the paths and roads almost impassable, Elena's mind parted the heavy barriers that blocked the terrible memories of her childhood, the Blackshirt and German invasions in the villages of Mitorna and Caterna. She sat on her stool next to the fire, hugging herself and sobbing. She shut the door to Andrea's room, leaving him safely sleeping with his hands flung wide as he settled on his back. She wanted to be alone with her misery and black thoughts so, when Bill came home, he had no inkling of these periods of unhappiness.

Elena settled into village life, making friends through the Young Mothers Group held each month in the village hall. Every fine day she put Andrea in his pushchair and walked around the village and the lanes, meeting local people. The grumpy old man, Mr Hastings, whom she had met in her first week, often sat and chatted with her on the wooden seat by the village green. He lived alone, his wife having died several years before. His clothes were grey and disreputable and his washing habits were dubious so Elena often took some items for washing. He called her 'Elena, my Italian beauty.' Elena had difficulty saying his name so called him 'Signor Asting.'

She was interested hearing of his time as a soldier in the First World War. Often the tales were sad and tragic when he remembered his 'trench mates' who'd been killed. Elena held his hand, understanding the trauma of war. Other times Signor Asting would relate stories of leave when his mates raided deserted orchards and farms and took fruit and chickens to supplement the miserly army food. Occasionally he would wink slyly at Elena and embroider tales of meeting beautiful young women on leave.

'You are an old rascal,' she told him one day, finding it difficult to understand how young girls had been attracted to him. She had always kept away from soldiers, disliking their language and the threat of unwanted advances.

Elena's friendship with Jo became close as they met regularly and took their children for walks together. Jo's youngest son was a year older, his brother three years older, than Andrea. They often met at weekends for shared picnics with their families, taking the bus out to the Gloucestershire countryside and finding a grassy field to lay out the picnic things. The boys chased around and sometimes fell into stinging nettle beds and needed comforting.

Jo's husband was an engineer and also worked at Filton Airfield. He had not fought in the war as his job was fitting airplane parts and considered essential. He and Jo had met before the war and married in the local church in the spring of 1940. Both their families lived in Bristol so they visited them infrequently. Elena found Jo to be an understanding listener and she told her about some of the tragedies of living in Italy during the war. Jo hugged her when told the story of the German invasions. She was a cheerful, kind person who had many friends, and adored her boys and husband. She helped Elena settle into village life and to continually improve her English when the lessons with Miss Stayt ceased after a year.

Elena matured and her skills at cooking English food improved through advice from friends, even though some items were rationed. She and Jo occasionally took the bus into Bristol for a shopping trip when the sales were held, looking for bargains for themselves and their children. They ate lunch at Lyons Corner House, relishing the different food.

Bill enjoyed his work as an aircraft engineer at Filton Airfield and occasionally invited a work colleague to lunch on a weekend. He talked to Elena about his work, leaving out the technicalities though she often asked intelligent questions, wanting to understand how the plane took off the ground and landed safely.

He arrived home early one evening just as the sun was setting in a haze of rosy clouds. He opened the cottage door and called out:

'Elena darling, I have a wonderful surprise. Come outside and bring Andrew. I have bought a car so we can drive to the seaside at Portishead or Weston-Super-Mare on the weekends. Andrew will love riding on a donkey on the beach and splashing in the sea. I'll buy him a strawberry ice-cream in a cone.'

Bill excitedly held Elena's hand as she picked up Andrea and they walked to the second-hand black Ford Prefect. Elena, speechless but happy, ran her hand over the shiny black metal, screening the car from bonnet to boot.

'Climb in,' Bill said.

She clutched Andrea. 'Where shall I sit?'

'In the front next to me and hold Andrea tight. We'll drive around the village and you can see the sunset over the hills and fields,' Bill replied, helping Elena into the seat. He was like a small boy with a new train set, proud and happy and keen to show off the car.

'I thought we could drive to Bristol to buy a kitchen table and chairs. We'll go tomorrow and you can look for materials for clothes and curtains you can make on your sewing machine.'

Elena enjoyed smartening up their home, using bright material to make curtains and flowery shawls to sling over the settee and beds. It was the first real home she had ever had and she took great pleasure in picking wild flowers for glass vases or jam jars. Bill put up shelves for books and the collection of mugs Elena had acquired at jumble sales in the local villages. She loved having Andrea's toys scattered around and, in his baby years, improved her English vocabulary by making words with wooden letters or drawing them on card with colourful crayons. Bill bought second-hand children's and adult books at church jumble sales and Elena improved her pronunciation of English as she read aloud to Andrea.

England – 1946 -1955

The years drifted by peaceably and life in the village was tranquil as people focused on family and the simple pleasures of country life. Elena, fascinated by the four changes of season each year and the variety of flowering plants and fruit that grew wild in the fields and hedgerows, foraged the country lanes with Andrea for wild plums and blackberries which she made into jam from an old recipe of Jo's mother. She picked wild herbs like mint, camomile and borage, and leaves to make salads. In Puglia there was little difference between the seasons, only in the temperature and the amount of rain. She took over their vegetable patch and successfully grew carrots, parsnips and potatoes, lettuce and cabbage. Bill planted apple and pear trees that flourished but the lone olive tree withered due to the thick clay earth and lack of sunshine. They bought an old wooden bench, which Elena painted bright blue, and placed by the two cherry trees so when they grew taller and more dense they would provide shelter for birds.

On Sunday afternoons after lunch Bill, Elena and Andrea usually walked around the local lanes looking for rabbits and the occasional squirrel. Bill showed Andrea how to identify the different trees by their shapes and leaves. In autumn, he pointed out the hazelnuts nestling in hedgerows, chestnuts falling to the ground in their distinctive spiky shells and two walnut trees at the crossroads. In spring, Elena picked pussy willow and catkin to put in a vase on the kitchen table. They walked through the beech woods smelling the strong perfume of bluebells covering the ground like a carpet. Andrea loved searching in the grass and hedgerows for primroses and violets sheltering from the strong March winds.

The little boy enjoyed playing hide and seek in the garden or chasing the birds, and he liked feeding the birds as they flew to the ground or landed on the bird bath. He was a contented child with dark brown eyes, and shiny brown hair that became curly when wet. He had a mischievous smile that tugged the corners of his mouth into dimples. He wrinkled his nose often and liked making faces, pretending he was a robber or an ogre. Elena read a story to him every night and Andrea snuggled under her arm, interrupting as he repeated the lines or pretended to be an animal by making lion or cat or dog noises.

Despite his cheery nature he was reserved in company and often preferred to play on his own in the garden, although he was friendly with Jo's boys. When Bill made Andrea a small sand patch, he liked to make shapes with his spade and bucket. They bought him a small blue bicycle which he rode when Elena went shopping in the village. He was intelligent and a fast learner, chattering in a mixture of English and Italian.

Elena and Bill's marriage developed into a close and passionate relationship, based on their shared wartime experiences and memories. They were happiest when doing things together with their child. They sat on the garden bench holding hands, talking of the miracle that they had met in war-torn Naples and survived; talking about the Italian cities that were being rebuilt using money from the Marshall Plan, organised by the USA. English newspapers carried photos of streets of bombed buildings and ragged starving children; women crouched in the ruins cradling tiny babies or helping gaunt old people to walk. The architectural beauty of Italy that had made it the wonder of the world over two thousand years had been destroyed in a few short years. Italians now emigrated in droves searching for a new life in America or Australia.

Elena became more fluent in English and more confident as an English wife. She enjoyed the social gatherings with the wives of Bill's workmates and had learnt to hide her dismay when people directed racist comments at her. At Bill's insistence, she let her hair grow down to her waist, tying it back with a ribbon when working or wrapping it in a French roll when they were socialising. Elena still needed her religion and they went as a family to the village church for Sunday morning services. Occasionally, Bill drove them into Bristol to attend mass at the Catholic cathedral and Elena could light candles for her Italian friends who were still struggling to get a decent home and life in war-torn Naples. She knew she would never hear from them as the Italian postal service was deficient due to war damage of the city infrastructure and she couldn't write to them because they had no fixed street address.

Elena received an occasional Christmas card from Marina, her childhood friend, who was now living in Fremantle, Australia. Marina wrote that she and Marco now had three children and had bought a small cottage. Marco worked for the town council and had tested a new improved prosthetic leg which gave him increased movement and less discomfort. Elena did not write back, Marina's betrayal still hurting.

Life was sweet, safe and happy. She had a comfortable home, a loving, hard-working husband and a delightful son. She started teaching part-time at the village school and enjoyed supervising the school playground. She decided to give music lessons at home, encouraging the village children to sing and play the recorder, instilling a love of music in them. Bill bought a record turntable in a second-hand shop and found some recordings of Franco Corelli and Maria Callas singing Italian operatic arias. Elena used the arias to teach Italian words and phrases to Andrea, singing along with the record.

When Andrea grew older, she bought him a recorder and he had lessons at school, joining a school musical group. Bill enjoyed hearing his wife and child singing together when he arrived home from work and often stood mesmerised in the doorway as they danced to the music. He felt so lucky to be surrounded by the love of his family and the joyous music that filled his mind and soul with tranquillity.

Bill enjoyed driving to watch Bristol City play football on Saturday afternoons. When Andrea grew older, he took him too and treated him to fish and chips afterwards. Bill bought Andrea a red and white striped football scarf to wear. Other times Bill met friends from Filton at the football ground and they went for a beer in the local pub after the match. They arrived on the bus at the village in happy spirits if their team had won or moping if they lost. Elena, Jo and the other wives often spent the afternoon over tea and cake where the conversation was mostly about childcare, the quality of children's clothes and limited budgets. They swapped recipes and occasionally clothes if they were bought on impulse or didn't fit when tried on at home.

Bill arranged on August 20 to take Andrea for his tenth birthday to a match of Bristol City Football Club against Swansea Town at their home ground. He and Andrea wound their striped red and white scarves round their necks even though it was a warm summer day. They left in the Ford Prefect at 2 pm as the 'kickoff' was planned for 3 pm. Andrea sat proudly in the front seat, wriggling with excitement. He liked to study the dials and tell Bill when to put the windscreen wipers on. Andrea's shoulders were broadening and his stance copied from his father. He also mimicked Bill's sayings which didn't go down well when he repeated simple swear words or comments about other drivers to his mother.

Elena stood in the doorway in the hot sunshine waving them goodbye, mentally planning the jobs she wanted to do at home in peace and quiet. 'Drive carefully,' she advised Bill. 'I will make spaghetti bolognaise for dinner.'

The day passed quickly as she cleaned the kitchen cupboards and swept and washed the floors. She sat outside on the garden bench to enjoy a mug of milky coffee — the closest she could get to a latte. The slight breeze was cooling and bird song filled the still air. She could hear a herd of cows lowing in a distant field. She daydreamed peacefully and planned more work in the garden and another family trip to the seaside. She vaguely heard a car stop outside on the road and the sound of male voices as they walked up the front path, then a solid banging on the front door. She leisurely finished her coffee then wandered back through the house to the front door to find out what the disturbance was about.

Two uniformed policemen stood on the doorstep ringing the doorbell.

'Mrs Whiteley?' the older policeman asked seriously.

'Yes, I am,' replied Elena, her stomach churning with anxiety and fear.

'We have some bad news. I think we should go inside so you can sit down. Here is my police identity. My name is Constable Poole and my colleague is Constable Webb. Let me help you into the kitchen and Constable Webb will make a cup of tea with your permission.'

Elena leant against the doorpost in paralytic shock, staring blankly past the policemen to the sunny view of the peaceful village green. Constable Poole gently took her arm and steered her inside, guiding her to a kitchen chair. He pulled out another chair and sat opposite Elena patting her trembling hands that were clenched in her lap. He cleared his throat and slowly told her about the car accident which had robbed her of her husband and son.

'Your husband was turning into the parking area opposite the football ground and a large truck that was travelling towards them veered to avoid a stray dog wandering in the road. The driver slammed on his brakes, lost control of the steering wheel and crashed into your husband's car. Both were killed immediately on impact. I am so sorry. You will need to identify them in the police morgue.'

Elena sat immobile on the chair. Her body had lost the ability to move; her brain had shut down. She couldn't respond to the Constable, her emotions too traumatised to comprehend the disaster that had just shattered her world.

Constable Webb put a steaming cup of deep brown tea in front of her and placed his hand on her shoulder to offer some comfort. The silence in the kitchen was profound, the policemen sitting quietly on either side of her. She shed no tears, sat like a statue staring out the kitchen window. She didn't touch her cup of tea, couldn't get the horrific image of her beautiful child, smashed against the broken windscreen and her loving husband thrown into the steering wheel.

Elena bowed her head to her chest and tried to breathe through the solid obstruction that clogged her lungs and throat. She touched her jumper, surprised to find her heart was beating normally beneath it; she looked down at her legs and felt the trousers covering them, her feet in her gardening shoes, her hands clasped together and was amazed that she appeared the same. She looked around her kitchen and wondered why nothing was destroyed as she herself felt destroyed. She had learnt over many experiences that life was precarious and fickle, pulled apart and shattered into ruins in an unexpected moment. She had fought to survive the tragedies of her childhood and the traumas of existing in war-torn southern Italy, but she knew completely that she was unable to continue fighting to survive.

The policemen sat with her for a while and asked if she had family who could support her. Elena shook her head, speechless with despair. Constable Poole said that he would return in the morning with his car as she needed to identify her family.

When the policemen left, she crawled into her bedroom, ferociously pulled the new curtains together to block out the sunlight and flung herself on the colourful patchwork quilt that she had patiently and lovingly made for Bill's and her marriage bed. She curled into a foetal ball, hugging Bill's pillow for comfort, absorbing his aroma, and clutched Andrea's ragged teddy bear that was left on the floor. Tears still wouldn't come, only a feeling that she lived in a nightmare that would never end.

She visited the morgue with Constable Poole the next morning and knew that living had no more meaning for her without her beloved husband and boy. It stretched bleak and bitter in front of her. She attended their funeral, arranged mostly by Jo then retreated for days into the darkened bedroom.

She lost interest in her comfortable home and could find no solace with her close friends or in the Catholic Church. Jo visited often and tried to console her, bringing special treats she had cooked. Her friends visited and brought meals they had cooked especially for her. Elena preferred to sit in a darkened room and think back on the happy sun-filled days of her marriage.

Spring and Summer 1955

Autumn and winter passed in a blur of wretchedness and bleakness. Christmas had no meaning without her family. She knew she was being irrational and self-indulgent by ignoring and distancing her friends. Their lives continued in careless happiness with their children and their kindness and interest in her gradually waned.

Elena felt there was a vast crater of grief inside her that couldn't be filled with endless tears but could only be patched up by time and reliving the happy memories of the past. For months she felt distraught and lifeless, longing for death to release her from this terrible loss, existing on the edge of life.

Jo tried to rekindle her interest in the patchwork group and the small church choir she had joined years before. Elena hardly ate and, as the weeks went by, sank deeper and deeper into a lonely despair. She was no longer interested in her appearance, her dark Italian beauty was dimmed, grey strands highlighted her black hair and lines of sorrow scoured her face. She mechanically kept the house clean and continued with the laundry. She repudiated her Catholic faith and was impolite to the local priest when he visited to offer words of consolation. Jo still visited and tried to understand how Elena's life had fallen apart but she and her family were talking about emigrating to Australia, fed up with English weather and austerity.

Soon Elena knew she would have no-one to care for and help her. She had to get on with life alone as she had done before in Puglia. She pulled back all the curtains in the house letting in the spring sunshine. She pulled out the cleaning materials and scoured her home from room to room, then, exhausted by the unaccustomed effort, made a cup of tea and sat on the floor as she searched out the family photos and gazed at them one by one, committing the faces of her husband and son to memory. She thumbed through the photos, carelessly thrown into shoe boxes, and sorted them into order, starting with her arrival in West Ashton, Andrea as a baby and riding his bike, going to school. She gazed at the cheerful scenes of visiting the seaside and playing in the garden. She cried a lot but felt a sense of peace surround her and knelt to thank God that she had been so blessed in her marriage and family life.

Elena packed the photos in the boxes and put them back in the dresser, washed her face and hands in the bathroom, changed into tidy clothes and left the house to walk to the church to light candles for Bill and Andrea. She went into the grocery shop and Mrs Franks looked up from the counter, her lined face crinkling with a smile. 'Welcome back, Mrs Whitely. The village has missed your friendly smile.'

Elena put her hand on the counter and Mrs Franks patted it gently. 'What would you like today – the bread and eggs are fresh and a present from me.' Mrs Franks packaged them and placed them in Elena's string bag. 'Pop next door to the Post Office. Mrs Wells will be pleased to see you out and about.'

Elena was comforted by the kindness of the villagers, especially when she saw Miss Stayt in the school playground and she walked over to greet Elena to ask when she was coming back to work at the school. She slept soundly that night for the first time since the accident and dreamt that she was planting fruit trees with Bill, and Andrea was running around getting in the way and covering himself with earth.

Elena awoke at dawn the next day and realised she had been unaware of the birdsong that drifted through the open bedroom window on a mild spring breeze. She leant out of the window and could see the soft green buds of the roses climbing the wall and reached out to touch their soft colourful petals and smell their enticing aroma. She realised the bleak despondency that had sat like a heavy blanket and suffocated her mind and body for months had lifted. She still felt hollow inside, her emotions ragged with grief but realised she had indulged her sorrow so that it had made a barrier to the future. A blackbird perched on the roses and, raising its beak, produced a beautiful plaintive song. Other birds fluttering in the garden chirped wholeheartedly announcing the promise of spring after the dead of winter. Elena was reminded of the hymn she had sung with the church choir.

'Morning has broken like the first morning,
Blackbird has spoken like the first bird,
Praise for the singing, praise for the morning … …'

She looked through her wardrobe and chose a flowered dress, throwing her worn old dressing gown into the bath. She walked through to the kitchen, made coffee and took it outside to drink under the soft flowering cherry tree. The strong perfume filled the air and she felt restored and ready to live on her own.

She knew it would be desperately hard but felt the resilience which had strengthened her through childhood and adolescent traumas resurge in her mind and body. She sat under the tree for hours thinking through the choices she had for her future. She could not return to Italy where the black shadows of early tragedies still lurked in hidden corners, nor could she stay in England where there was no-one to detain her.

She remembered she had received a postcard weeks before from her Puglian childhood friend, Marina, who had emigrated to Perth after World War II and had taken the same boat as Elena from Naples to Southampton. Marina had suggested that Elena could start a new life in Western Australia as the climate was similar to Italy and there were more and more Italians moving into Fremantle, a port city. Jo had talked to her a few months ago that she and her family were emigrating to Australia using a British government scheme. Jo said that Australia was a new country full of promise and opportunities and a better place for her children to grow up in. Her husband was already investigating job options.

Bubbles of excitement and anticipation filled the hollow spaces in her body left by the deaths of her beloved husband

and son. Energy tingled through her veins and her mind raced with ideas for the future. She looked around and her small enclosed world seemed to sparkle, the dew twinkling on grass and birds hopping around chortling their spring chorus.

Elena spent the day sorting out the house and cupboards, throwing away uneaten food and stale bread, mouldy cheese and fruit that her friends had bought her. She felt strong enough to look through the wardrobe at Bills' clothes and pack them into plastic bags to dispose of. It was heartbreaking sorting through Andrea's room but she put his clothes and toys into plastic sacks also, hastily tying the tops so she couldn't pull them out and hold them against her face and body to inhale his smell.

After a quick snack she started sorting her own clothes, throwing old ones away and keeping the special ones Bill had bought her for Christmas and birthdays. She stood in front of the bedroom mirror and held them against her emaciated figure and pulled her long hair from its plastic band, spreading it around her shoulders. Her face was pale and thin with new lines spreading from her eyes and mouth. The bedroom was empty and silent.

Suddenly Elena felt exhausted by her emotional whirlwind of sorting out the belongings of her husband and child. She collapsed onto the bed and the tears fell in a waterfall through her fingers on her cheeks, onto her clothes and spotting the floor. Her body felt hollow and insubstantial, a thin covering of flesh over her bones. She curled her hands into fists and banged the quilt cover in a mixture of despair, anger and sadness. She rose to pace to and fro in her room, from the door to the window to the bed and round again several times. She picked up the photos of Bill in his RAF uniform that she kept by her bedside and the photos of Andrea as a baby and small child sitting on her chest of drawers. She flung them onto the bed and slumped down again, sobbing with a breaking heart.

That was the last time Elena felt sorry for herself. The next morning, she walked to Jo's house and asked her if she could tell her about the process for emigrating to Australia. Jo turned around from the sink where she was washing up and hugged Elena tightly.

'The papers are on the dining room table and we are going to fill them in tonight when Martin gets home. There is also last Saturday's Evening Post which had the notice from the Australian Government advertising that the country had a financial scheme to aid young families to emigrate to Australia. We wrote to Australia House in the Strand in London to request the application forms. We'll probably need to be interviewed in London or maybe Bristol to check if we are suitable. We're so excited about it and Martin is looking forward to new work opportunities.' Jo made a little dance and pulled Elena to her chest so they could jig together.

'Will they accept me if I'm a widow?' Elena asked cautiously.

'I don't know. Write to them and find out. Mention that you'll be with us,' Jo replied. 'I'll tell you about our plans and that will give you a good idea of how you could manage. Martin has been thinking about going to Australia for a long time because some of his work mates have found aviation or engineering work in Perth and Melbourne. They have kept in touch with us and sent photos of the beaches and lifestyle, the houses are single storey, like bungalows. Their children love the outdoor life and sports, especially the beach. The education system seems similar to British schools and there are more and more British migrating to Perth especially. The Australians call them Poms.

'I think you would like the warmer sunny weather and there are many Italians living in Fremantle,' Jo chattered on excitedly, obviously looking forward to her family migration and a new kind of life.

Elena felt caught up in Jo's excitement and borrowed the *Bristol Evening Post* to read the advertisement thoroughly. She sat on the blue bench, listening to the birds trilling their evening songs while the sun set and dusk crept slowly in shades of gold over the garden and house. She made dinner and spent the rest of the evening thinking over the pros and cons of emigration. She had grown weary of the bleakness of war damage in Gloucestershire and Bristol. She disliked the long damp winters and the bitter cold winds when she had to stay indoors most of the time. She felt the dreary days wearing her down, blanketing her lively spirit and energy. As a widow with no children she felt she needed a more outdoor life where she could easily meet people and join community activities. She had no family in Italy or England and few friends in the village to keep her in England now Bill and Andrea had passed away.

Elena went to bed later than normal but still couldn't sleep as she mused over what kind of future she would have in Australia. She had a contact there with her childhood friends Marina and Marco who were living in Fremantle. It might be possible after all this time to heal the hurt of rejection by them during the German invasion. She longed to talk about the memories and adventures they had shared in their childhood. She had almost forgotten her emotional connection to Puglia and the boisterous passionate Italian way of life. She had allowed her deep religious conviction in the Catholic faith to lapse during the war years and because she had adopted the formal Anglican religion that Bill believed in. Also, she would be sharing her new life with her close friends Jo and Martin who had supported her through the death of Bill.

Elena finally slept for a few hours until daybreak then decided to complete her application letter to the Australian Government offices in London. She enclosed the documents of identification they had requested and stipulated on the forms that she had become a British citizen through her marriage to Flight Lieutenant Bill Whitely who had been on active service in Italy flying RAF bombers. Bill and her son Andrea had been tragically killed in a car accident in Bristol one year ago. She emphasised that she spoke fluent English as well as Italian and had never been in a combative position during the war but a Naples refugee when she met and later married the Flight Lieutenant. She entered her work experience as teacher in Italy and England. Using the stamped addressed envelope they had sent her, she sealed it and, whispering a prayer for luck, walked across the village green to the Post Office.

Mrs Wells looked at the address on the envelope and smiled at Elena saying, 'I think that will give you a new start and certainly the weather will be more like Italy, with lots of sunshine. Good luck for your new adventure. I know that Jo and Martin and their sons are also planning to emigrate so you should have company on the journey.'

One month later, Elena received a reply that she was required to attend an interview with an Australian Government agent in Bristol who needed to view identification papers and evidence of good health. Elena took the bus from Filton to the village centre. Bill had taught her to drive but she hadn't bought a car since the Ford Prefect had been smashed in the accident. The formal interview was a harrowing process for her as she had to give details of her life in Italy, information about her marriage to Bill, and her reasons for migrating to Australia.

Several months later when the Australian government's final approvals arrived for Elena and Jo's family, they celebrated with a picnic on the village green, inviting the locals to share their excitement and to wish them good fortune in the new world. Elena had been shopping in Bristol with Jo the week before to buy suitable clothes for Australia's weather, including swimming costumes. She sold or gave away her furniture to local people, keeping her special items – photos and presents from Bill.

She carefully packed these treasures and keepsakes in a wooden tea chest, placing the handmade quilt on top, wrapped in a clean bedsheet. Her clothes, shoes and other personal items were packed in another tea chest. These would be collected from her home to be loaded and stored separately on the ship as she could carry limited personal belongings on board. She had been allocated a cabin to share with Jo.

In the week before sailing, Elena wandered around her home, now empty of belongings and memories. There was no aura of the happy home it had been, no echoes of Andrea's laughter and the music they had played and danced to. She wandered out to sit on the weathered blue bench under the cherry tree and, closing her eyes, felt Bill's presence behind her and heard the calls of Andrea. 'Goodbye, my darlings,' she whispered, wiping away her tears. 'I couldn't say a real goodbye and I will never see you again but you are tucked into my heart and fill my mind every day. I will never forget you.' Elena placed two gentle kisses on the bench seat, looked around her garden one last time and went into the kitchen to collect her hand luggage and documents.

She firmly closed the front door walked to Jo's house to join her family and ride in the hired car that Martin drove to Tilbury where they would stay overnight before embarking on the Orion passenger ship.

Jo's sons were jumping with excitement when they reached the docks and saw the size of the ship they would travel on. There was only one funnel and a single mast and the vast hull carried the name *Orion*. They queued to show their boarding tickets at the exit of the terminal and were directed to the rear gangway. Elena looked around as she climbed the gangway, her feelings an overwhelming mixture of sadness to be leaving her connections with her husband and son and anticipation of the future in Australia. They were directed to their cabins, Jo's boys and husband going to a different cabin. They arranged to meet in the dining room for lunch after unpacking. With the cabin door shut, Elena and Jo shared a hug and a few tears for the friends and family left behind.

Sailing to Fremantle 1955

Elena stood alone on the deck of the *RMS Orion* passenger ship sailing for Fremantle, Western Australia, which she had boarded at Tilbury with Jo and her family three weeks earlier. Entranced by the clarity of the night, and the star constellations of the Southern sky, she felt the fresh sea breeze bringing the promise of a new world with plenty of opportunities and a different future. The ship was due to dock early the next morning and Elena flung her arms out with exhilaration as the burdens of her past, the dark tragedies and the bleakness of war-damaged Europe that had pushed her to the edge of life, were dissipated by the fresh ocean wind. She returned to her cabin and packed her belongings ready to disembark with Jo and her family in the morning.

There had been plenty of things to do on-board ship, including deck games which Jo's sons had enjoyed. There had been an outdoor celebration for crossing the equator and tug boats accompanied them into every port the ship stopped. Elena had enjoyed the voyage, marvelling at the luxury of the Orion's interior fittings and furnishings. There was air conditioning in all the public rooms located on Deck 6 and polished wooden floors in the lounges with armchairs and desks. There was a café and library, and an outdoor swimming pool. The cabin she shared with Jo had cold water on tap, a wardrobe, chest of drawers and two single bunks. A rug lay on the floor between them.

The immigrants had been given a booklet – *Information for the Guidance of Passengers arriving in Australia* – produced by the Australian Department of Trade and Customs and were urged to read it carefully. Another booklet – *Facts about Housing in Australia* – advised immigrants there was a shortage of rental flats and houses, but they could build a house themselves. Elena, Jo and Martin had many lively discussions in the evening after the boys had gone to bed about the merits of renting versus building. Jo and Martin had owned their home in West Ashton so were keen to buy land and build. Elena and Bill had bought their small flat so the money from this and her regular income from the RAF as Bill's widow would fund Elena's life in Australia.

Many of the passengers assembled early on deck the morning of disembarkation to look at the stunning Australian dawn, the sky full of rainbow colours. Big black and white birds landed on the rails their chorus ringing round the quay. Large seagulls raucously called to each other as they squabbled over the detritus fishermen had thrown on the water. Tug boats had left the quay and were moving into position to nudge this huge liner into its allocated dock. Passengers peered over the rails to watch even though they'd been instructed to queue in the lounge area for a final check by the Australian authorities that their passports or documents of identification were correct, their embarkation cards stamped and officially authorised. The *Orion* edged into the dockside and mooring ropes were thrown to the decks from the quay, and finally two gangplanks were lowered into place. The quay was crowded with transport vehicles ready to load and unload supplies, packages and crates. Huge dockside cranes raised their metal arms against the brilliant blue sky and started lifting goods from the hold onto the quay. People crowded behind the terminal windows, waving and gesturing at passengers.

Excitement and anticipation filled the air as small groups and families were guided to the gangways which led to the crowded dock below. The new emigrants were officially checked by Immigration Officers before being guided through Customs to the baggage collection area in the Passenger Terminal on Victoria Quay.

Elena had arrived in Western Australia, near the capital of Perth, a city on the edge of the world and the most isolated. She walked with Jo and her family out into Fremantle's brilliant sunshine. Crowds of people craned their necks and pushed to find their relatives or friends. A fleet of buses parked in the road awaited the emigrants to transport them to government-provided temporary accommodation. Elena was about to board a bus when she saw someone waving frantically at her, flashing a piece of white paper. It was Marina; Marina pushing her way through the crowds with a huge grin on her face.

'Welcome, Elena. I will visit you soon so we can restore our friendship, and you can meet my family and friends. *Benvenuto a Perth. Como esta.*' Elena blew Marina a kiss and climbed on the bus to sit in a vacant space, astonished that Marina had thought to meet her.

The buses drove through the centre of Fremantle, past the old covered market and through a busy shopping area. Elena was amazed at the selection of goods for sale, the displays of colourful clothes and street cafes thronging with people. She noticed that many people dressed casually, often in shorts and sandals. The bus drove alongside the Swan River and the passengers excitedly pointed out large pelicans sitting on lamp posts and other aquatic birds flying to and fro.

They were taken to Graylands, a riverside suburb of Perth where Nissan huts had been erected, intended for short-term stays by British Migrants while they looked for work and accommodation. The migrants, on arrival in Fremantle, had given up their passports or Documents of Identification to officials and were informed that their hold baggage would be delivered to their allocated hut.

Elena thought it strange that the group of huts was inhabited by migrants from other ships and countries as well as those from Britain arriving on the *Orion*. After the enforced intimacy of shipboard life where every action and event on board had been discussed around the whole ship, everyday life at Graylands seemed relaxed and informal, with people excitedly mingling with other migrants, exchanging information and future prospects. Her world had been constrained in childhood by living in a remote hillside Puglian village, then hiding in Neapolitan caves with other refugees from the bombing, then living in an insular country village in England.

Now Elena was alone and free of the constraints of isolation, war and family, free to make her own decisions about where and how she could live and work. She walked around the settlement on her own after unpacking her belongings and thought about her work experience to date – teaching, waitressing and cooking. How could she make a living and where could find accommodation? She was healthy, fluent in speaking Italian and English, and interested in all aspects of Australian life.

A few days later, Marina invited Elena to her house to meet her family. She and Marco drove their Holden sedan to Graylands, bringing their family of one girl and two boys. Elena introduced her childhood friend to Jo and Martin, and their boys, Jimmy and Johnny. They went to the onsite café and exchanged news and migration stories over cups of tea.

Then Marina stood up and said they must be leaving as there was a barbeque planned for lunch. Elena noticed that apart from a slight limp, Marco was managing well using his artificial leg. He had developed a method of playing football with his sons and still keeping his balance. After the initial strain of meeting again after many years, Elena looked forward to visiting Marina's home and her first Australian barbecue.

The weather was warm with a stunning blue sky arching across the river and city as they drove towards Fremantle. Marina's daughter, Tina, sat next to Elena in the car and put out her hand to be held, looking at her with trusting eyes. The boys, Tomaso and Mateo, sat squashed in the back seat also and excitedly pointed out the boats on the river and the ocean in the distance. They drove to a narrow street in the middle of Fremantle bordered by wooden houses, many painted white. Marco drew the car to a halt outside a pretty board house with a wide wooden veranda and a towering native gum tree to provide shade in the summer.

Marina showed Elena into the house while Marco parked the car on the grassy driveway. She walked down the central hallway and pointed out the rooms on either side, two bedrooms and a living room, and out the back entrance where another wooden veranda had colourful plants climbing up the structural poles and across the tin roof. Elena was surprised to see the house also had a tin roof, rusting in places. In the back garden was an area for vegetables, a few fruit trees and an umbrella like clothes line on which children's clothes swung in the wind as the line twirled round. The barbecue stood in one corner, smoke and enticing smells rising as a young man stood turning the food over on the grill. Another couple sat chatting, while a boy and girl played in the garden on a tree swing.

Marina introduced Elena to her friends and told her to sit in a comfortable cane chair. Elena felt a little shy as the group all seemed so relaxed and comfortable with each other. Marina brought out some salads and Marco carried some beer. While the drinks were being poured, a latecomer arrived and stood in the doorway. Marina pulled him over and asked him to shake hands with Elena, her childhood friend from Puglia. Elena took his warm strong hand and, looking up, saw his broad smiling face, tanned to a soft brown. Paolo was handsome, and tall for an Italian. He wore tailored brown shorts and a blue T-shirt that showed his muscular arms and legs. He said he managed a café in Fremantle and had told Marina that he needed another Italian-speaking waitress. Elena couldn't resist his sparkling brown eyes and huge smile. She found out later that Paolo had lost his whole family in the ruins of Naples.

The barbecue was a wonderful way to spend a Saturday and Elena enjoyed the food and the non-stop conversation, changing between Italian and Australian. The children were content to run around the garden and use the clothesline to swing on. A large black dog that had been sleeping in the shade under the veranda appeared to chase them.

Elena took the bus back to Graylands and talked that evening with Jo and Martin about their plans. Martin had been offered work at the State Engineering Works in North Fremantle so they had decided to search for somewhere to live around Rockingham as it was near the beach for the boys to enjoy. They had found a small cottage to rent while they decided whether to build a home or buy an existing one.

'There are so many opportunities here,' Jo told Elena excitedly. We drove down the coast and stopped for fish and chips at the café on Cottesloe beach. It's wonderful with soft yellow sand and the sea is warm. The boys loved splashing about and running in and out of the water. Martin was teaching them to swim. Then I suppose the next thing will be they will want surf boards which are popular here. There is so much freedom for children with this weather allowing so many outdoor activities. The beach was busy – families picnicking everywhere – but there was plenty of parking and no mud like the beach at Clevedon. There weren't any donkeys but we all had delicious ice-creams in different flavours. Everyone is so relaxed and friendly.'

Martin smiled. 'I intend to try out surfing and fishing. We drove down after lunch to Rockingham and looked at a few houses for sale and even some plots of land. We have lots of ideas and are keen to find a home near to the local school.'

They parted a week later as Jo and Martin packed their belongings into the car Martin had bought. They exchanged addresses with Elena who used Marina's home address and vowed to keep in touch.

The migrants' settlement felt lonely without them so a few days later Elena moved into a single room above Paolo's café, sharing a bathroom and kitchen with two other waitresses, both Italian. Her tea chests had been delivered to Graylands so Paolo came in his Holden car and loaded them into the boot and stored them in the basement of his café until they were needed.

Elena loved working in the café – she enjoyed speaking Italian again and talking with the customers. She bought a black skirt and blouse and sensible black shoes to wear when working, and added a frilly white apron. She had her hair trimmed to shoulder length and wore it tied back at work. She went to events at the Italian Club with either Marina and Marco or Paolo when he had time and also regularly to the Catholic Church to take mass.

Elena helped out with the cooking when the chef had days off and, with encouragement from Paolo, produced new dishes based on Puglian cooking which the patrons enjoyed. Paolo loved using Italian endearments to his friends and called Elena, 'la bella.' Her relationship with him developed from boss and employee to friendship, and he often took her to late night picnics at Fremantle to watch the sun sink behind the waves. It felt completely different for Elena to be sitting in the sand on a rug, with no barbed wire or gun emplacements marring the view as there had been in Naples. Her trips to the coast with Bill had to be carefully organised between bombing raids and to small bays where coastal defences were minimal.

One late summer evening Paolo took Elena's hand, knelt in the sand and said, 'Will you marry me? I know that you lost your husband and son tragically last year so I'm no pressing you to commit at this time. I fell in love with you when we first met and decided to wait for you to settle into Australian life before proposing. I'd like to share my plans for the future with you and help to soften the tragic past. I love you dearly, Elena, and know you are the right person for me. I want to hug you tightly and kiss you in the moonlight.'

Elena moved into Paolo's arms and once again felt safe and comforted that she had met someone who cared about her. It felt like a miracle: the warm sea breeze wafting through her hair, the sea lapping over her feet and Paolo's body close to hers. They sat entwined until darkness fell, and became lovers, sheltering behind the beach jetty.

Six months later, Paolo handed over the management of the café to an Italian friend and he and Elena moved out to Roleystone where Paolo wanted to run a fruit orchard and market garden business. Elena was content living on the land in the country and, when nine months later, she gave birth to a beautiful little girl, it seemed her life was settled; her home a small paradise.

Author's Notes

I am aware from the research I have done on the events of World War Two in southern Italy that the RAF did not fly Lancaster planes on bombing missions there. However, I wanted to include in my story my long-term friend and mentor Bill Gilliam who bravely flew Lancaster bombers over Germany. Hence, I have invented a special mission for Elena's Bill in Naples so he can meet and marry her.

I started writing this story several years ago when I met a beautiful old Italian lady on a cruise ship. She was walking slowly and painfully, using a walking frame. My husband helped her to a chair where she sat alone, self-contained, remarkable, and listened intently to the piano music. She was smartly and expensively dressed in a silk blouse and plain skirt. When she arrived the next evening and sat in the same place, we recognised each other and she invited us to sit with her. Her name was Anna and she wanted to tell us her story.

'I was born in Puglia in the southern tip of Italy. It was a very poor area. When I was seventeen, I started working in a nearby village just before the Germans invaded. After some incident in the village I was captured by the Germans with about twenty other villagers. We were held in the cellar of the town hall for a day then, with no trial, were sentenced to be shot. We heard that our village priest tried to bargain with the German soldiers and offered himself instead. He and all the other villagers were shot but, miraculously, I managed to escape.'

Anna didn't explain how. The memory was obviously too painful even after sixty years. After a long silence, she continued with her story.

'I walked back alone to my home village that night. I was terrified that I would be caught and shot. When I reached my home village and asked my friend for help and safety, she told me to leave so there would be no repercussions on her family. I couldn't talk about this with anyone for years, not even to my family.'

Anna sat quietly while the trite piano music continued in the background. 'After the war, I met and married an Englishman in Italy and moved to England.' Anna quietly finished her story and rose to dance.

Internet Reference Sources

University of Exeter, Centre for the Study of War and Society – Bombing Italy: Allied Strategies, 1940-1945 Exhibition.

Miriam Mafai – Pane nero. Donne e vita quotidiana nella seconda Guerra mondiale. Milan: Mondadori, 1987. The author wrote about Italian women living in fear due to bombing and hunger.

Jolanda di Benigno – Occasioni mancate. Roma in un diario segreto, 1943-1944. Rome: S.E.I, 1945. The author wrote about civilians living in Rome in the summer of 1943.

The Italian Campaign by Robert Wallace and the Editors of Time-Life Books. This is a volume of the - World War II - Time-Life Books - Alexandria, Virginia, copyright 1978.

<u>Wikipedia sites for information on the period 1943-1955</u>

Eruption of Mount Etna, March 1944

World War II in southern Italy

Military airfields and ports in southern Italy

German invasion, bombing raids and shelters

Mussolini's Blackshirts in Puglia

Photos and descriptions of WWII bombing and war damage in Naples

Photos of street kids and information about assistance by priests

Agriculture, food and cooking in Puglia

Filton airfield, near Bristol and data of war damage in the city

Personal diary entries of visit to Naples in 1960 and sighting of people living in caves in the surrounding hills

About the Author

Louise Croft has recently returned to live in Perth after spending eleven years living in a small village in rural southern France. She says this was a positive life-changing experience, speaking French continuously, absorbing and adapting to the customs and culture of French country life and renovating a 300-year-old stone house. She has lived in seven countries and has enjoyed the challenges and adventures of each one.

She was born in a small country village near Oxford, spent her childhood in Bristol and college years at Brighton. She migrated to Australia under the Government sponsored Business Migration Scheme in April 1989. She organised her own business in IT and Management Consultancy in the UK and Australia from 1986 to 2002 and has worked in sixteen countries in Europe, Asia, Australia and the USA. These include working at a Swedish shipyard and an English naval dockyard, and providing onsite services to the mining and offshore resource industries.

She has four grandchildren, and two sons from a former marriage who live in England.

www.ingramcontent.com/pod-product-compliance
Lightning Source LLC
Chambersburg PA
CBHW070623170726
48291CB00003B/851